J. A. ROOT

SECRETS IN THE HIGH RISE

River Falls Mystery Series | Book One

ISBN: 978-0999175118

Scripture taken from THE HOLY BIBLE, THE NEW INTERNATIONAL VERSION ® Copyright © 1973, 1978, 1984 by International Bible Society. Used by permission of Zondervan. All rights reserved.

Scripture taken from THE HOLY BIBLE, KING JAMES VERSION.

This book is a work of fiction and any resemblance to any person, living or dead, any place, events or occurrences, is purely coincidental. The characters and story lines are created from the author's imagination and are used fictitiously.

Cover Design and Interior Formatting by Crystal L Barnes
Building cover photography by J.A. Rost

DEDICATION

To my husband, Leonard, who has been supportive to the point of forcing me to finish this novel. I did my best writing burning the midnight oil, and he never complained. His support and inspiration have made my first novel possible.

ACKNOWLEDGEMENTS

Officer Cindy Rost of the St. Paul, Minnesota, Police Department for her help in researching the forensics and legal views of law enforcement.

To my editor, Janie Goltz, for editing this book with patience and kindness.

To my two daughters and special friends, who acted as my critics, and to my Women of Words critique group for their guidance through this novel.

I give credit to my Lord and Savior, Jesus Christ, who gave me the courage to write again. I know He was there with me during this entire process, giving me strength and forbearance to continue.

CHAPTER ONE

Dogs come out at night to hunt prey—sometimes animals—sometimes humans.

For the residents living in the rural area of River Falls it was a common occurrence to hear the dogs late at night.

Four Vietnam veterans, recently returned from fighting in the jungles, had been hunting with their dogs when they spotted a few Mexicans at The Last Stop, an out-of-the-way bar tucked in among the tall pines. The owner of the bar was friendly with the cheap labor hired to construct a high rise for the elderly.

The vets had been drinking heavily while thoughts of animosity got them all wound up over the Mexican workers who took jobs meant for them.

Work was hard to find in their small town even with the construction of a new high rise and low-income housing.

President Lyndon B. Johnson designated billions of dollars to help end poverty, and thus began construction of high rises and low-income housing for elderly and families throughout the United States.

The four hunters, afraid to start a ruckus at the bar, decided to frighten the workers after the bar closed. They gathered up their dogs and muzzled them to keep them quiet.

Because of its remote location, the bar's typical customers were tourists and weekend residents during the summer months. It could not be seen directly from the main road, except for a small sign by its driveway entrance. Customers needed to travel a short tree-shaded one-way road that opened into a clearing where an old converted log house blended in with the pine and oak trees. Vehicles parked under one of the low-hanging pines could be easily camouflaged.

The Mexican workers frequented the bar because of its remote location to avoid fights with the locals after working hours. Law enforcement turned a blind eye toward the harassment, so the migrants avoided food and bar establishments in town.

The lights of the bar dimmed to reveal it closed for the night. Five Hispanic men staggered out the door; each carried a bottle of beer.

Their two pickups tucked out of the way under the pines, the four veterans watched quietly, their dogs muzzled in the front seat, unseen in the dark by the staggering silhouetted figures.

All five tried to pack their bodies into the bench seat of a rusty 1950's pickup. Two ended up in the back, where they stretched out leaning against the wheel wells. The driver stumbled several times as he attempted to step into the pickup to get behind the steering wheel.

With the lights from the old pickup and the full moon, it was easy for the two newer pickups to follow and not use their headlights. Like outlaws from the old west, the four men covered their lower faces with bandanas. The Hispanics did not realize anyone followed them. They drove unhurriedly with the music on the radio blaring and continued to drink and sing their way back toward town. The slow drive frustrated the four vets.

The old rusty pickup turned off the main road and started down a narrow graveled road toward the thicker woods and closer to the river. They planned to camp in the woods for the night and sleep off the booze.

Tired of the slow pace, the two newer pickups boldly crept forward to where they could easily be seen. Suddenly one of the Mexicans noticed they were followed. He shouted to his friends and pointed to the vehicles. The driver turned the steering wheel abruptly and the old pickup ended up in the ditch.

Unable to back out because the other two pickups blocked their path, the terrified Mexicans emerged and scattered in different directions. They had no way to realize the men meant them no harm, but just wanted to frighten them out of town. Surprised to see them on the run, the men turned their pickup lights on bright, and scanned the area to see the direction the Mexicans ran into the woods.

"Let's go get 'em," came a slurred shout from the tall skinny man in the first pickup as he emerged with shotgun in hand. He seemed to be the one in authority as the others started to follow his command.

"No, just let 'em go!" shouted the other driver. Smaller in stature with a wiry body, he moved swiftly around the truck. "We'll get 'em some other time. I don't feel like chasing 'em into the woods."

"Yeah, let the dogs find them and give them a good scare," shouted a shorter, stocky man who jumped out of the pickup and held the two hunting dogs by their leashes. He walked briskly to the back of the old truck where he stretched to grab an old shirt one of the Mexicans left behind. He removed the dogs' muzzles, gave each a whiff of the shirt, and gave the command to "Go hunt!" He released the dogs, and the men grabbed flashlights and shotguns from their pickup.

The dogs raced into the woods toward the river where two of the hunted already went into hiding. Their shrill bark clearly marked where the dogs were headed.

"You can't do this!" shouted the one hunter who did not agree. "I don't want any part of this."

The tall man spoke up spitting his disdain in the face of the shorter man, "We're in this together. We agreed to get them outa here, and we gotta stick to our plan. What if they go to the sheriff tomorrow and report this? They saw our trucks. I don't want to end up in jail over a bunch of Mexicans. I've been through enough in Nam."

They agreed they had gone too far with their plan and needed to continue the chase.

"Can't you keep those dogs quiet? We don't need the entire town wonderin' what's goin' on," growled the tall man. Even though they were far enough out of town, the dogs' barks carried and echoed so close to the river.

"Let's break up into pairs and see if we can find 'em," he suggested. "We've got our shotguns, and can always say we were huntin', and they attacked us. Don't fire your guns unless you absolutely have to."

One pair, with their flashlights, followed the sounds of the dogs. The other two headed in the opposite direction. The two hunters with the dogs could hear the rushing waters as they neared Witchikoochi Falls. They knew the Mexicans would soon be cornered with nowhere else to go but into the river.

Because of the recent rains, the river flowed high against its banks and splashed treacherously against the ragged rocks and fallen trees. The water, blackened by the night, rushed on to carry broken branches and tree stumps until it reached another rock-filled widening in the river. It became more ferocious as it dropped more than forty feet to the roaring water and perilous jagged reef below.

It surprised the seventeen-year-old to hear barking dogs in the woods as he drove the winding road in his 1957 sports coupe. It was after 1 a.m. and usually too late for hunters to be out this time of night. A friend, who lived on a farm miles from town, invited a bunch of guys to a keg party. Intoxicated and dizzy from the cheap beer, he decided to take the less traveled roads home to avoid being stopped by a squad car.

He needed to relieve himself and pulled over to the shoulder. He stayed on the main road and never noticed the pickups parked down the narrow gravel road.

While he stood outside close to the trees he could still hear dogs. Even though it was faint, he believed he also heard men's voices. Curiosity got the best of him.

Not too far from the falls, the full moon guided his way as he followed a deer path toward the voices and barking dogs. He stayed back in the trees as the moonlight outlined the figures of the men near the river. Several men wore bandanas over their faces as they pointed shotguns at two others who had been forced toward the river's edge by the dogs.

The two cornered men backed closer to the river's edge as the dogs showed their teeth and lunged toward them. He saw the frightened features of the hunted men. They pleaded in broken English, and he heard the words *no perros* as the animals came closer.

One of the cornered men nearest the water's edge bent down and pulled a knife from his boot. The sharp blade glimmered brightly and startled one of the vets with a shotgun. He pulled the trigger. Bang! The young Mexican lost his balance and fell backwards. He struggled in the current of the river, and started to float toward Witchikoochi Falls. The other man shouted, "José," and dove into the cold river to save his friend before he went over the falls.

The teenager stood there paralyzed in fear as several more men with shotguns arrived on the scene.

The young Mexican, who jumped in to save José, grabbed hold of his friend's arm and attempted to swim toward the shore. The bandana-wearing men raced to help. However, the two in the water were too close to the edge of the falls. Their screams were muffled by the roar of the water as they dropped over the falls.

The teenager continued to stand motionless as he saw the four men weave their way down to the bottom of the falls and search for the two Mexicans. After they reached the base of the falls and shined their flashlights into the river, he decided to get out of there. He knew the large rocks at the bottom could be disastrous.

He turned around and staggered back toward the car when he heard the dogs bark again and this time in his direction. He picked up his pace as he thrashed through the woods.

What a nightmare! Maybe I'll wake up and find this was just a dream. I'm feeling sick.

He started to wretch not far from his car.

"What's going on with your dogs?" one of the men shouted. "Can't you keep them quiet?"

"Don't know!" shouted the short, stocky owner of the

dogs. "They must be on another scent. Maybe the other Mexicans saw what happened. Someone better go check it out."

The teenager made it back to his car. He could hear the dogs close behind and decided to get out of there pronto. The adrenalin rush sobered him as he started his vehicle and gunned the engine.

Several men arrived at the edge of the woods and quieted the dogs. They did not see a vehicle, but they could hear the roar of an engine down the road. One of the men turned around to head back to the falls while the other ran down the road to their pickups. He backed up and drove as fast as he could to catch up to the other vehicle.

The young man prayed they did not see his license plate or get a look at the sports coupe. He heard the distant roar of the truck behind him and looked for a place to hide before the truck closed in on him.

He remembered a cabin surrounded by trees just around the curve on the right side of the road. With his lights off, he turned in the narrow grassy driveway and hid his car along the far end of the cabin, just enough so he could see if the truck would drive by and miss his tracks to the cabin. It passed by without slowing down.

In a short amount of time, the truck returned and again passed by his hiding place.

He waited several more minutes before he inched his way out to the road and looked both directions. No other vehicles in sight. His hands trembled on the steering wheel, but he sighed in relief that he was safe for now. He turned the lights on as he drove toward the town of River Falls.

I'm dead meat if they ever find out who I am.

CHAPTER TWO

Over Forty Years Later

The words on the "Welcome to River Falls" sign read population 12,030. The town nearly doubled in population since Stephanie Runnell last visited almost twenty years ago. Growing up in a quaint little tourist town close to the Minnesota River and Witchikoochi Falls brought floods of good memories of her brother and parents. She needed those good memories right now.

After graduation, she moved out of state to attend college in North Dakota and never returned. Her parents moved shortly after her high school graduation, so there never seemed a need to go back to something no longer there.

Even after all those years she felt the desire to look for familiar buildings as she turned off the main highway and started driving toward the downtown area.

Nothing looked familiar anymore. She noticed a huge Walmart sign as soon as she turned off the exit. Target, Menards, Fleet Farm, hotels, and gas stations dotted the area that used to be farming fields and wildlife areas.

Even though it was only April, the state was experiencing exceptionally warm and rainy weather. After a two-hour drive from the Minneapolis airport, her legs felt cramped in the leased car. Steph needed a bathroom break. She planned to freshen up before arrival at her ultimate destination and her final job interview. With several convenience stores to choose from, she finally decided on the Holiday gas station.

The humid sultry heat hit her as she exited the car. Her lightweight business suit felt heavy and damp on her slim body as she made her way into the store with her purse and makeup kit.

The air-conditioning felt wonderful after the hot trek from the car. Her eyes blinked while she adjusted from the sunlight to fluorescents to survey the store. Customers and employees wandered around, but she focused on the restroom signs.

That employee looks familiar. I'll check it out as soon as I finish in the restroom. I wish I would have kept in touch with some of my high school classmates.

She sighed with relief that the restroom provided privacy.

Steph recently cut her long auburn hair into a more fashionable shorter style that barely came below her chin, and her bangs covered a small scar on her forehead. Her new hairstyle accented her narrow face and showed off her hazel eyes and straight nose. She had been blessed with nice clear skin and required very little makeup. She applied fresh perfume, used the bathroom facilities, and felt ready for her appointment.

As she stepped out of the restroom and wove her way around the displays, a voice called, "Stephanie, is that you?"

She turned around.

I thought she looked familiar. It is Azalea Rose.

Azalea's body jiggled as she crossed the store. She smiled,

and with her arms open wide gave Steph a quick hug. Steph noticed a few wrinkles around her eyes, and her tucked-in red Holiday polo shirt showed several extra pounds around her midsection. Otherwise, she was the same energetic classmate Steph remembered from high school.

"Azalea Rose, how nice to see you again," she exclaimed as she awkwardly stepped into the brief hug. Pleased to see a familiar face, Stephanie did not want to appear anxious, but she did have an appointment and no extra time for chitchat. Remembering Azalea's penchant for gossip, she was not quite sure this was the right time to run into her.

"What brings you to River Falls after all these years?"

Steph knew as soon as she told Azalea why she came back to River Falls, the rest of the town would also know. The local newspaper already contacted her regarding an interview, so the locals would know soon enough. She glanced at her watch. She hoped Azalea would notice her impatience. It proved to be a useless gesture.

I might as well be blunt and to the point; otherwise, I'll be here forever.

Taking a deep breath she answered, "I've just been through a divorce." She hesitated, and waited for Azalea to reply, but she said nothing. "I'm returning to River Falls to start a new job reconstructing some housing projects for the city. In fact, I'm on my way now for the final job interview. I'm a little anxious, and needed a break before the interview."

"Don't worry about the interview. You'll do great!" Azalea smiled, as she grabbed her hand and gave it a pat to offer her encouragement. "I'll say a prayer everything goes well for you, and God will be with you. It's wonderful to see you back," she replied, and not blinking an eye continued. "I'm so sorry to hear about your divorce." She bit her lip, and looked down at the floor. "It's been five years for me now."

"Really?" Steph raised her eyebrows. "I didn't know."

Azalea lowered her voice to above a whisper. "I married Jake Leddering right after college. Best thing I ever did was to get rid of him and take my last name back. The Lord has changed my life and led me down a whole new path. I'm manager of this place now and it keeps me busy. I don't have much time for a social life, but I attend a wonderful church and make time for God and my little girl."

Steph remembered Azalea Rose and Jake Leddering being together since high school, and it was no surprise to her they married. Azalea was a cheerleader and Jake the football hero. But divorced? She would have to find out the details later. Azalea, with her wild nature, turned into a God-fearing woman was new to Steph. She would need to absorb that information very carefully as she felt God had not dealt her a good hand. She wanted no part of any church.

"We'll have to get together for coffee sometime soon," Steph offered, as she wanted to get out of there without any more personal revelations. Her divorce remained a sore spot in her mind. "I still don't have a place to live so I'll be staying in a motel until I can find something. Everything's back in Chicago and should arrive within the next week or two once I finalize my contract with the city. A friend will ship my stuff when I find a place to live."

"I would love to help you look. Let's get together tomorrow for lunch and put our heads together. I think there's a small house for rent near me. Here's my number and my address." She jotted the number and address quickly on the back of a sticky note she kept in the pocket of her polo shirt and handed it to Steph.

Stephanie was surprised she could get away from Azalea

15

so quickly.

This isn't like the Azalea I remember.

"Sounds great to me," Steph exclaimed, as she grabbed the sticky note and headed for the door.

"We can catch up on all the latest gossip while we're house hunting," Azalea shouted as Steph walked out the door. She turned and waved at Azalea as the door closed.

Sure enough, Azalea was still a gossip. Here I thought maybe she changed.

She wondered how many other familiar faces she would meet within a short time.

CHAPTER THREE

From the highway turnoff Steph drove several miles to the high-rise building where she hoped to start work immediately. She parked on a side street and stepped warily out of her car.

The original sign out front read River View Towers, a federally funded HUD project. HUD was short for the federal department of Housing and Urban Development. The building, situated right smack in the middle of the town, was home to many of the elderly in the community, and still the tallest building in the area.

Steph stretched her neck back to observe the entire building and counted the rows of windows—thirteen floors. Questions floated in her mind.

Who on earth would put up a building with thirteen floors? Would they actually have a thirteenth floor? Why do they call it River View Towers? It's not even near the river.

She discerned the building looked run down and definitely in need of renovations. The landscape was dying; the grass bare in many spots. The cement and brick building seemed to leer at her as she noticed rust stains and black streaks that ran down the cement, and gave it an eerie if not cynical look.

Everything around the building appeared neglected except for the small, well-kept tree-lined city park located next to the property. The park was the only thing that took away the stark nakedness of the building and brought some color to the area with the flower gardens immersed among the trees. The building certainly was not new when Steph left for college, but the neglect over the past years left an indelible mark of shocking disrepair.

Her analytical mind started to add up costs. Then it turned cynical as she thought about turning around and walking away from this job. She hesitated to take the position for several reasons.

As far back as she could remember, some mystery surrounded the building construction back in the 1970s. She was also concerned about funding for the project. She previously renovated HUD projects, and HUD was not one of her favorite government agencies. They needed every "i" dotted and "t" crossed before they released any funds. However, the Board of Directors at the Housing Authority informed her the money was available for the renovations.

I really don't want to be here. I've been let down so many times this past year. I'm not sure I want to come back to my hometown and face old friends with my failures. God let me down so many times that I'm not sure I can pick myself back up and go on.

According to the Board of Directors, money and poor management had been an issue. The federal government gave an ultimatum to the housing authority to remodel or shut down.

Steph vaguely remembered an old rumor about the building being cursed. She never paid much attention to the story, but her dad—who was in high school at that time—also worked the summer of his senior year as a laborer on the project. Now she returned to manage the very same building. It seemed like déjà vu that she should be here.

However, she again remembered she did not have much choice. Her ex-husband put her in that situation.

I sure hope the inside looks better than the outside. If my parents were still here, they would tell me to believe in God's help and ask for guidance to get through the interview. Well, God is no longer in the picture for me. My prayers haven't been answered for years. I'll do this by myself. I don't need any help.

She shook her head, squared her shoulders, and entered the secured building.

Even though she did not want to be in this situation, she still felt lucky to find a position so soon after her divorce. Her first priority was to get out of the same city where her ex-husband lived. She came from a luxurious lifestyle and this job would not come close to provide that same income. It would be a start to get back on her feet and build a new future.

Inside the entrance was an antiquated telephone security system. She pushed the button to contact the office and announce her arrival. A cheery sing-song voice answered, "River View Towers. How may I help you?"

Steph announced herself. "We've been expecting you. I'll buzz you into the building." The lock on the glass door clicked. As Steph entered, she was hit with a worse heatwave than what was outside.

Oh, my goodness. No air conditioning.

Fans sat on the floor and blew the hot air around. She

19

noticed the offices on the left, and quickly walked through the closed door.

Thanks heavens, air conditioned offices.

Beads of sweat showed on her face even with the short walk to the office.

A lot of good it did to freshen up.

An elderly woman with short, gray, permed hair sat behind the reception counter. She had difficulty rising from her chair as her feet barely reached the floor, and she ended up hopping off the chair because of the high counter. Steph felt like a giant as the older lady walked around the counter. Her five-foot-eight frame dwarfed the older woman, who was less than five feet and almost as wide as she was tall. Her round, friendly face held a pair of bifocals that looked like they were about ready to fall off her nose.

"I'm Lola, the part-time senior worker," she explained, as she extended her short pudgy hand. It felt clammy to the touch, but Steph firmly clasped her hand and shook it. "The Senior Work Program is funded by the government, and that pays my salary here at the Housing Authority."

Even though she was not familiar with the program, she did know of its existence.

Steph nodded. "It's nice to meet you."

She looked around the group of offices for some of the other employees. There was no one else in sight—or at least that she could see without going into each office. She thought it odd, especially when the board knew her arrival time.

"I'm so sorry for the problems we are experiencing with the chillers in the community room area." She explained, "They got it to work in the office, but not the community room. Maintenance is working on them now."

"Chillers—I haven't heard that word used in reference to

air conditioning in a long time. I understand things like that happen at the most inopportune time," she answered, while she wished for a nice, cool hotel room. "I am meeting the board members at two. Please point me in the right direction for the boardroom?"

"Sure, follow me," answered Lola. Steph noticed Lola's slight limp as she waddled to the door.

She followed Lola through the community area where the residents would normally meet and gather (no one around today), past the dining room, and down a short hallway to a larger room with still more fans. Grouped around the long rectangular table sat five people. Steph always attempted to maintain punctuality for any type of meeting. She hated being late.

Lola left her at the door without making any introductions, and scurried back to the air-conditioned comfort of the offices. The five turned to stare at her. She could feel tension in the air as she looked around the room. She gave them a tense smile, hoped they did not notice how her hands trembled, and walked into the room.

After many years of dealing with boards and large corporations, meeting people for the first time still made her a bit nervous and apprehensive. Even though she was one of the few female reconstruction developers in her field, the first initial social contact with people gave her the jitters.

She never considered herself an ambitious person or social climber. That job went to her ex-husband. She considered herself the person with the vision, but not the social skills to close the deal. He did all the deal closings, while she acted as construction manager and designer. Probably just the opposite for most couples, but it seemed to work for them.

The telephone interview three weeks ago gave her the

opportunity to accept the position of Director of Housing in River Falls, a place she thought she knew so well. They needed a complete reconstruction of their housing for the elderly or over 100 people would lose their homes. There would be no place for these seniors to relocate except to move out of town. She did not want people to suffer unnecessarily, so to come back to face many of the citizens she had not seen in years would, hopefully, not be as difficult as she originally thought.

Clarence Larsvig, chairman of the board, stood to greet her. Steph remembered him as the local banker at the State Bank. She set up her first savings account there while in high school. Hunched over, he leaned heavily on his cane. He walked with an unsteady gait to stand in front of her and extend a rheumatic, shaky hand. She remembered him as being taller. His eyes were watery and full of emotion as he greeted her.

"It is so good to see you again after all these years," he exclaimed as he shook her hand. He pulled a handkerchief from his back pocket and wiped his sweaty brow.

Stephanie recognized Jake Leddering, Azalea's ex-husband. Jake still looked the same with his broad shoulders and muscular build. His long dark blond hair tied back in a ponytail looked the same except for a few gray hairs along his sideburns. A few lines in his tanned face enhanced his virile yet sleazy appearance. His eyes took in her appearance from top to bottom. She felt a shiver go through her body as he ogled her.

She never could understand what Azalea saw in him. Steph cringed as he took her offered hand in both of his and tried to caress it instead of shaking it. She pulled her hand away as soon as she could so it did not seem like she was insulted by his gesture. After all, he would be one of her new bosses, and she wanted no problems in this new job.

"It is so good to see you again, Stephanie," he exclaimed. "You haven't changed a bit since high school."

"Oh, yes, I have," she retorted. "I got rid of my braces and my long hair. I have a few more wrinkles and bulges in places I don't want to admit." They all laughed.

The tension seemed to ease out of the boardroom after the attempt at humor.

Clarence introduced the remainder of the Board.

Donald Hanson, a retired sheriff's deputy, looked at her with a flat, steady gaze. Steph remembered him at least fifty pounds lighter. His reddened nose and ruddy complexion indicated liquor had taken over his life. From her past experience with property management, Steph recognized the signs of alcoholism. She also noticed the bulge under his vest as he stood to shake her hand. He carried a pistol.

The other two were overweight middle-aged women. Steph noticed no wedding bands on either of their brightly colored, manicured hands as they giggled and laughed together. She assumed Colette Finegan and Wendy Benjamin were friends. They reminded her of pampered women who did not bother to get to the gym very often. Their long nails and expensively tailored suits gave away their propensity to live the good life. She wondered what they were doing on a board for low-income families.

Steph made a mental note to be very vigilant around these women. They looked too chummy to be neutral board members. She assumed with their first meeting that each woman would agree with whatever the other had to say.

Even though a phone call from Clarence Larsvig confirmed the job, it was still contingent on the final contract negotiations.

This position would be easy for her as it involved 150 low-income units around the town, which included the high-rise complex. She used to manage several thousand units with help from staff. This job would give her a new start, and help her forget her former life.

The board wanted to get the final negotiations over as soon as possible. She concurred with the final settlement for salary and what her duties would entail. They agreed to give her a tour of the high rise after the meeting, and she could see the other complexes within the next few days.

As she toured with the five members of the board, she was reminded of a gaggle of people, each tried to be more important than the other.

Clarence seemed to be the person most familiar with the building. He worked across the street during its construction. He was the oldest member of the board, and the longest incumbent member of over fifteen years.

They discussed repairs to the building, which Steph agreed were badly needed. He wanted her to start making plans immediately.

Clarence explained that the federal Housing and Urban Development gave them grant money to cover most of the renovations needed, but—he hesitated—it would not cover all the repairs needed.

Why didn't they tell me this before they offered me the position?

She believed through their previous phone conversations that all the money would be in place to use for the renovations. Now she would need to find additional finances to complete the project, bring it up to code and HUD approval—or to start cutting parts out of the renovation schedule.

The federal government offices located in Minneapolis approves all the final renovations needed, so she needed to work with this board as well as the federal government. It would involve innovative politics to get the project completed.

"You can get started on the bidding process immediately. You know what we need to do," declared Clarence Larsvig.

"Just a minute, Mr. Larsvig," Steph interrupted and held up her index finger to get his attention.

"Call me Clarence!"

"Thank you," she hesitated to use his first name. "Clarence ... I need to get situated first. Finding a place to live will be my first priority," she stated, as she held up one finger and then her middle finger. "Meeting my office staff and going through the financial statements will be the next priority. This building has stood for all these years. Surely several more days won't hurt it."

"Hmmm," he mumbled. Then he exclaimed in a slightly higher pitched voice, "I understand your priorities, but you need to understand these repairs should have been made years ago. Even though the former director was a friend, he did not know how to organize. The board wasn't aware of this until he passed away, and then a short time later HUD showed up for the inspections."

"This is what you hired me to do, and it will get done. It takes time." She walked away to join the other board members.

River View Towers was octagon-shaped with the elevator in the center of the building. When they exited the elevator, they walked to the left and circled around the building. They toured each floor.

Donald Hanson stumbled along with the group, wiping his brow. When they finally made it to the last floor of the apartments, the thirteenth floor, he mumbled, "It's too hot for all this walking." His handkerchief soaked up the perspiration as it dripped down his face.

Steph's once-crisp suit felt damp and chafed her body as they moved through the building.

She walked around the circle and noticed a door marked Private.

"Where does this door lead?"

"That door leads to the roof and a large windowless room used for storage. We consider it a partial fourteenth floor."

"So the elevator only goes up to the thirteenth floor."

"Yes, you need to climb another set of stairs to get to the roof and storage room. The door is locked to keep the residents off the roof, and can only be opened with a master key," he responded.

"Let me look at the storage room another day." They all agreed. "It's only a storage room and not important to see right now."

She continued her walk on the thirteenth floor and stood in front of an apartment marked 1313. Stunned, she stared at the door.

How odd! Having a thirteenth floor in buildings is bad luck, but an apartment marked 1313 is even worse.

She shook her head, but said nothing to the members of the board.

Clarence opened an empty apartment with a view of the river. They all stepped inside the small apartment, less than 500 square feet, cooled by a wall-mounted air conditioner, and breathed a sigh of relief. Steph walked over to one of the windows and looked out.

I still wonder why they called the building River View Towers? You can only get a glimpse of the river from the last three or four floors, and only because those floors stretched over the trees and the rest of the town.

Collette and Wendy walked together and chatted, offering no information to Steph in regards to the building. They started to look as uncomfortable as Mr. Hanson.

When they arrived back on the main floor, Clarence pressed the renovation plans into her arms. After the others left the building, Jake's clammy hand grabbed her by the elbow and maneuvered her off to the side outside the office while she tried to balance the rolled-up plans in her arms. "You've hardly changed since high school," he flirted, leaning his arm against the wall to keep her from walking away.

Steph listened and remained at arm's length, while he mentioned their high school days. It did not seem to matter to him that she never ran around with his group of friends. He tried to play the sympathy game of how his college football career ended abruptly with a back injury. Jake bragged about his success in the real estate business.

"Since you just returned after all these years, why don't we get together for a drink or coffee tomorrow to talk about the renovations?" He did not mention his failed marriage.

"Thank you, but I need to find a place to live."

"I've got connections and can get you into a place right away."

"Again, thank you, Jake, but I talked to Azalea earlier and she volunteered to help me find a place." His face turned a light shade of red as he realized she knew about their divorce.

"Okay, but if you need help, just give me a call." He handed her his business card. She put it in her pocket and walked out the door to her car, leaving him behind in the building.

Steph checked into the air-conditioned Holiday Inn located close to the main highway. It felt good to take a shower and go over the renovation plans Clarence forced on her before she left the building.

She'd tried to remember stories heard in the past about the building. She knew her father talked about his job during his senior year. She was too young then to understand their conversations. Right now, she just wanted to lie down and get some rest before going down to the hotel restaurant.

CHAPTER FOUR

The next morning Steph woke up to the radio. The announcer said the weather would be another hot and humid day. She detested the thought of getting up and going into a hot office building. Depression hit her. She curled up in a ball and pulled the covers over her head. She wished she could go back home, but there was no more home—just reality.

Steph spent the last fifteen years working with her ex-husband, Larry, in a property management and development company. She started as his draft designer for several years before they married. Larry and Steph managed the company together. It prospered under her expertise, especially when it came to reconstruction and remodeling of large office buildings and apartments.

It all fell apart when her husband announced for the past several years he had a mistress and he would be a new father.

Both of them had been career oriented, or so she thought. During the first years of their marriage, Steph and Larry wanted to start a family. After five years, she gave up and devoted her entire energy to building what she considered their company. Both talked about saving for early retirement, so when they reached the age of fifty they could easily retire and spend their time travelling. If they wanted to take on an extra project or two, it would be up to them.

As she expended her energy working with the business, she believed they lived an ideal lifestyle. Afterwards, as she looked back, the late nights out, the separate business trips, the extra drinking when home, and the quietness on his part that last year all seemed to fall into place. And she didn't even see it. What a fool!

She felt God failed her. First, she was not able to conceive a child. Second, Larry left her for another woman. Third, she lost the business in the divorce battle. *Three strikes and you're out.*

Her now ex-husband retained the business. He owned the company before they married; and he claimed pre-marital assets during the divorce. All the hours and stress she put into the business did not make a difference in the final settlement. Her ex-husband hid most of their other assets. He always handled the financials in the business, so before he asked for a divorce he started to move the company's assets into a blind corporation in his new girlfriend's name.

When Stephanie found out about the affair, there were very few liquid assets left in the company to divide, but she fought long and hard and only ended up with their house and a small settlement from the company. After she sold the house, which Larry mortgaged without her prior knowledge, and paid off the mortgage, she had very little left. She needed to downsize and move to another neighborhood where the houses were still out of her price range for a woman with a new divorce and no prospects for a good paying job.

Even after the divorce, her ex-husband made it impossible for her to continue to live in the same city. She seemed to run into him and his new younger pregnant wife wherever she went. It hurt too much to see them together. She hated her life and found herself in a deep depression. Then the stress headaches started. She had nowhere to turn—very few friends left, no family around. The few friends who supported her during the divorce could not help her establish a new career.

She felt God deserted her, and she refused to attend church or seek help from her fellow church members. Even though she and Larry were members of a church, they seldom attended. Word of the divorce traveled fast, and several women from church tried to get her involved in activities and divorce-care groups, but she refused. She wanted to wallow in her own self-pity.

Her skills were no longer in demand by most of their former friends and business acquaintances. Her husband had been the socializer and she the dutiful wife, too busy to attend parties and gatherings after working sixty hours every week. Steph knew everyone thought he had been the brains behind the success of the company. She never made many lasting friendships because she devoted her entire married life to the business. She needed to find employment before all her money ran out.

Now thirty-six years old and alone, she still hurt with a lot of animosity toward her ex-husband.

She could move to Texas where her parents retired, but to her it was a last resort. They never liked Larry and told her so after she called to tell them about the divorce.

After seeing the job notice from the Housing Authority on the internet, she decided to reclaim her life. It surprised her to be offered the position so soon after the phone interview. Her depression disappeared, and she felt a new lease on life—until this morning. She could feel it trying to take over again and control her.

No, this is not going to happen. I need to get back to my old self and be in control. I cannot let this feeling take me over. Be strong, Steph, be strong. No more depression.

Not her own boss anymore, she dragged herself out of bed. By the time she showered and dressed, there was no time for breakfast. She dressed casually as she had no idea if the old chiller in the building had been repaired yet. She would grab something at Azalea's convenience store on the way to River View Towers, and make a date for lunch with her.

Arriving shortly after 8 a.m. with a hot coffee in her hand and a double-chocolate-chip muffin in a bag, she noticed the old chillers cooled the main floor of the building as well as the offices. Residents moved around on the main floor and relaxed in the air-conditioned rooms.

She walked through the main office door and met another employee.

Through a stiff, forced smile, showing nicotine-stained teeth a woman around fortyish greeted her.

"I'm Callie Weber." Her voice sounded deep and gravelly. She smelled of cigarette smoke, which permeated the air around her. Steph noticed her brown-stained finger tips. Callie made no effort to welcome her.

Even though she stood only a few inches over five feet, she could have easily passed for a man. Callie's selection of clothing did not impress Steph. She wore faded black jeans and a short-sleeved polo shirt with River View Towers embroidered over the pocket. It looked like a man's shirt, too small for her as it hugged her frame and showed the bulges around her waist. Her long hair pulled back from her face in a ponytail held by a rubber band showed she made no effort to wear makeup over her pale freckled face.

She wondered what this employee did at the housing authority, and noted professionalism must not be a priority at the agency. This was so different from the employees back at her former company.

Steph asked about her office, and Callie pointed to the last office. She noticed another woman in the office next to hers talked animatedly on the phone, and waved her other hand in the air as she held the receiver. As soon as she noticed Steph in the doorway, she said, "Call you back," and hung up the phone.

She surmised this must be Karen Mueller, who managed the agency while the board searched for a new director. She heard a lot of good feedback about Karen from the board. She had been at the agency longer than any other employee, including the previous director. Steph found out during the interview that Karen also applied for the director position, but she did not have the construction experience needed to do the renovations.

"It will be so nice to have a new director. I'm Karen," stated the middle-aged woman with deep-set eyes covered by a pair of thick glasses. "We've been waiting a long time to finally have the board make a decision. Welcome to our agency!"

Wearing a white blouse with River View Towers embroidered above the pocket, she dressed more professionally, but still wore a pair of tight-fitting jeans over her heavier figure. Shaking hands, Steph noted she and Karen were about the same height. Close up, her eyes looked tired and weary.

"Thank you very much," smiled Steph. The handshake felt soft and limp in Steph's firm grip. The smile she first thought genuine did not extend to the limp handshake.

I wonder if she's upset about not being offered the director's position.

So far she had negative vibes from the first two employees this morning.

Sure hope the remainder of the employees are friendlier.

She walked back to her office and closed the door. Steph drank her coffee and ate her muffin in privacy while again reviewing the plans for renovations.

Later that morning, Karen introduced Steph to Darrin Waltz, the head maintenance person, and his young assistant, Derek Olson.

Darrin, a short stocky fiftyish man with a craggy deep-wrinkled face and a thick mat of greying hair, worked at the facility almost twenty years. He ran his hand nervously over his oiled hair and pushed his black-framed glasses back on his nose where they would slip back down a short while later. Steph asked for a tour of the boiler room and maintenance area where some of the renovations would take place.

"I don't allow anyone in the boiler room. The instruments are too delicate and old and need to be babied to keep running," he gruffly responded.

Derek, in his early twenties, newly hired, greeted her with enthusiasm. After Darrin's gruff retort he nodded his blond head and smirked. "You should have seen him my first week here. He wouldn't let me touch anything."

"Well, I've many years of experience with commercial renovations, and an old boiler system does not deter me," Steph replied. "I promise I won't touch anything."

Darrin's eyes glared as he dared her to usurp his authority.

Steph continued to stare back until he finally turned away. "Oh, all right. Just make sure you keep your promise not to touch anything."

During the tour Steph observed Derek's uniform shirts were definitely too tight fitting. His biceps bulged out of the sleeves almost to the point of tearing, and the snaps on the shirt were ready to pop.

We are definitely hard up for new uniform shirts.

Steph noticed several older men and women doing miscellaneous jobs around the building. Karen commented earlier that they volunteered to help with morning coffee and social functions for the residents.

Steph decided to call an employee meeting before she scheduled an appointment with the architect. She hoped the architect could be instrumental in obtaining extra funds for the renovations. Since there were three buildings scheduled for renovations, and River View Towers, the largest and the most costly, she needed to move on this project first.

Steph met Azalea for lunch at The Nest, a cozy, vintage-style restaurant serving breakfast and lunch. She was enthralled with the garish design of its bright raspberry-colored walls accented with large-flowered wallpaper on alternating walls. The antique-like tables and chairs were an odd collection of various shabby chic designs and colors. The centerpieces of flower vases color-matched each table. Steph complimented Azalea for her suggestion of the restaurant.

A restaurant this unique and eclectic would go over well in Chicago. I love it.

"Well, how's the first day going?" Azalea asked quizzically, while seated around a turquoise-themed table.

Steph shrugged her shoulders. "Just as I thought it would. Met pretty much all the staff, except for a few volunteers. Not sure what all their jobs are yet, but I will find out more this afternoon during the staff meeting." She let out a little snort. "I think they were surprised I called a staff meeting so soon."

Azalea frowned. "You have a big job ahead of yourself. I don't envy you the position you've been put in. I heard through the grapevine they didn't get enough funding for the entire project."

"I found that out yesterday at the board meeting. We'll make some cuts or otherwise raise more funds." She took a drink from her water glass, then asked, "Any ideas?"

"Let me do some thinking. You know I don't want to stick my nose into your business especially since Jake's on the board. I avoid him whenever I can, but I can put on my thinking cap and see if there are any other people who might be able to help."

"I don't mean to make you feel uncomfortable with your ex on the board," replied Steph, her face hot with embarrassment. "Just forget I asked."

"No, I want to help," she replied, "but not sure how much help I can give you."

"You know more people right now than I do, so that alone would help."

"I've lived here most of my life. It's hard to believe when we graduated from high school there were less than 100 graduates and now there's over 250. Businesses have started up hiring many locals. Jennifer Williams, one of the owners of Pearl Candy Company, now employs over 200. She's been a big philanthropist around town and might be willing to donate or help to do some fundraising."

"She'd be one I would like to meet."

"She has her own personal assistant who does all her errands, including filling her car with gas. She's so busy with her company that it's hard to get an appointment with her."

I don't want Azalea obligated to help when it's my job to raise any extra funds. I don't have any idea, at this point, how much extra we'll need.

"Let's order and talk about living quarters. You know Jake offered to help me find a place. When I mentioned your offer to help, he just walked away and didn't say a word."

"Well, our divorce wasn't amicable, but at least we try to stay on speaking terms. He's still mad I divorced him."

"Why?"

"I guess I outgrew his childish and selfish behavior. We have a teenage daughter, Becca, and I didn't want her to grow up without her dad, so I just kept ignoring his behavior," she explained. "He would come home some nights after drinking at different bars claiming he was with a client. I started to question whether a client existed. He would lose his temper and then hit me. He would apologize the next day, but it happened more and more often. After years of feeling inadequate, and then with the physical abuse, I needed to get out for Becca and myself."

"You've been through a lot," Steph commiserated. Her mind going back to when Larry deserted their marriage making her feel like the worst kind of failure.

Failure makes you speculate what type of person you truly are in the sense of what others see in you. Then you are by yourself, not knowing what to do next.

"Not too many people know about the reason for the divorce." Azalea continued to talk, not noticing Steph's inattentiveness. "I never reported the abuse because of Jake's position in the community. I'd appreciate it if you would keep it to yourself," Azalea requested.

"Ah…of course. No problem," her reply sounded aloof.

"If it wasn't for my relationship with my church and praying to God to give me the strength to leave, I don't know if I could have made it through the divorce. Jake never wanted me to work after we married. Even with a college degree I couldn't find a job," she explained. "But I prayed and left everything up to God, and God answered my prayers. The job keeps me busy, and I put smiles on people's faces every day. It makes it worthwhile." Her voice turned wistful, "I still dream of owning my own business one day."

Steph envied Azalea's enthusiasm, and her determination to make her life work for her again. "I'm glad things worked out for you." Her voice changed to cynicism. "I've given up on church and God. I don't feel He has been in my court for a long time. Too many bad things happened this past year."

"Don't give up, Steph. God is just waiting for you to accept Him again, to do good things for you. Just believe and give it time. Put everything in His hands and things will work out."

"Could we talk about something else? I don't feel comfortable with this subject," Steph exclaimed. Her head started to hurt with the direction of the conversation.

I hope Azalea doesn't try to convert me to her church.

She gave Azalea the glossed-over version of her divorce situation, and left out the problem of her inability to find work after the divorce. They both sympathized over each other's problem with men.

Steph was hungry. She ordered a large hamburger and fries. Since she walked to the restaurant, Steph decided to walk off some of the calories going back to the office.

She made plans with Azalea to look for a place that

weekend.

Because of the tense introductions to the staff earlier, the afternoon meeting was not something she looked forward to, but it needed to take place.

All the full-time staff members showed up in the board room: Callie, Karen, Darrin, and Derek. Lola was there on behalf of the residents. She wanted to purposely seek out each staff member's requests so none of them felt left out of the decision making process.

Steph went over the renovation list with each employee, how it would affect their jobs, and to get their reaction.

Earlier in the day when Darrin reluctantly gave her a tour of the boiler and maintenance areas, he explained the system had been babied for many years and fickle.

"I'm excited about the new boiler system for the entire building and especially the new air conditioning units. The only thing I don't like is the installation of a sprinkler system. It's going to be hard to maintain as it needs to be at a certain pressure on a constant basis. I know…I know", he threw his hands in the air, "HUD mandated the installation, but I think it stinks."

Derek shook his head in agreement, and then added, "The plumbing and electrical is so old and overused, it's no longer functioning properly. Since I started this job, several leaks in the pipes caused flooding on other floors and did a lot of damage to the walls and ceilings."

Steph noted Derek's laid-back attitude, and sticky situations did not bother him quite as easily as it did Darrin.

She jotted down notes during the meeting as each person took a turn to state their requests.

Karen presented her thoughts for repairs. "The apartments in this building are so hot in the summertime and many of the residents don't have money for an air conditioner. I think we should consider new air conditioners in all the apartments at no charge to the residents. The community kitchen needs to be updated, and we need new tables and chairs in the dining room. The sitting area needs new chairs." Her list was almost as long as the maintenance department. Steph put most of Karen's list on the "want" list, if there were funds left.

Since she had not yet been able to view the apartments, Steph continued to jot down notes as Lola spoke up. She seemed to be the grandmother to all the staff, and they listened to everything she said as she represented the residents. She found out earlier that Lola also lived at River View.

"I would like to see some money put into activities for the residents. They get bored. I find many of them don't leave their apartments. Some I only see when it gets so hot, and they come down to sit in the community area to cool off," she offered. "I know all of the residents are going to be uncomfortable with the renovations, so we need to keep them busy."

Her ardent appeal and concern for the residents touched Steph's heart.

Callie did most of the inspections, which included turnovers when residents moved and the annual federal inspections, processed all work orders, plus played receptionist when Lola was not there. She sat through the meeting with her arms crossed over her chest. "We've passed inspections from the federal government, and it should be good enough. Besides, the residents here are not happy with all the work that is going to be done," she snarkily replied.

No wonder I got bad vibes from her when I first walked in

the door.

Steph raised her eyebrows. "Okay, Callie, tell me why did the federal officials say they will shut down the building if repairs are not made?"

No answer from Callie.

"The building passed federal inspections," Steph continued. "But it's up to each state to make sure renovations are completed, especially on the oldest buildings. They give each agency so many years to complete the work. If it's not done, the buildings are closed. The former director knew this information and did nothing. Now he's gone, and we're stuck with a deadline." She stopped for a moment. "From what I understand very little has been done for major renovations for many years. And besides, looking at the last several federal inspections, this building passed by only a few points."

"I think you should talk to the residents," Callie exclaimed belligerently. "They don't want this!"

"I'm sorry you feel this way, Callie, but the work is going to get done. I'll be meeting with the architect tomorrow, and bid requirements will be put out in the papers by next week."

Steph tried to hold back her anger at Callie's outburst. She needed to hold it together and not let the staff overrun her authority. If she let Callie get away with her callous disregard for her authority, then the other employees might follow and more trouble would ensue. She thought about Darrin's reluctance to show her the maintenance area.

She began to realize the employees might not want to be cooperative, and there would be protests if she could not get things under control.

However, she did, under the circumstances, agree with Callie.

Why did HUD threaten to shut down the building when

they did pass the inspections? Even though the inspection score was low, only the necessary repairs should be made instead of a full renovation.

It confused Steph as it did not make any sense, but she could not let the staff know her concern. She adjourned the meeting before a staff uprising her first day on the job.

As the staff left the board room, Karen stayed behind.

"Thank you so much for not causing a scene with Callie. She can be a handful and is very opinionated," she stated quietly.

Steph shrugged her shoulders, "Yes, I noticed that."

"Just be careful with her. She was a favorite with the former director. If she doesn't get her way, she will find a way to get it. I've learned to stay away from her when she has her tantrums. She can have a vicious side when pushed."

"Oh, I see," replied Steph thoughtfully.

I will have to watch my back.

"Thank you for the information."

"Just wanted you to know," replied Karen.

Did she just attempt to ingratiate herself to me? Should I watch out for her, too?

CHAPTER FIVE

The next day an early morning meeting with Reinhold Architects gave Steph the chance to walk the few blocks to their office. She received glares that morning from Callie when she showed up for work. The chill in the office came not only from the air conditioning but from some of the staff.

As she walked into the office building at 9 a.m., a friendly receptionist greeted her.

"Right on time," she commented after Steph introduced herself.

Even though Todd was only a few years older, she did not know if he would remember her. Still tall and slender as a rail, his thinning brown hair with a smattering of gray and thick wire-rimmed glasses reminded her of his dad.

An easy smile played at the corners of his mouth as he greeted Steph with a handshake. "So glad to finally meet you. I don't know if you remember me, but I hung out with your brother," he volunteered.

"I do," she managed to grin as she remembered a shy boy

who very rarely said anything to her while he hung out at their home.

By the time Steph left his office, she was impressed with his organization skills. He completed the work write-ups for the bidding process. She perused them and gave a final approval. They set the date for the opening of the bids. Todd suggested they sit down together again and see what renovations needed to be cut or modified.

Even though Steph gathered estimated figures for each project, she knew there was a need for additional funds over and above the grants given to the agency.

"I'd like to get the community involved in raising funds so we can get some of our wants met and not cut too much of the work that needs to be completed. I hope some organizations or businesses might come forward with donations."

"I have some contacts, but let's wait until bids are opened. Then we can do some modifications and see where we stand."

Karen had warned Steph earlier that there would be a meet-and-greet coffee time in the afternoon to introduce Steph to the residents.

She picked up a sandwich for lunch on the way back from the architect's office. As she walked toward River View Towers she noticed an elderly lady with a pair of pruning shears clipping some bushes behind a bench in the nearby park. She mumbled incoherently to herself as she clipped away at the bushes. As Steph warily walked closer to her, she could hear the lady speak to herself.

"Need to make room to hide. Gotta hide and get away."

"Excuse me. Would you please explain what you are doing with the pruning shears?"

Startled, the elderly lady turned around, and almost lost her balance. Steph dropped her briefcase and sandwich and reached out to catch her, but the elderly lady grabbed the arm of the park bench to keep from falling.

"Who are you? What are you doing here? Don't you know you can't be here?" Her voice sunk to a whisper. "Shhh…I'm trying to get into my house, and they put all these bushes in front of it. I can't get in."

Steph, flabbergasted by her response, recognized she was hallucinating and needed help. Just as she was about to offer her services, a county sheriff's car pulled up close to the curb.

A tall, well-built man dressed in a tan uniform with his full-gear utility belt strapped around his waist emerged. His controlled body movement spoke of power and strength. Steph recognized him immediately. "Goodness gracious, Mitch DeVries." Steph stood and gaped at the man. "It's been years!"

"Good to see you again, Steph," his facial expression softened and relaxed. Mitch stood at least half a foot taller. He was the boy next door, her second big brother, her first puppy love, and always her friend until he left for college. Then she never heard from him again. She left town a few years later. "I heard you were back in town."

She remembered how his deep azure eyes used to twinkle as a teenager. They were still dark, but she did not notice any twinkling in them anymore.

Life must have dealt him some blows to be able to take that twinkle out of his eyes.

His thick black hair was cut shorter than the last time she saw him—over twenty years ago. His chiseled nose with a slight slope still flared at the nostrils when he talked. That always intrigued her. She could always tell when he was angry or nervous by the way his nostrils flared.

Funny how a person remembers little things even after many years.

The DeVries lived next door to her family. Her older brother, Aaron, and Mitch were best friends all through high school, until Aaron died his senior year in a car accident.

After the funeral Mitch stopped coming over. At the age of fifteen it left Steph with excruciating pain—the loss of her brother and the loss of seeing Mitch every day.

She forced a smile and extended her hand, "Nice to see you again."

Couldn't I think of anything better to say after all these years?

Mitch took her hand in both of his for a brief moment, but then turned his attention to the elderly lady. His eyes gave the impression he would have liked to talk more with Steph.

"Miss Mattie, what you are trying to do here?" he said softly, and attempted not to upset the older woman any further.

"Can't you see, officer?" She whispered close to his ear as he bent his head. "I'm trying to get into my house, and those people put these bushes in the way so I can't get to my door." She pointed her pruners at the bushes.

"Well, Miss Mattie, how about I take you home, and have your sister give you some medicine. When was the last time you took your medicine?"

"I don't remember," she shrugged her shoulders. Tears started to form in her eyes and run down her cheeks. Mitch put his arm around her. Steph found her walker behind the park bench and brought it over to her.

"Thank you, dearie," she replied.

"You remember Miss Mattie, don't you, Steph?" He raised his eyebrows. "She used to work in the library until she retired. Now she lives with her sister at River View. I think she probably hasn't taken her meds for several days," he explained. "This happened before. She starts hallucinating and making up stories. Sometimes we've had search parties looking for her when she wanders too far from here. Good thing she stayed close by this time."

Yes, now that Mitch mentioned it, I do remember Miss Mattie Turnborn. Everyone called her Miss Mattie because she never married, and she always tried to teach the young girls at the library proper etiquette.

As a teenager, Steph thought she was a sweet soft-spoken very proper older lady. A few more pounds, wrinkles, and a walker did not change her.

Miss Mattie worked for the city library her entire adult life, and her sister, Maude, worked at the elementary school. Steph thought both should have decent retirement benefits and wondered why they lived in low-income housing.

She helped Mitch put Miss Mattie into the car. Steph's heart skipped a beat as she watched Mitch's large frame slide into the squad car to drive Miss Mattie around the block to the high rise.

"Do you want to ride along? As long as I'm going in the same direction I'd be happy to give you a lift." He smiled, showing a set of gleaming white teeth, and she thought maybe she saw a small twinkle in his eyes again.

"No. Thanks anyway." Her face flushed red, her heart pounded, and the feeling of being a teenager again overcame her. "I…I need the exercise," she stuttered.

As he drove off Steph realized he still brought a flutter to her heart. She noticed no wedding ring on his finger. Her teenage crush returned with just one sight of him.

She picked up her briefcase and sandwich, and walked to her office with a skip and a smile on her face.

CHAPTER SIX

On Saturday Azalea accompanied Steph to look at several apartments and houses available for rent. The slim inventory of housing gave her few choices. Steph knew houses and apartments became more available after the month of May, but still hoped she could find something reasonable. Azalea called in a favor from a local contractor who recently renovated his mother's home. His mother was in a nursing home, and he did not want to sell the house.

She signed a month-to-month lease on a quaint two-story 1950s house with a single car garage several blocks from Azalea's home. The two upstairs bedrooms and bath worked perfectly for her needs. The downstairs had an eat-in kitchen, new appliances, and a nice-sized living room with a small den. The small basement came with a washer and dryer. Both agreed the den would make a perfect office away from the high rise.

Even though the rooms smelled of fresh paint and the wood floor newly refinished, the selling point was the small back yard with a back alley that gave her access to the garage. Landscaped with a large old gnarled oak tree and beds of perennial flowers lined up against a white picket fence gave it a homey atmosphere. The perennials poked their heads out of the ground and would bloom soon with the warm weather. A large white-painted cushioned bench under the oak tree added to the ambiance. She could see herself with a good book as she sipped a glass of wine under the shade of the tree—an idyllic scene.

She moved in right away. The remainder of her few assets, arrived via UPS, and ended up stored in the garage until she could go through everything. Steph did not want many reminders of her marriage and sold all the furniture except for a few keepsakes.

She kept her original paintings purchased on various vacations and business trips. Shopping at small art shops and perusing through their displays of hopeful artist originals brought a sense of tranquility to her former hectic lifestyle. She spent many shopping trips purchasing artwork for the properties she renovated.

Azalea volunteered to help pick out furnishings. Steph wanted to keep things simple and opted to go to re-sale stores for used furniture she could refurbish.

Some vintage inexpensive things that could accentuate the quaintness and uniqueness of the house. Don't need to tell Azalea my funds are limited.

The next week, during their lunch hours, they spent shopping at various thrift and used furniture stores finding just the right pieces to fit into the tiny house. Her bedroom set she purchased new. Azalea had an eye for decorating, and Steph was happy to have her along for support.

While they shopped, Azalea brought her up to date on most

of their classmates still around the area. What they were doing, how many children they had, and who was divorced, etc. Azalea had an endless array of knowledge about the community.

During her outings, they saw Mitch drive around in his squad car. He waved but never stopped. Still every time she noticed him, her heart did a little flip-flop. She wanted to see more of him.

The following Saturday, a week after she signed her lease and moved in, Azalea and Steph shopped at several garage sales in the morning and stopped for a late lunch at The Nest. Mitch, his back to them, sat at one of the corner tables with several deputies.

While both were deep in conversation over different ideas for furniture color schemes she recently purchased, Steph noticed a shadow hovered behind her and looked up. Mitch's tall frame stood behind her and looked ruggedly handsome in his uniform. Again, her heart started a little flutter.

"Good to see you again," Steph tried not to show her excitement.

He grinned. "Looks like you ladies are having a deep discussion," and pointed to the different color swatches laid out on the table.

"Come, sit and join us. We'll even let you give us advice," Steph offered teasingly.

"Yes, please do," Azalea also offered, although not as enthusiastic as Steph.

"No, thanks," said Mitch, as he looked directly at Steph. "I'm on duty right now, but I sure would like to take a rain check. Can I buy you dinner one evening soon."

"That sounds great!" Steph exclaimed. "I would love to catch up on the past years."

"Well, my life is an open book. Being a public official offers no privacy. So you can ask away when we have dinner. How about tomorrow evening? I usually get off around five if we don't have any emergencies. I'll pick you up at six."

"Sounds good to me," said Steph. "I'm working around my house getting a few things settled. Here's the address." She jotted it on a napkin and handed it to him. "I also listed my cell phone number just in case," she explained.

Being several years older, he was way out of her league of friends during high school. He never noticed a gangly teenager who made cat eyes at him when he came to her house with Aaron.

Wow! I'm going to be as nervous as if it were my first date. In fact, this is my first date since the divorce.

Her mind wandered as she remembered it had been years since she needed to impress any man except for a business presentation.

"Earth to Stephanie!" Azalea exclaimed, as she snapped her fingers in the air. Steph looked startled as she came back to reality.

"Just remembering things from the past."

"Good or bad?"

"It's hard to say. My life's been such a jumble over the past year, and then seeing Mitch again brought back old memories. He never came back much during his college days, so I figured he didn't want to be friends anymore since Aaron died. I remembered how much I missed talking to him," she sighed. "Oh, well! I guess it will be like starting over again."

"Mitch has become a loner since his wife left," Azalea confided. "They'd been married for less than five years. You don't see him out in public anymore except when it concerns his job as sheriff." Azalea folded her hands together on the table and took a deep breath. "I guess I might as well tell you that we dated for a while after my divorce and his wife left. It didn't amount to anything more than friendship. He put himself in a shell, and no one could get in. I worried about Becca, and didn't quite know how to cope with his daughter."

"His daughter?" Steph looked puzzled.

"Yes, his little girl, Natalia. She's about ten years old now. She was only four when her mother left. Mitch tries to be both mom and dad to her and literally does not date—at least not in public anymore."

"Why did his wife leave?" She eagerly questioned Azalea, wanting to know as much as possible before seeing Mitch again.

"I don't really know all the details except he shouldn't have married her in the first place. Soon after they were married, Mitch and his wife, Susan, moved back to River Falls. Mitch started at the Sheriff's Department. She just didn't fit in, especially with the other deputies' wives. She liked to party. You know how gossip goes around in small towns. She wasn't good for Mitch. Rumors went around she got involved doing drugs with some of those swinging couples."

Azalea lowered her voice and whispered, "Apparently Mitch found out because they had several fights where he actually moved out. She would promise never to do drugs again, and he would move back in. That happened several times that I know about, but there could be more to the story. I was too busy trying to keep my own marriage alive. Then one day she disappeared, and hasn't been heard from since."

"She left her husband and little girl!" Steph exclaimed. "I can't believe anyone would pack up and leave," she snapped her fingers, "just like that…and leave a child behind. Doesn't seem like much of a mother."

"While we dated, whenever I would stop to bring a meal or to visit, Natalia would run and hide in her room. Mitch tried to talk her out of her room, but she wouldn't budge. It was so sad to see both of them pining away. I even brought Becca with me hoping she could get Natalia to come out of her shell." Azalea sighed. "I didn't know how to handle it anymore, so I told him it wasn't going to work between us. I want you to know in case anyone ever mentions anything to you about it."

Steph shook her head sadly. "I am so sorry to hear about Mitch. I had no idea what's been going on in his life. It's worse than mine these past few years. Do you know if he heard anything from Susan since she left?"

"Mitch never said anything to me about it," she shrugged her shoulders. A flush crept across her cheeks while she continued, "I've been afraid to ask. I considered it none of my business once we broke up. He's never sought me out with any more information. All I've been able to do is pray for him. I truly care for him as a friend, and I know he needs God more than ever right now. I'm just not sure how to approach him on it. If you noticed, he's working on a Sunday, too. As sheriff he really doesn't have to schedule himself to work."

Maybe it would be better not to have dinner with Mitch. I don't need any more distractions in my life at the moment either.

Her relationship with her ex, still fresh in her mind, wounded her soul. A therapist friend said she should dig into a new work project, but stay away from any type of involvement until she healed.

"Give it at least two years," her friend Cynthia said. "It will take that long to heal where you feel you can trust people again. Getting involved too quickly will only lead to the same disaster again."

Was Cynthia right in this respect? Should I stay away from Mitch and his daughter until I feel a little more secure? Her attraction to Mitch took over. *I'm a risk taker. I'll have dinner and see what happens.*

"Instead of working on your house Sunday morning, why don't you attend church with me and Becca?" Azalea suggested, as she interrupted Steph's thoughts. "I would like you to meet our minister and see all the changes in our church."

"Thanks, but no thanks." She shook her head. "Not right now. I'm not in the right place to start going to church again. I've given up on any religion at this point in my life."

"Steph, you know God is always here for us. You just need to call on Him and ask Him back into your life." Azalea laid her hands on top of Steph's folded hands. "Maybe things will change for you soon. I'm not going to give up on you." She sat back and sipped her drink. "I still want you to meet our minister. He's really hot for a minister," she giggled and rolled her eyes.

Steph could not help but smile at Azalea's enthusiasm for her church—and her minister.

"Just not yet," she replied, as she shook her head and set her mouth in an uncompromising line.

Azalea let the subject drop. They decided to get together after church instead, and Azalea and Becca would help Steph move a few things into the house.

Becca carried a heavy picnic basket up the walk to Steph's house after church. The warm weather made it nice enough to

eat outside in the back yard under the oak tree. The remainder
of the afternoon they sanded and painted furniture. The day
became oppressively warm until a slight breeze gave them
some relief as they toiled in the garage with the doors open.

Becca was a miniature of Azalea, and her sweet disposition
drew Steph to her right away. By the time five o'clock rolled
around Steph fell captivated to Becca's girlish charms, and
wished she could be a part of their lives. They laughed and
teased Becca about a new boy in school, and then gave her
advice on teenage boy-girl relationships. The paint splattered
on their clothing to their hands, face, and even a little in their
hair.

"I'm not going to wash my hair, but wear it this way to
make a statement at school." She paraded around with her
hand on her hip.

"You better think twice about that, young lady," her
mother giggled.

Steph needed to clean up before her date with Mitch, so
Azalea and Becca left early enough so she took her time to
shower and scrub off all the paint. She decided to dress
casually in a sleeveless dress and matching shoes.

Mitch arrived promptly at six, and he drove to a new hotel
and restaurant with a view of the river.

"This is one of the prettiest views of the river," she
commented as they sat by the large windows that faced the
river.

"I've never dined here for a private dinner," mentioned
Mitch. "It's only in an official capacity or for a meeting. Their
meeting rooms are just as nice and most face the river."

The waitress brought menus and it surprised her to see the
expensive prices. He noticed the distress in her eyes as he
watched her look at the menu.

"Don't worry about the prices," he assured her. "I don't get to take a lovely lady out too often, so once in a while it's worth it." He smiled.

All the physical work that afternoon made her hungry and she decided to order filet mignon well done. Mitch ordered the same, only rare.

During their leisurely meal, they caught up on their pasts. Steph did not want Mitch to know about her previous depression, but she did hastily explain about her divorce. She figured Mitch would understand. She did not mention his marital situation, but hoped he would share the information freely. His nostrils flared while he stumbled through the story of his divorce and how it devastated him and Natalia.

"It's not as if she just left me, she left our little girl alone without a mother. But I guess she thought drugs and getting high were more important. She refused to go to therapy and we fought all the time. Then she just left," he shrugged his shoulders.

Okay, now is the time to ask him.

She finally burst with curiosity and asked, "Have you heard from her...or know where she is right now?"

He hesitated and clenched his mouth tighter. "Yes, I finally found her." He sighed and flared his nostrils. "She's actually in prison. She got involved with selling and dealing drugs in Minneapolis. I'm glad she's there, and not laying on a slab somewhere." He ran his hand through his hair and pulled on his ear. Steph remembered his flaring nostrils when excited and how he pulled on his ear when upset. "I expected her to overdose or get involved in a bad drug deal and end up dead. Of course, maybe prison is not much better than being dead, but at least I know where she is."

"How many people know this?"

"No one...except for a few close friends," he painfully exclaimed. "It's been difficult for me not being able to tell anyone about her," he stumbled for words, "but for Natalia I think it's the best way to handle it. She's not tried to contact us, so I know she doesn't care about her own daughter." He brushed a corner of one eye, as if wiping a tear away.

"I...I understand...but, Mitch, you need to talk to someone other than me. I can see it's eating you up inside," she sympathized.

"When I ran for sheriff several years ago, I thought for sure I would lose the election if word got out about her whereabouts, but I guess the divorce wasn't an issue and I did win—even though by a slight margin. As for talking to someone, I prefer to have as few people know as possible. I hope you understand where I'm coming from."

"Yes, I do. We all have skeletons in the closet. It's best to lay them to rest."

The evening went by faster than she realized. Mitch wanted to be home early to make sure Natalia went to bed on time. "She always tries to talk the sitter into a later bedtime," he explained.

On the way back from the restaurant, Mitch drove in silence. Steph relished the silence as it gave her time to think about the mind-altering evening where both of them rehashed their personal relationship failures. Small talk did not seem necessary.

Her heart raced when they wandered slowly up the sidewalk to her front door. He turned to face her, put his large hands on her shoulders, and gave her a light kiss on the forehead. She raised her face to him, hungry for something more than a casual peck, but it did not come.

"Let's get together again," he suggested. "I'd like you to

meet my daughter."

"Sure," she nodded. He slowly turned and walked to his car. She felt adrift in a mire of her own making.

Surely, he could have kissed me a little more passionately than a peck on the forehead.

She walked into the house dreaming of possibilities.

CHAPTER SEVEN

The following month went by swiftly for Steph as she continued to work on the high-rise renovation project. With the bidding process over, Todd Reinhold, the architect, and Steph diligently looked over each bid to make sure it followed all the guidelines from the federal government.

After careful consideration, they selected Johnson & Wieber Construction from the Minneapolis area as the low bidder for the majority of the project. Renovations would begin immediately upon approval by the board.

Disappointment showed on Steph's and Todd's faces as they perused through each bid. Cuts needed to be made in the 'wants' part of the project. The renovations needed to be scaled back due to budget restraints.

The board meeting scheduled for early morning, before any of the regular staff arrived at River View Towers, brought the board members in one by one with the exception of the two women who arrived together five minutes after Clarence called the meeting to order. Both Collette and Wendy looked as if they just jumped out of bed with messy hair and dressed in sweats. Both explained they came from the gym. Steph put her hand up to her face to stifle a giggle.

Todd Reinhold attended the board meeting as an observer. Steph, in charge of the bidding process, needed Todd's quiet support.

"I'm sorry but the grant money set aside for River View Towers will not cover the entire renovation costs. We need to settle for the minimum needed to pass federal guidelines. Whatever is left over after the renovations, we can put into our 'wants' bucket."

A few groans sounded from the board. The meeting lasted less than an hour with unanimous approval of all awards.

Clarence, the board chair, adjourned the meeting with a sigh of relief and a final remark. "I'm so glad this is finally coming to fruition. I think I can speak for the entire board: we never thought to see this day. We need to give both Stephanie and Todd a big thank you for their many hours of work to get this done."

The board members nodded in agreement as they rose from their seats to leave the board room. Steph smiled to herself because she could actually see the excitement on their faces.

Donald Hanson lagged behind after the other members of the board left the room.

His voice stammered as he looked at her with raised questioning eyebrows. "Um, Ms. Runnell, I...I would like to hang around when the work actually starts."

"Why would you want to do that, Mr. Hanson?" Steph inquired, her eyes narrowed. "There's no reason for it. In fact, with all my experience with renovations, you'll just get in the way."

Oh, Steph, why did you have to be so blunt and put your foot in your mouth?

He insisted. "I think it would be in the best interests of the City of River Falls to have someone on the board present during the renovations."

From the short distance where she stood facing him, she could smell the liquor on his breath. His lips closed in a tight line, and the veins in his forehead bulged.

He might actually injure himself at the jobsite if he showed up intoxicated, and he'll be a hindrance. Not that it would happen, but it is still my responsibility to see all the safety requirements are followed and progress continues smoothly. I also need to fix it with this board member.

"But…" An idea came to her, and she needed to act before he lost his temper. "How about if you come by periodically to check on the progress?" she spoke in a soothing, placating voice. "I don't think the contractor would mind if you did. With my experience, the contractors want as little interference as possible." She hoped it would ease his mind.

She breathed a sigh of relief when he agreed to only come by periodically.

Now another thing to try and monitor. Maybe we could agree on certain days and times, so I can accompany him and make sure he wears a hardhat.

"How about Tuesdays and Thursdays between nine and ten in the morning?" she suggested, and held her breath as she waited for an answer.

After he thought about it for a minute, he agreed. She bit her lips to keep from smiling and said goodbye before he asked for any more considerations.

After the meeting, to make the process more efficient, Steph decided to call the general contractor and schedule a start date for as soon as possible.

Arnold Johnson, the owner of Johnson & Wieber Construction, appeared very receptive to her suggestion to hire some of the local contractors as subcontractors. He already contacted several of them during the bidding process and would hire them if she agreed. Steph, satisfied Johnson and Wieber would work well within the community, promised to send him an acceptance letter the same day.

She then called a staff meeting and gave them the news of the awards.

After she explained to them what happened during the board meeting and the bids accepted, she continued to discuss what she expected from them.

"I also want to make you aware after the bids were opened we needed to cut certain items off the bid list, so not all renovations can be completed," she explained. She expected some dispute from them. No one said anything. It was so quiet in the room you could hear a pin drop.

"There will be contractors here next week," she looked at each employee individually. "I expect all of you to give them the courtesy and any help they need. The first thing replaced will be the heating system and then the new air conditioning system. It should not affect us except for a shutdown of air conditioning for a day or two while they replace the old 'chiller' system. The current boiler system is huge and this new system will be more compact. It will take less than half the space of the old system. However, they will need to remove the old boiler system piece-by-piece to get it out of the lower level."

Darrin's eyes glowed with eagerness. "I look forward to a new heating and air conditioning system."

"I know it will be hot in here on those days. Since it is still the beginning of summer I advise we work shorter days while the transfer is made. You can make up the hours once the system is up and running again."

She looked around the room for agreement. Both Karen and Callie nodded their heads. Darrin and Derek looked at them and then at each other. Even though they were completely opposite in age and stature, they seemed to complement each other and know each other's thoughts.

"If you don't mind, Ms. Runnell, both Derek and me would like to stay around and watch the entire installation of the system since we'll be workin' with it afterwards," suggested Darrin.

Steph's jaw dropped open at his announcement. He had been so hesitant to allow anyone in the basement boiler room. Now he actually sounded happy.

"Absolutely. I'm glad to see you take the upper hand to learn the new system."

"How about notice to the residents with the work schedule?" questioned Karen.

"Good idea!" Steph agreed. "Why don't you get notices out to the residents? When the boilers are removed and replaced, they will have the inconvenience of no hot water for a short time period…and also the noise when they tear apart the old boilers. The air conditioning is for the main floor, but they can change that out within a few days." She added, "Make sure and advise them to stay away from any of the construction areas. It will be hard-hat areas only. You might even suggest they stay in their apartments where most of them do have their own air conditioning units."

"I will take care of it," Callie interjected. Karen looked at her quizzically, and wondered why she interfered when Steph gave the direction to her and not Callie.

Steph did not want to cause any dissension between the two women. "Karen can work on the notices, and Callie, you'll make sure they get delivered to all the residents?"

By the scowling look Karen gave Callie, Steph knew Karen was upset.

Since none of the other employees had anything else to add, she adjourned the meeting.

Steph spent so much time the past month at work, and she wanted some quiet time at home. Mitch met her several times for lunch in the past month, but she also refused several dinner dates with him.

I think I'll give Mitch a call, and see if we can arrange a nice quiet dinner. I'd also like to meet his daughter. Maybe I'll offer to pick him up this time, and disguise this as a celebratory dinner, and pick up the tab. After all, this is the age of women's lib.

After the employees left for the day, Steph remained behind to answer some emails. Her dinner date with Mitch was at seven, so she had time to drive home and take a shower.

She stood in the front office by the counter ready to lock the office doors when a soft knock sounded on the door. A middle-aged man dressed in faded blue jeans and red T-shirt entered. The tight t-shirt, embellished with words 'Team Jesus' in large white letters, accentuated his biceps and tight chest muscles.

"I'm looking for a Ms. Runnell?" he explained politely and gave her a wide grin.

"Yes, I'm her," she responded, entranced by his dark, almost black eyes.

I wonder if he's here to apply for a job or an apartment.

He stepped closer to the counter, and she could smell his earthy aftershave.

"I just wanted to introduce myself," he extended his hand over the counter. "I'm Reverend Rafael McGowan from the River Falls Christian Church." He smiled, and his teeth gleamed white, in contrast with his tanned skin. "Azalea Rose asked that I stop by when visiting some of your residents here. I noticed the office light on and decided to take a chance."

"Oh," the only response Steph could give. His eyes mesmerized her, so dark and kind of squinted when he smiled.

An Irish last name, yet his skin's darker.

"You certainly don't look like a reverend."

I actually said that!

Embarrassed, she covered her mouth with her hand instead of shaking his hand. "I'm so sorry. I shouldn't have said that," she swallowed and cleared her throat. "I've heard a lot about you from Azalea, but I expected someone who looked like a super hero in minister's garb, and not dressed in blue jeans and a T-shirt."

He glanced down at the clothes he wore and then back at her. "I work with a very diverse congregation, and they feel intimidated if I dress in a suit and tie or even in clerical clothes," he shrugged his shoulders, "so I choose to dress for the people I serve."

Steph could now understand why Azalea was so mesmerized by this man. He eluded masculinity in his own way.

"Ahh... You still don't look the reverend type to me," she felt like biting her tongue.

Again, foot in mouth. What a stupid thing to say!

She could not take her gaze away from his eyes.

"My mother's Hispanic and my dad's Irish and German, so

you could say I'm a mutt." He laughed and a dimple popped in his chin and made him look more striking. He did not seem offended by her remark.

Now that he mentioned his nationality, she definitely saw the Hispanic ancestry. The combination of nationalities made him quite handsome. He did not have the short rounded nose of a typical Hispanic, but a narrower aquiline nose, and his short coal-black hair curled where it grew out on his neck. His well-built muscular frame did not portray what Steph thought a minister should look like. The longer she looked at him, the more he intrigued her. His eyes evenly met hers.

Azalea never mentioned if he was married.

"How can I help you?" she nervously twirled the office keys in her hand to keep her mind off his eyes.

He noticed her uneasy action with the keys. "I wanted to stop in and introduce myself. Like I said, I visit some of the residents here who don't get out very much. I also wanted to invite you to attend church service if you have a Sunday open soon."

"Well, thank you very much for the offer, but I'm not ready to attend a church anytime soon," she replied, regretful she did not feel the urge to attend his church—or any church.

"You're welcome anytime," he answered, not offended at all by her rebuff.

I'm sure he's used to being turned down when inviting people to his church. I bet anything Azalea told him about my aversion for any church right now.

"Thank you. May I take a raincheck?"

"Anytime you're ready, I will be there," he said, still smiling. "Nice meeting you."

He extended his hand again. This time she reached across the narrow counter to shake his hand. Heat and a slight tingle went through her body as their hands touched. She did not want to let go and held the handshake a bit too long while their eyes met across the counter.

There is no way I could be attracted to a minister, of all people, but his hand is so gentle, almost caressing.

As he removed his hand, she noticed a slight blush on his face.

Okay, it affected him, too.

As he left the office, he turned toward the closed door, and she could see through the window that he smiled to himself.

Steph waited until he left the building and then locked the door.

CHAPTER EIGHT

Since this was to be a celebratory dinner, she dressed in a black-and-white striped, simple sheath dress that hugged her figure. A white clunky necklace with matching earrings and white high heeled sandals completed her outfit.

Time to get out the white shoes.

She drove over to Mitch's house, about a mile away.

This car lease is too expensive. Maybe this would be a good time to ask Mitch to help me pick out a nice used car.

She knocked and a young girl around ten years old answered the door. Her hair was dark brown, not black like her dad's, but her azure eyes matched her father's.

He couldn't deny this one.

The young girl smiled shyly.

"You must be Stephanie, my dad's friend," she opened the door wider. "My dad's in the back by the grill cooking some steaks. My name's Natalia."

"Yes, I am an old friend, and it's nice to meet you, Natalia," responded Steph. "Why is your dad by the grill? I offered to take him out to dinner tonight."

Mitch walked through the patio door dressed in shorts and sandals and over his t-shirt he wore an apron with "Beware of the Cook" on the front.

"Hi," his eyes lit up as he smiled and then looked at his daughter. "I see you've met Natalia. We just thought it might be fun for you to come over for a nice quiet barbeque. I hope you don't mind." His eyes rested on her dressed-up appearance. "I know you're dressed for something fancier, but hardly anyone dresses up anymore around here during the summer."

"No, I certainly don't mind. It's been a hectic day and winding down with two nice people would be just fine with me." She grinned at the family of two. An emptiness filled her chest.

This could have been my family.

She removed her heels and followed both of them to the backyard where Mitch already set places for three on the patio.

"Besides," he added, "I couldn't find a sitter for Natalia tonight, so instead of breaking our date I thought this would be much better."

"It's great!" she readily agreed. "I wondered when I would meet your daughter."

"She's a great kid. It was rather rough going when her mother left, but we're surviving quite nicely now. I certainly don't look forward to the teen years though."

Steph laughed. "Yes, I can still remember my teen years. I don't envy you."

"How do you like your steaks?"

"Well done. Can I help?" she offered.

"Nothing at the moment. Just keep me company. Natalia is putting the dressing on the salad. We went to the market and purchased ice cream and all the fixings for sundaes–her idea for the dessert."

Mitch turned out to be an excellent chef. Steph helped clear the patio table and put the dishes in the dishwasher.

"Daddy, I promised the boys I would come to the park and play softball tonight. Can I go now?" Natalia pleaded as they put the last dish in the dishwasher.

"Okay." He threw up his arms in defeat and gave her a hug. "Just make sure you are home before dark…which isn't very long."

"The ball game's already started, so I'll be home as soon as it's over." She grabbed her baseball cap and plopped it on her head. "I'm their best hitter, and they weren't happy when I told them I couldn't come earlier."

"Natalia," he frowned, "you know we talked about this earlier. I don't like you being out at night. The park is only two blocks away, but you make sure you're back as soon as the game is over."

"All…right…Dad!" she pouted, and stomped her feet in her sneakers as she walked over to pick up her baseball mitt and bat from the hall closet.

"I think she should have been a boy," Mitch responded shaking his head as she went out the door. "She loves baseball in the summer, and last fall I caught her playing football with the neighbor boys."

Steph smiled. "Sounds like she's a regular tomboy. Remember when I used to follow you and Aaron around?"

"Yeah, you were a pain in the butt if I remember correctly," he teased. "I purchased a bottle of wine to celebrate the milestone of getting the board to agree on a contractor. I'll pour us each a glass and then give me all the details."

Steph explained how eagerly the board approved the

contracts, and how Mr. Hanson wanted to immerse himself into the project.

"Things aren't going to go well if the board members think they can start to follow the contractors around," she stated emphatically. "I don't normally work with the board members. My ex-husband always kept them away so the work could proceed normally. I'll probably get a little cranky if any of them try to interfere."

"Well, I remember Hanson as a cop with the city. He always tried to push his weight around, and bullied people, both town folks and other officers." He stopped and scratched his head and continued, "I never had any trouble with him because I started with the sheriff's department and not the police department. Being a hometown boy and a lot bigger, he kinda left me alone. After the retirement of the police chief and sheriff within the same year, the city council and county commissioners decided to combine the two departments because of budget restraints. Instead of the police and sheriff's departments, we now call it the Law Enforcement Center. He retired shortly after the election, so I didn't have of a chance to interact with him."

"So he actually was a police officer and then a deputy."

"Yep," he replied, and tipped his head back to drain his glass of wine. He refilled both their glasses even though she drank only half her wine.

"I'm concerned about him being intoxicated while on the site. Every time I've been around him I smell liquor," she confessed. "I also don't like the idea that he carries a gun when he drinks."

"If he gives you any trouble, give us a call. We'll escort him off the premises."

"I hope I don't have to do that, but thanks for the offer."

She let out a sigh of relief. "As long as we're talking about renovations, do you remember hearing about any problems when they built the high rise?"

"Yeah...I do remember my dad talking about the Mexican workers and the local men getting into fights. I heard a bunch of them ran off most of the Mexican workers one night. Hearsay is they chased them all over the county, and a bunch of them got fed up and moved on. They hired more local workers after that. I remember both our dads saying they got hired even though they were still in high school just to get the job completed."

"I remember Dad said it helped him pay his college tuition the next year."

She lifted up her glass of wine to get the last remaining drops and then set the glass down, stretched her body, and let out a yawn. "I've got another busy day tomorrow, so I need to get to bed early." She stood to leave. "Thanks so much for the delicious steaks. This was much more relaxing than going to a restaurant."

"You're welcome." He walked her to the door and then to the car.

"Say, when are you going to get your own car?" He looked at her vehicle. "It's expensive to keep up a lease."

"I negotiated a three-month lease, but it's almost up. I can go month-to-month after that if needed. Would you be able to help me pick out a nice used one?" She raised her eyebrows and gave him a helpless girl smile.

"Sure. Any time. Just call."

Steph felt awkward but wanted him to kiss her goodnight. She dreamed of how his kisses would feel, but until this point in their relationship it was always a peck on the cheek.

He pulled her in his arms, lifted her chin with his thumb,

and lowered his head to give her the kiss she waited for when they heard a little voice coming in the back door.

"Hi, I'm home, Dad. Did you hear me … Dad? I'm home." That seemed to break the spell. He gave Steph a hug and a kiss on the forehead and said "Goodnight," and "We'll pick this up later."

It gave her at least some encouragement as she drove home.

CHAPTER NINE

The following week the crew from Johnson & Wieber arrived from Minneapolis with the new boilers and air conditioning units. The tear down of the old system began immediately. Everyone heard banging and hammering throughout the building as men worked relentlessly to remove the old system and install the new one.

Mr. Johnson, the general contractor, stayed on site to oversee the project. Darrin and Derek hovered near the boiler room as the men worked. They watched and asked questions during the entire process. Steph periodically checked on the progress and shook her head at the two.

They are like two boys in a candy shop.

The new above-ground piping and equipment were set in place when Mr. Johnson walked into the office late in the week. He took off his hat and started to roll it in his hands.

"Um...there is a small problem...with the boiler system," he started to explain to Steph. "We're unable to get sufficient pressure for enough steam to get full use of the system. I think we might have an underground leak." He nervously stroked his chin. "We'll need to dig up the old piping in the concrete and replace it."

"Well, that doesn't surprise me," she said as she wrinkled up her nose. "I expected a problem, but hoped it wouldn't happen this soon."

"We'll get busy and start on the floor tomorrow. I need to rent a big enough jackhammer to dig up the concrete. You know...this wasn't...um, in my bid...to dig up the floor." He stammered. "But...I'll do my best...to keep the cost down."

"I appreciate that," replied Steph as she rubbed her temples.

Well, I can start re-working the budget.

The next morning the rat-a-tat-tat of the jackhammer echoed throughout the building. Even though the residents knew the contractors would be using jackhammers, they still came down to the office to complain. The office staff headed off the complaints. Steph felt more relaxed and was able to go through the bids to see where they could cut more expenses.

Shortly after lunch, Steph left her office door open to get air circulating. The main door slammed as Derek ran into her office. Out of breath, his eyes wild and terrified.

"Ms. Runnell...come with me now!" he shouted in between trying to catch his breath. "We need you in the boiler room!" He stood in front of her desk, his body shook from the adrenalin.

"Calm down, Derek. What's the problem?"

"You gotta come see what they found diggin' up the floor," he ran his fingers through his hair, agitated by her calm demeanor.

Instead of taking the elevator to the lower level, Steph followed him down the one flight of stairs to the boiler room area. Darrin and several workers were gathered at the jackhammer site. All work stopped.

The boiler room was not well lit, and there were only a few shop lights throughout the huge room. The crew hung portable quartz lights pointed toward the digging site. The jackhammer produced a floating haze of dirt that permeated the atmosphere. It reminded her of a scene from a horror movie. All the men wore face masks to cover their mouths and noses, and she clasped her hand over her nose and mouth to keep from breathing in the dirt.

The men started to jackhammer at one end of the boiler room going down at least eighteen inches to two feet below the cement floor. Pieces of cement laid on one side of the trench and sand and dirt on the other. The old pipe had been cut out to the middle of the room. Dread stuck in her heart as she moved closer to where the men stood.

"What's the problem?" quizzed Steph through her covered mouth. The men moved back, and she stepped up to the edge next to Darrin, and looked down at one of the workers in the trench. Steph followed his gaze.

Her mouth dropped open, and she could feel the blood drain from her face. She gasped, and her hand flew to her chest.

Chunks of bone laid in the trench uncovered. The man who operated the jackhammer reached down into the hole and in the loosened dirt pulled up a skull. He started to brush the dirt away from the eye sockets.

"This is what we found," his hand shook. "I think there's more than one body in this trench."

"Don't touch anything else!" Steph nervously raised her

voice. "Darrin, call the sheriff. Tell him to come here immediately...but no sirens. Make sure it's the sheriff you talk to and no one else."

He rushed out anxious to leave the boiler room.

Steph turned to Derek, who stood close to the door. "Please make sure nothing else is touched until the sheriff arrives."

Derek inched closer to the trench in short, jerky movements. Steph noticed the perspiration on his face as he rubbed the back of his neck. Steph left to wait for Mitch.

Mitch arrived within minutes of the phone call. Steph met him outside the main entrance to the high rise. She explained what the workers found, and asked him to keep everything quiet until they could figure out what was going on.

"I can't guarantee that, Steph," he stated, anxious to see the possible crime scene.

"But...this can't be good," Steph sniffed. "This can't be good!" she repeated, as she shook her head in nervous tension.

"Calm down!" he whispered as he held her by the shoulders. "Let's take a look. This is a potential crime scene, Steph. A possible homicide. We need to take precautions." He paused and pulled on his ear, a now familiar nervous gesture. "I need to involve the county coroner. It's almost impossible to keep this hushed in this small town."

She knew he was right, but in her heart she dreaded what all the publicity would bring to the agency.

"I know... I know," she nodded her head in agreement. He followed her down the stairs to the boiler room. The men continued to lean against their shovels, and stare into the trench. Since the jackhammering subsided some particles of dust still floated in the air, though not as much as when she first entered the room. It did not look or feel as creepy as it did a few minutes before.

The sheriff did not want to touch any of the evidence, and did not want any of the workers to disturb anymore of the remains.

He requested Darrin and Derek stand by the door to the boiler room until he could get additional officers to secure the room. Mitch and Steph then walked up the flight of stairs to the main floor.

There was no cell phone service in the lower level of the building so Mitch called the coroner from her office. The minutes ticked by as they waited for him to arrive from the hospital where he worked as an emergency room physician. Steph tried to keep busy with paperwork already on her desk, but could not concentrate; while Mitch made phone calls to his office and gave orders to secure the area.

It seemed like hours, but actually less than a half hour, when the coroner arrived. Mitch noticed his arrival from the office window and walked out to greet Dr. Sanderson. While Mitch informed the doctor of the situation, Steph filled in the office staff on what the workers found.

Mitch walked in the building with Dr. Sanderson, a short balding man in his sixties with thick glasses. He looked familiar to Steph.

"Doctor Sanderson, this is Stephanie Runnell, the new director for the housing agency."

"Ahh...I remember Stephanie as a child. Wasn't it Thomas? I remember your parents. I was a new doctor in town when I first met them and their lovely children."

"Well, yes, it was Thomas," she responded, surprised he would remember her after all these years.

Dr. Sanderson turned to the sheriff. "Okay, Mitch, let's see what you got!"

A deputy already secured the boiler room door. Another deputy inside the boiler room kept an eye on the workers who stood quietly in a corner. The coroner asked everyone else to leave the room except for Mitch and Steph. Before they vacated the room Mitch reminded each person they needed to make a statement for the case record.

The doctor's deep authoritative voice echoed throughout the boiler room now that everyone else vacated it. "So sorry about this distressful situation, Mrs. Runnell."

"I am too, Doctor," she replied. "Also, it's Ms. Runnell... not Mrs."

What a stupid thing to say.

Steph's face reddened with embarrassment.

"Hum...," he replied as he knelt on one knee to examine the skull one of the men pulled from the trench and laid on top of the dirt piled on the cement floor. He opened his medical bag to take out a magnifying glass. He briefly examined the skull and then laid it back on the dirt pile.

"We'll need to have a few deputies help dig up what remains we can find. We'll have to reassemble what we can at one of the mortuaries in town. We don't have the facilities here in the county to handle this sort of crime. I'll have to call in the state officials for help on this," he stated emphatically. "This may take a few days to get everything dug up." His gaze circled the room and then the length of the trench. "We'll have to jackhammer some more of the floor to see if there are any more bodies."

"Oh, no!" anguished Steph. "This can't be happening!" She put her fingers to her temples and started to massage on both sides. The stress headache that started to form would leave her unable to think straight if it got any worse. After less than a minute, she gained control again as both men waited patiently for an answer. "We will cooperate as best we can, but I need to continue with the renovations."

"Everything down here will have to stop for now," the coroner gruffly retorted as he looked at Mitch for cooperation. "We're short-handed at the ER right now. I'm very limited on the time I can spend on this case," he continued to explain, as he wiped his brow with a white handkerchief he drew out of his pocket.

The dust continued to settle and delicately cover everything. Steph could feel the damp grime from the dirt on her skin, and it made her want to go home and wash away the nastiness of the find. She never covered her mouth when she re-entered the room and now the feel of fine sand played on her lips. She shivered and turned her back to the trench.

"We'll do whatever needs to be done to assist you," agreed Mitch. He needed to go back to the main level to use his cell phone to call in more officers. Several off-duty deputies were called to bring picks and shovels to the high rise for a digging operation, and a deputy was requested to stand guard throughout the day and night. After he completed that task, he left to question the workers as witnesses.

Mr. Johnson, the contractor, cooperated and allowed his men to jackhammer the cement floor as long as an officer and the coroner stayed on site to oversee the operation. Dr. Sanderson watched over the operation and treated each body part with kid gloves trying to keep as much intact as possible.

However, after several days of careful digging, and no more skeletal remains found, the coroner put a stop to the intricate excavation. The contractor replaced the pipe, but did not cover the excavation area yet.

The remains had been delivered to the River Falls Funeral Home where Dr. Sanderson reassembled the body parts in order to see what could be missing, and if they needed to continue to excavate the area where the original remains were found.

Through his best examination, he concluded there were only two bodies buried in the basement of the high rise. The remains pieced together and the bone density analyzed, the coroner indicated both bodies had been young males, probably in their twenties. One had a bullet hole in the left scapula. The workers found the fragments of a bullet in the pit. One of the workers said it looked like buckshot from a shotgun. The coroner did not find any other bullet holes, but did find some broken bones among the remains. He was unsure if the broken bones were due to the excavation or if there was other trauma involved. The exact cause of death could not be determined because the coroner did not have the equipment or the expertise to continue with the case.

Dr. Sanderson made arrangements with the Law Enforcement Center to have the skeletal remains shipped to the Bureau of Criminal Apprehension in St. Paul, or BCA as he called it. A few remaining pieces of clothing, still intact, parts of blue jeans, a red t-shirt, and a necklace with a cross found in the trench were sent for testing. He did his best diligence on the case, but he wondered who else knew of this secret in River View Towers?

There was no mistaking the time of death for these two unfortunate individuals. Everyone knew it had to be during the initial construction of the building back in the early 1970s. Dr. Sanderson did not have the forensic experience to involve himself further in the case and sighed with relief when the sheriff finally removed the remains from the funeral home. Each body was wrapped in separate body bags and put in a squad car to be delivered to the BCA Forensic Lab.

CHAPTER TEN

Over the next week Lola called Reverend McGowan to come by every day to comfort the residents who felt disturbed by the entire scenario. He prayed with them in his soothing voice and talked gently to gain their confidence and wash away their fears with passages from the Bible.

During this time Lola suggested to the residents who met for prayer that they start a Bible study group. They wanted to hear more about the Word and agreed to meet every day during the week for a short prayer meeting and then a Bible reading.

"Reverend," began Lola, "you've been an inspiration to us over this past week. Won't you please consider guiding us through this stressful time and teach us more about the Bible?" All eyes focused on the reverend as he sat there, mouth opened, and did not know what to say to the flattery the residents handed out.

"I'm humbled that you want me to lead your new group, but I wouldn't be able to do it on a day-to-day basis. There would be emergencies, meetings, and others from my congregation that need my attention. I'll certainly do what I can to help. There's a book by Max Lucado that gives a daily devotion and Bible passage to read. You can start with that, and if I can't be here, it will get you started for the day."

They all clapped and cheered.

"Let's bow our heads and pray," he suggested.

The coroner could not officially release any information about the two remains, so the residents prayed for the sheriff and the forensic team to put a name to the bodies, so the families, if any, would find closure.

"Before I leave I want to emphasize that you need to use God as your refuge and strength. Don't rely solely on me for your support."

Steph watched from outside the dining room as Reverend McGowan prayed with the residents and later talked with each of them. He turned and looked at her several times. When their eyes met, she could see the compassion he felt for his followers. She observed the residents hung on his every word. She looked forward to his daily visits as a welcome distraction.

Miss Mattie Turnborn and her sister, Maude, were present every day for prayer. Miss Mattie sat and nervously wrung her hands. Each day the reverend would take her aside and listen intently in an attempt to comfort her.

Steph never believed herself to be a detective, but she found Miss Mattie's reaction disturbing, and tried to piece together why Miss Mattie would be so upset.

She heard rumors of Miss Mattie's engagement many years ago and her fiancé disappearance one night. He never returned.

Could it be that one of the remains belonged Miss Mattie's fiancé?

Steph's thoughts jumped around as she continued to run questions through her mind.

Why would Miss Mattie and her sister live in low-income housing when I'm sure they could well afford to live a more comfortable life? Some things just don't make any sense.

Steph stood by the community room door when Reverend McGowan walked by on his way out. His head was down and eyes focused on the floor.

"Thank you so much for coming here the last few days." He jumped and turned, and almost dropped his Bible. Her lips curved in a slight grin. "You've been a good influence during this situation."

He noticed the dark circles under her eyes. His mouth went dry and nothing came out. "You...are...welcome," he finally replied and grinned.

There's that dimple again.

"A minister with nothing more to say," she laughed.

"Could you take a few minutes for a cup of coffee?" he proposed. "You look like you need a break."

"I sure do."

"Let me treat you to coffee and pie at The Nest," he put his hand behind her back to lead her away from the dining room. The heat of his hand burned into her back, and she felt a warm glow through her body.

She was thankful for the small reprieve from local reporters and the Twin Cities newspapers. Plus, television reporters from all sorts of networks still attempted to get a story. She said nothing, as she knew nothing at this point, but they continued to be relentless. She referred everything to the Law Enforcement Center. Still, they hovered around the building like vultures.

"We have the whole place to ourselves," he commented as

they entered the restaurant.

I need to remind myself that even in t-shirt and jeans he is still a minister.

The waitress walked over to take their order. Steph noticed she kept her eyes on the reverend while she took their order.

"Thank you. I guess I really needed to get out of there—away from the reporters. I can't seem to get any work done as phone calls come in constantly and the television reporters are camped outside on the street waiting for answers." She took a deep breath and sighed.

"It's taking its toll on everyone. Even the residents are frightened, but I've tried to assure them with prayer that everything will be all right. They are all making guesses, which actually makes everything worse for them."

Their order of pie and coffee arrived. Steph at first didn't feel like she could eat anything, but the coconut crème pie looked so delicious she ran her tongue over her lips.

"Again, I appreciate you counseling everyone who wants help even though it's only with prayer. Do you feel prayer will give them the answers they need?" She hesitated and did not want to offend him. He offered his services to the residents, and it meant the staff did not have to act as counselors. "I mean, I haven't had much luck with prayer. My life has been in a shambles for over a year, and prayer never helped me."

"Do you believe in God?" he asked.

I don't know if I can answer that question. What can I say to him?

She glanced up and surveyed him for a brief second before she decided to answer him as truthful as she could at that time.

"I thought I did, but with all the unhealthy things going on in my life I just gave up. At first, when I went through my divorce I kept my faith, but then the depression set in. It pulled me down to where I couldn't function," she confessed. "Life became a bitter part of me until I couldn't dig myself out. That's one of the reasons I came back to River Falls. I grew up here with my parents and a brother. Life was good then," she explained, smiling as memories of her childhood came flooding back.

"Where are your parents now?"

"Retired and living in Texas," she replied, taking a sip of the rich aromatic coffee.

"Your brother?"

Her hand shook with that question and she set her coffee down. "My brother died in a car accident outside of town when I was a teenager," she sniffed, tears starting to fill her eyes as she remembered the day so clearly.

"I am so sorry for your loss," he sympathized, and reached for her hand on the table. "It seems like a lot of joy and happiness have been taken from you. But again, I ask if you believe in God."

She hesitated and then stammered, "I was brought up to believe there is a higher power called God. But I'm not sure I believe in God. Not that it's done me a lot of good as you can see by my past life. I always feel as though He's out of reach for me."

"God is never out of reach." Her gaze centered on the lights over Reverend Rafael's head as he continued to talk. "When you feel God is far away, He is actually the closest to you. You just need to realize that God gave you the gift of joy. In the book of James it says 'Consider it pure joy, my brothers, whenever you face trials of many kinds, because you know that the testing of your faith develops perseverance.'"

"So what you're telling me is when bad things happen to me that I should consider it as a joyful gift from God?"

"Well, no and yes."

"What do you mean—no and yes?" she quizzed him. "That's really a double standard."

"God can give you trials to test your faith in Him. Look at the Apostle Paul. Despite his circumstances being under house arrest and chained to a Roman guard, he wrote passionate letters to the church at Philippi and expressed his joy in Christ. Half our lessons on increasing our joy are written by Paul, who was constantly persecuted."

"I guess I never looked at the Bible that way before." She raised her coffee cup toward the reverend as in a toast, "Well, here's to trying to find joy in my life again."

At least he made me feel better about myself. Maybe I need to reassess my outlook on life and find peace within myself again. It would be wonderful to feel peace and joy again.

"My life hasn't always been a bed of roses either, but I put my faith in God no matter how bad it gets. I thank God every time a road block is set before me. It challenges me to keep my faith strong. So don't give up."

He sipped his coffee and dug into his piece of pie.

"So what is your story?' she finally inquired.

His almost black eyes glanced at her apprehensively. "Both my parents were Catholic, so when I decided to become a minister, but didn't want to be a priest, my family was quite upset with me. I grew up as a military brat. My mother and dad met in Texas, and I grew up living in all parts of the country. My mom was an illegal immigrant and became a citizen after they married." He paused in his story.

"So, how is that a sad story?" she interjected, and wanted him to continue.

He lowered his voice in a mysterious manner, and continued, "Not too many people know my story, so I would appreciate it if you would not tell anyone why I'm here in this part of the country."

Curious now, she agreed.

"Like I said before, I grew up as a military brat," he continued after a tiny pause, "but my mom had relatives from all over, including Mexico. Her family traveled together as migrant workers working the peach crops and picking grapes for the wineries. She remembers as a young child several years of drought down south, and there wasn't much work for the migrants. Her brother and several of his friends decided to head up north to find work. They never heard from them again. The family figured they found work and decided to stay in the United States. The families gradually drifted apart, each going their own way. My mom wanted something better than being a migrant worker, so as she grew up she saved her money, worked hard and long hours, and put herself through college."

"Very commendable of your mother to put herself through college," she replied. "I can imagine how hard it was for her as a minority and an immigrant to get that far." She thought back to when she was one of the few women taking architectural design in college, and how the male students constantly harassed the females.

"Well, I'm really proud of my mom. She got her nursing degree and always found work wherever they stationed Dad."

"I can see you're proud of your mother, but why don't you want others to know about her status?"

"Well...," he hesitated, "when I first arrived in River Falls, I was not welcomed with open arms. The former minister once taught at the bible college I attended. I was hired with only phone interviews, and never asked about my heritage. Because of my last name they hired me without any qualms based on his recommendation."

Steph put her elbows on the table and her hands under her chin as she listened intently to his story.

"When I arrived the older congregation was not happy with my Hispanic background. It took over a year to gain their confidence. Our church is open to everyone, and they eventually accepted the fact we are all children of God whatever nationality or lot in life. A few did leave the congregation at first, but most of them returned. I don't want to rattle any more cages than necessary."

Steph never quite met anyone like Reverend McGowan before. She liked him immediately. Now she felt she liked him even more. He was kindness and goodness all rolled into one person. Steph, puzzled why he confided in her, did not know how to comment back to him. Looking into his eyes tongue-tied her. She needed to think of something to say—and fast—without getting gushy and thus sound ineffective.

Her throat constricted as if she just ate a piece of shoe leather. She felt choked up he would confide in her. "I guess I don't know what to say…except…I respect your privacy in your family affairs, but I'm still curious as to why you want to keep it a secret…and why you confided in me?"

"Not really a secret," he stated. "Just quiet for now. My mom wanted to start a family tree. She got me started on family ancestry since ours is so diverse, and I got hooked on it. In my spare time I do research for both sides of the family. Since I live in Minnesota, I take time off to travel to different towns to search for my uncle. My grandma lost the last letters received from him, but she remembered he wrote from Minnesota. It's surprising how many Hispanics live here. So far—no luck, but I'm still researching, and hope to find him or someone who would know where he is now."

"All my roots have been here for generations. That's one

of the reasons I came back, but no one is left. It just doesn't feel the same anymore."

I'd like to tell him about Mitch, but it's not the right time or place. Even Mitch changed, and his feelings were up for grabs. At least Azalea welcomed her back as a friend.

He smiled and put his hand over hers. "We all have our demons, but will all eventually find our place in the world. If this isn't your place to settle you'll know it in time. Just give it time and give your time up to God and ask for His help."

"Thank you so much, Reverend McGowan. I appreciate the chat even though I didn't think I needed it," she remarked. Her eyes sparkled for the first time since her divorce with hope there might be some bright promises ahead for her. She could not wait to get home to call Azalea and tell her about their visit.

"Why don't you call me Rafael or even Rafe? Most of my parishioners call me Reverend Rafe. Please feel free to call me by my first name."

"Thank you again, for the friendly conversation" she said, grateful for the time he spent with her. "Please call me Stephanie or better yet…Steph. I would really appreciate it." She reached across a vacant chair for her purse.

He enjoyed their conversation and wanted more. "Tell me, Steph, how did you get your experience with renovations?"

"My father. I always tagged along with him in his construction business. He taught me how to read blueprints and construction codes. Math's my favorite subject, so as a teenager I started to figure his bids. It only seemed right to take up architecture and drafting in college."

"I heard you and your ex-husband ran a business together."

Every time Larry's name came up, it felt like bile in her throat. "Yes," she swallowed, "but that's not the case anymore.

He deserted me and left me with very little. I find it hard to talk about it."

He hit a sore spot and knew it. "Again, I am so sorry." She nodded, and accepted his apology.

Steph decided she did not want to talk any more about her former marriage. She reached in her purse to take out money to pay for the coffee, but he shook his head and grabbed the ticket. They parted at the restaurant door with Rafael headed toward his church while Steph walked back to the high rise.

CHAPTER ELEVEN

Since the restaurant was less than six blocks from the high rise, Steph preferred to walk back to work. Rafe offered her a ride back, but it turned out to be a beautiful sun-filled day, and she did not look forward to the unwelcome and stifling atmosphere at the office. Instead of going directly to the front door she decided to cut across the small park located next to the building and started down the narrow asphalt path.

Large trees, planted upon completion of the high rise, stood tall and majestic and shaded most of the park. The benches were empty as she strolled through the winding path shaded by the canopies of the trees. Where the sun peeked through the trees, the flowers planted by the city employees showed their colors. She slowly strolled through the park admiring the colors and reminiscing over her conversation with Reverend Rafe.

As she drew closer to the building she noticed Callie in an argument with an elderly man. Callie pushed him on his shoulders, and he tripped backwards, almost losing his balance. Steph did not recognize him, so did not know if he lived in the building. With everything that happened so quickly after her arrival, she never met all the residents.

The back side of the building gave more privacy with the heavily wooded park, and they did not notice her approach. She found a large tree to stand behind and eavesdrop, but still observe their behavior. She heard a portion of their conversation.

Callie's deep voice radiated into the wooded area. "I don't want you around here. Don't you understand?"

She attempted to move her head around the tree to get a better look at the man without being too obvious. He looked to be in his late sixties or early seventies—short and thin as a rail. His stooped figure made him look only slightly taller than Callie. His hands in his pockets and head lowered, Callie continued to scold him. She could barely hear him speak, but he did raise his voice once. "I only wanted to know what was going on, and what the cops found out."

"No one knows, old man," she gruffly replied as she shook her finger at him. "Now I'm telling you to get out of here before anyone else see you."

She turned toward the front of the building, stormed angrily away and entered the complex. He stood there a moment, then turned away as if to follow, stopped, shrugged his shoulders and staggered to the side street to an old dilapidated pickup and drove off.

Steph looked around to make sure no one saw her come out from behind the tree and head toward the office. 'Old man' Callie called him. She wondered if Callie had more family here. She never talked about anyone except a husband and a son. Her antisocial attitude never changed from the moment Steph arrived. What Steph gathered from others, her marriage was not happy. Instead of divorce, they each decided to go their own way, but still live in the same house.

Her son remained unemployed and did not seem ambitious enough to look for work. Steph's believed he used his mother as a pocketbook. She overheard their heated conversations several times when he stopped by to demand money from Callie. The last time Steph heard their angry voices, she stepped out of her office and glared at him. He gave her an embarrassed look as if he got caught with his hand in the cookie jar, turned around, and left without another comment.

Callie turned away from Steph, and started to fiddle with her computer. She refused to apologize or say anything about his attitude.

This irritated Steph, and she folded her hands on her hips as if she spoke to a child. "This is a business office, Callie. If your son can't control his temper, he is not welcome here anymore."

Callie just stared at her, pinched her lips together, and continued to say nothing.

She wanted to know more about this man Callie called 'old man' and why he came skulking around the high rise.

Was his visit just curiosity or something else? He looked the age where he could have lived in town during the high rise construction. I wonder if he knew anything or heard any gossip around that time period. Mitch would know.

CHAPTER TWELVE

T en days and not a word from the sheriff about their investigative progress. Under normal circumstances Mitch would meet Steph for lunch several times a week. Since the discovery of the remains, he fell off the face of the earth. Her curiosity peaked, Steph decided to his secretary.

"He's tied up in meetings right now," said Sally. "Can he call you back?"

"Yes, please ask him to call Stephanie Runnell at River View Towers. I'd like to know if there's any progress on the investigation."

Johnson and Wieber finished with the new boiler system and waited for the state inspector to rubber stamp the project. The completion of the new air conditioning units put the work schedule back to normal.

Mitch received her message. He strode into the housing authority office later in the day.

"We are searching through all the records we can find for reported missing persons," he explained to Steph. "With no computers over forty years ago everything is on paper in file boxes stored in the basement of our building. It's going to take time to go through all the records for that year." He paused and started to fiddle with his ear. "It gets more confusing because the city and county departments were separate at that time. Our investigator already put in a lot of his time on the case, but he has other cases to handle besides this one."

When he mentioned missing persons, Steph remained quiet about Miss Mattie and her sister, Maude. She did not know when Miss Mattie became engaged or when her fiancé left, and did not want to stir up a hornet's nest. She decided to bring it up only if she thought it would help the investigation.

She rose from her desk, walked out of her office, and asked Callie to run an errand for a few office supplies. She needed Callie out of the office so she could talk more freely to Mitch. Several times over the past couple weeks Steph noticed Callie outside her office door, eavesdropping on her conversations. She did not feel comfortable with Callie skulking around.

Karen looked up from her desk and raised her eyebrows. Steph winked at her, walked back into her office and closed the door.

"I witnessed something odd over a week ago and wanted to run it by you to hear what you think." She relayed what she saw outside the high rise between Callie and the older man.

"Old Eddie Barkley." Mitch looked at her, his curiosity piqued. "I guess I never thought too much about him. He's been an old drunk for many years and gets thrown in jail periodically to sober up. After a day or so we just let him go. Callie's his only family. His wife left him years ago and moved out of the area." A few moments went by before he spoke again. "He does have a temper though. I think it might be a good idea to question Eddie." He paused again and then leaned forward. "We need to start questioning anyone who lived here around that time."

"This is getting to be more complicated," he continued, and started to rub his ear. "I guess our small department is not equipped to handle all the inquiries. Our office is inundated with phone calls from curiosity seekers, plus the news media. It's occurred to me that one or more of those callers may actually know something."

"Is your staff taking down names of who's called or stopped by?" Steph inquired.

"I'm sure all callers are identified—either by name or caller ID."

"It seems to me, if they're that curious, you may want to find out if they lived here during the time the construction of the high rise."

Steph did not know if she would overstep her boundaries with law enforcement, but she continued, "We even get inquiries here at our office. I've informed the staff to say we know nothing and to call the Law Enforcement Center if they have any questions."

At first she hesitated, then volunteered, "Maybe I should have the calls referred to me. I can get their names and find out if they lived around here during that time."

Mitch stiffened his posture. He knew Steph wanted some answers, but he did not want her involved in the investigation. Their department needed to follow up on any calls. "Thanks for the offer, but I'd rather you direct all the calls to the Law Enforcement Center. That way we can get more of a handle on who's called right away."

He cautiously watched her reaction. Steph took a deep breath and relaxed her shoulders.

His eyes lit up. "I went to college with an investigator who works cold cases in St. Paul. I think I'll give him a call and elicit some advice from him. In the meantime, I think I'll pay Eddie a visit this afternoon."

He stood to leave. A loud hollow rap sounded, the door swung open and Donald Hanson walked into her office. Mitch noticed Steph roll her eyes.

That's all I need, a board member to check up on me. It's not Tuesday or Thursday.

Mitch stood by the door and deliberately blocked his entrance. Don stopped and looked from Mitch to Steph. "Howdy, Sheriff," he held out his chubby hand for a handshake. Mitch shook his hand briefly. "How's the investigation going?" he inquired, his speech somewhat slurred.

"Not a whole lot to report," replied Mitch. He realized Donald was a tad inebriated.

"Well, I'm just checkin' in to see what I can do to help. I… bet you guys down at the…department are snowed under right now…." His voice dragged. "Anything I can do to help speed…things along."

"Not right now, Don." Agitated by the older man's behavior, Mitch struggled to keep his voice casual. "But I'll let you know if we need any more help. Right now we need to question people who worked or lived here at the time this building was constructed."

"Don't forget your folder you left on my desk," Steph reminded him.

Mitch turned to pick up his paperwork, smiled, and winked mischievously at her. "Say, Don, you lived here during the construction of this building. Why don't you stop by my office later this afternoon? Maybe you might remember any scuttlebutt going on during that time? We can take any sort of statement you care to give us."

Donald's eyes grew large after Mitch's statement. He seemed flustered at first, threw his shoulders back, and almost lost his balance. "Don't know if I can remember that far back, but I'll put on my thinkin' cap and see what I come up with," he murmured, turned, and walked out of the office.

Steph put her hand over her mouth to keep from laughing. "Mitch, what are you doing?" her curiosity peaked.

"Well, you said it yourself. We need to question as many people as possible who lived here during the early seventies. He lived in town, probably not on the force at the time, but still may have some memory of what happened." He paused and then gave a slight chuckle which surprised Steph. "Did you notice how fast he sobered up when I mentioned coming in to make a statement?"

"Yes, I did," she smiled. "But I don't see how that makes him a suspect."

"He may not have been a cop at the time, but became one a short time later. Cops can be crooked too," he interjected as he left the office. Steph's mouth dropped open until she realized he willingly teased her.

Steph left her office door open since Callie had not returned, and within a span of a few minutes, Karen walked in.

"You know we didn't need those office supplies. We have plenty in the downstairs storage by the boiler room."

"I know," Steph replied. "Callie just needed to be out of the office."

Karen nodded and shook her finger. "Just be careful of her."

"I will," Steph said, aware of Karen's sudden friendliness. *I wonder if I need to be wary of her, too.*

She shook her head.

I'm getting too paranoid. Maybe she's just a nice person.

Steph called a short staff meeting to update the employees on the investigation progress. She reiterated the importance to the employees not to give out any information about the skeletal remains or to speculate with the residents about the victims. Then she requested they continue to forward all phone inquiries to the Law Enforcement Center.

"Darrin, you and Derek are among the residents most of the day. If any of them start to question you, give me their names, and I'll pass the names to the sheriff. Is that clear?"

"Yes, ma'am," both of them chirped at once.

"Karen, Callie, Lola, do you have questions?"

They all shook their heads.

"Okay, let's get back to work." With that last remark, they all broke away back to their work areas.

Thank goodness for Friday. What a stressful week!

CHAPTER THIRTEEN

Later that evening three men met in an alley behind a local bar. Their faces blurred by the low lighting outside so only obscure shadows could be seen. Their dark clothing hid their identities.

Nervous and agitated, the shorter man lit a cigarette.

"Put that cigarette out," whispered one of the men. "We don't want to draw attention to ourselves out here. We don't need anyone seeing us together." The short man stomped the cigarette on a garbage can lid and stuck it back in his shirt pocket. He wanted to quit, but with his nervous energy he needed something in his hands to keep him busy. He stuck his hands in his blue jean pockets to keep from grabbing another cigarette.

"I'm gettin' worried what's goin' on with the sheriff's department. Can't seem to find anything out from anyone," he wrung his hands and walked back and forth in short strokes circling the other two. "Heard the sheriff's goin' around questioning people who lived here during the building of the high rise."

"Nothing we can do right now," came the raspy voice from another. "We just need to keep our cool."

"Cool—keep our cool!" the shorter man almost shouted. "Are you kidding me? My stomach's doing flip flops, and you say to keep our cool! Saw an unmarked squad drive by this afternoon."

"Look," said the third man agitated by the shorter man, "Even if they find out who we buried in that building, they can't pin point it to us. It's been over forty years. How are they going to get enough evidence to point their fingers at any of us?"

"We need to get our stories straight," the raspy voice spoke again. "We basically know nothing. They aren't going to be able to determine when and how it happened. There shouldn't be a problem if we just keep our cool. If we're questioned, we know nothing. Right?"

"Right," the other two nodded in response.

"All they're going to be able to determine is the approximate date, so in essence we are free and clear as long we don't get nervous if questioned, and I say if," the raspy voice spoke condescendingly to the other two.

"I don't know if I can keep this secret too much longer," the shorter man complained. "Why can't we turn ourselves in and tell what happened?" He paced back and forth. "Throw ourselves on the mercy of the court. I can't sleep nights since they found those bodies."

"We're all in the same boat," the third man spoke. "After all these years, how many people know what actually happened? Hopefully, no one else. Skeeter left town soon after, and who knows where he is right now? He's the only one besides us that knows what happened." He walked over to the shorter man, grabbed hold of his shirt so he could look him in the eyes. "And you're not goin' anywhere or tell anyone anything," he threatened. "Understood?"

"Yep, I understand," he gulped, and removed the other man's tight grasp from his shirt with shaking hands. "Just don't you ever touch me like that again!" he returned threat for threat. "I'm goin' in for a drink. Anyone care to join me?" No one else moved. "I didn't think so."

He turned, walked out of the alley, and headed toward the front door of the bar.

"I'm worried about that one. He's getting too jittery and he's makin' me nervous."

"Yeah, I know what you mean," replied the raspy voice. "I just wish I knew what to do." They both shook their heads and walked slowly out of the alley, each going a separate direction.

On Sunday morning the sun attempted to shine through the foggy haze of humidity. The day showed a promise of no rain for a change. Steph lounged in bed ready for a quiet day at home when the phone rang.

"Hey, Steph." Azalea's perky voice sounded a little too cheery over the phone. "How about attending church with Becca and me?"

Steph yawned. "I just woke up and didn't think about doing anything but lie around today."

"Oh, come on. Reverend Rafe always gives a good sermon. You need to put God back in your life again," Azalea replied, not put off by Steph's initial reaction.

"Oh, okay…I'll go," she relented. "Give me a half hour to shower and get dressed."

"We'll stop by and pick you up. We can all go together."

"Sounds good." After hanging up the phone, she smiled to herself, grateful for a good friend in town like Azalea—even though she called too early in the morning.

She showered, dressed and waited by the front door a half hour before the church service. Azalea and Becca arrived on time to pick her up for the ten o'clock service.

The church, filled to capacity when they arrived, showed the diversity of the congregation—from residents at the high rise to professional people throughout the community.

Four men stood in front with guitars, drums and a keyboard. Azalea led them toward the front of the church where all three could sit together.

A few minutes before the service the music started. A young woman stepped up to the microphone and started to sing in a soulful soprano voice and one of the guitarists joined her at the microphone. The congregation joined in and raised their arms in praise and worship. Moved by the music, Steph found herself swaying to its beat. Even though she was not familiar with the songs, she joined in, especially when the congregation started clapping their hands to keep in time with the music.

The young soprano's voice carried them through several songs before Reverend Rafe came up to the stage. Steph noticed him earlier as he stood on the side and waited for the music to end before he walked to the lectern.

Their eyes met and he smiled, as he acknowledged her presence. She returned the smile and looked quickly away.

Azalea nudged her, and her face turned a light shade of pink. She also noticed Reverend Rafe looking at Steph.

After he stepped up to the lectern he acknowledged the musicians and thanked them for the beautiful praise music presented to God that morning.

"God is good. God is great. Can I get an 'Amen'?" The congregation shouted with a hearty "Amen!"

Reverend Rafe started his sermon from behind the lectern, but within a short time he walked down among the congregation. His gave a sermon on joy. The same joy he talked to her about during coffee at The Nest.

"What gives us true happiness and contentment in life? I want to quote from John, chapter fifteen, verse eleven, 'I have told you this so that my joy may be in you and that your joy may be complete'. Again I ask you, what gives us true happiness and contentment in life? A person can have money, all the possessions they desire, health, and even good looks, but if they don't have joy, life can be a challenge."

He looked around at the crowd as if he were assessing everyone, wondering if he was getting through to them.

He continued, "It's easy to find joy when things are going well, yet some people struggle to experience this virtue even then. Christ offers us joy, no matter what our circumstances. True joy is believing the one true God is a personal God who is involved in and cares about our daily lives. He loves us and is working out a good plan for us. When we confidently believe this in our hearts, we can rise above our circumstances and find joy in Christ alone."

Steph sat mesmerized.

He is talking directly to me. Joy has been out of my life for a long time, ever since I turned away from God and quit going to church.

The reverend continued his powerful and energetic sermon with examples from the Bible from the birth of Jesus Christ to quoting from the books of James, Peter, and Philippians. When he quoted from Philippians chapter four, verses four through eight, about rejoicing in the Lord always and not to be anxious about anything, she vowed to read Philippians, and hoped it would calm her heart and soul.

All these sources of joy made Steph's mind turn in a whirlwind of emotion. She remembered things from her childhood: happy things, sad things, her brother's death, marriage, and then the divorce. There was happiness and joy and sadness, and God stayed around her during those times because she made it through. But she never took the time to thank God for giving His only son as a sacrifice so that she could again rejoice in the Lord.

Now in the presence of God, she could feel a flutter in her heart and wanted more of what Reverend Rafe preached. Her eyes moistened with tears, she tried to inconspicuously wipe them, but the reverend noticed and held that picture in his heart.

"I want to close the service today with two quotes that I would like you all to remember. The first one from James, chapter one, verse two, 'Consider it pure joy, my brothers, whenever you face trials of many kinds, because you know that the testing of your faith develops perseverance', and then from First Peter, chapter five, verse six, 'Humble yourselves, therefore, under God's mighty hand, that he may lift you up in due time. Cast all your anxiety on him because he cares for you'."

He paused for a moment as he bowed his head. "Let us pray as we end this service with prayers for those who are ill or need God's help in other ways."

The reverend guided his congregation down a spiritual path, and she could hear people speaking in low tones "Yes, Lord," "Amen, Lord," "Praise the Lord," "The Lord is good," as he led them through a final prayer. After the prayer ended, he raised his arms toward the congregation and spoke enthusiastically. "Go in Peace and find joy in everything you do this week."

The musicians sang a final hymn as the congregation filed slowly out of the church speaking to one another as they moved along toward the doors. Steph noticed many gathered in small groups to visit among themselves. It reminded her of her growing-up years when after church her parents would always visit with many of the congregation. She could see the fellowship at this church, and understood the reverend's happiness with his growing congregation.

She recognized many of the older men and women who stood around after the service and visited with each other. The diversity of ages, from the young to middle-age and older generations, all brought together in one common goal, made Steph realize she could be part of this family.

Since Azalea drove, Steph didn't want to leave their side to visit. Becca wanted to say hi to some of her friends, so Azalea excused herself to follow Becca. She said she would be right back, and that gave Steph the opportunity to walk over and talk to a few of her parents' acquaintances.

Her first stop was to acknowledge the Ledderings, Jake's parents and Azalea's former in-laws. Both Charles and Beth knew her as a teenager and lived less than a block from her parents' house. Being in his seventies, Charles stood slightly stooped as he leaned on a cane. She noticed his clothes hung loosely on his once heavy frame. Beth, first to recognize her, moved quickly to reach up and give her a hug. Steph bent over to return the hug barely getting her arms around Mrs. Leddering's rotund figure.

"Stephanie, lieben," she exclaimed in her slight German accent. (Beth married Charles in Germany during the Vietnam War. She met him in the hospital after he was injured in the

Army.) "By golly, I hardly recognized you. Of course, we've read about you in the paper and heard vhat happened at the high rise. It's so gut to see you again. How are your parents?" She tried to get everything out in one breath.

"Mom and Dad are doing fine," she said, smiling. "In fact, I'm going to call them today. I'll mention that I saw you."

"Wunderbar!" Beth exclaimed. "I still miss them even after all these years."

Charles remained quiet while Steph and Beth exchanged small talk. He started to waiver on his cane. Beth quickly moved to his side and held on to his elbow.

"Charles just went through another round of chemo on Thursday," she explained, as she looked at Steph but steadied her husband's balance. "It takes a few days to really feel the side effects. He feels a little lightheaded and veak right now, but he insisted to come to church. I didn't vant him to go, but he said it vas gut for him to get out."

She frowned with concern for her husband of over forty years.

"I'll be fine in a few minutes," he said in a weak, scratchy voice. "I just need to sit down." Steph stepped up to hold on to his other elbow and lead him to a nearby bench. She remembered him as a strong, well-muscled man who did hard physical work as a carpenter. "I'm sorry, ladies."

"That's all right, Mr. Leddering. I'm so sorry to hear about the chemo," she commiserated with him.

He gave her a timid smile and tried to make light of it for his wife. Steph could see the pain in his red-rimmed eyes.

"It's all right, my dear," Beth clucked as she moved around Charles, adjusting his shirt and tie. She put her arm around his shoulders to comfort him. "Charlie got throat cancer and taking chemo and radiation. The radiation damaged his throat so he doesn't talk a whole lot right now as it hurts. The doctor says it vill heal in time, but the chemo makes him veak right now."

Rafe noticed Charles's distress and walked over to where they stood. "What can I do to help?" he inquired, concern apparent on his face.

"I'll be okay in a few minutes," Charles repeated in a weak throaty voice.

"Do you mind if I say a special prayer?" Charles nodded his consent. Rafe put his hands on Charles's shoulders, both bowed their heads, and the reverend prayed for Charles's recovery and for his soul.

Steph and Beth silently observed his prayer. Again, Steph, awed by the concern Rafe had for his congregation, brushed the corner of one eye, and wiped away a tear, as she watched Rafe shower God's love on one of his parishioners.

Azalea and Becca waited for her by the car. She wished she could spend more time with the Ledderings and others still milling around after church, but she needed to join Azalea and Becca. After she said her goodbyes, Beth invited her to stop by soon.

Becca ran up to give her grandparents a hug before Steph gave Beth an answer. She noticed Azalea stayed by the car and waited while Becca talked to her grandparents.

Steph offered to buy lunch. Becca jumped up and down and clapped her hands when given the choice of where to go. She chose pizza. As they stepped into the car, Rafe hurriedly walked over to them.

"Thank you for helping with Charles," he said. "He suffered for a long time, so I hope with prayer and the good doctors in town he can beat this thing."

"I sure hope so, too," she replied and shook her head. "I

knew them many years ago, and to see the change from a strong healthy man is sad. Not to change the subject, but I've offered to buy lunch. Would you care to join us for pizza?"

"Thank you so much for the offer but I've been invited to have lunch at another parishioner's house this afternoon." He sounded disappointed. "May I take a raincheck?"

"Sure, not a problem. I'll probably see you at the high rise this week. I was enlightened by your sermon and enjoyed it."

"Thank you. I hope you come back again." He gave her an irresistible devastating grin.

"You can count on it!" She blushed as she closed the car door.

Azalea gave her a playful nudge. "I think you have someone that likes you," she teased. Steph did not say a word, but looked dreamingly out the window.

Azalea and Becca dropped Steph off at home shortly after lunch. Steph missed her talks with her parents so decided to give them a call. As she walked in the front door, her phone rang.

"Hi, sweetie," said her mom, as she answered the phone. "We've tried to call you several times around lunch and didn't get an answer."

"I took Azalea and Becca out for lunch and shut off my phone," she replied, happy to hear their voices. "I'm so glad you called. I thought about calling you this afternoon."

"We tried to get the news from up there on the Internet. Did they find any more information about the remains found in the boiler room?" her mom inquired.

"Nothing really yet, Mom, but, hopefully this week we'll hear something from the BCA."

"Dad and I think you need some moral support as well as physical support," she stated, and then hesitated for a moment before she continued. "So...we're going to drive up there and stay with you for a while until this crime comes to some sort of solution."

"Mom, I know you and Dad mean well, but you don't really need to concern yourselves. Mitch is doing a fine job with the investigation, and I'm kept busy with my job."

"Well, dear, I think this is the excuse we needed to see you and spend some time with you. We haven't seen you for a long time." Her mother persisted, "Do you have room for us, or do we need to stay in a hotel?"

"I've got plenty of room with a second bedroom, but no furniture in it–just storage boxes. I can certainly accommodate you. But really, you don't need to come and babysit me. I'm fine...really I am."

She noticed a hesitation on the phone, and then her father took over the conversation.

"Now, Steph, we know you're trying to be independent, but it's always good to have family around in a crisis situation," he emphatically stated. "We know this is a situation where you need your family. We're coming whether you like it or not."

"Yes, Dad," she humbly replied. She knew better than to disagree with her father.

"We'll be there by the end of the week." He hung up the phone.

Just like dad. He always gets the last word. Now to get a room ready for them.

Part of the afternoon, which she planned for her relaxation time, was spent at the local furniture store to purchase another bedroom set. The remainder of the day she moved boxes to the basement and to the garage.

So much for my stress-free day. I think I'll get a glass of wine and enjoy the sunset.

Even though she did not want to admit it, she wanted to see her parents again. Since her separation and divorce they only corresponded with phone calls back and forth. They never liked Larry, so they were not surprised when she called them and informed them of his infidelity.

I hope they don't get in my face again like they did after I told them about the divorce.

They did not believe in divorce. They never knew the difficulty she went through during the divorce.

CHAPTER FOURTEEN

Wednesday morning Steph woke up to birds singing outside her bedroom window. She noticed a pair of finches made a nest in the oak tree in her backyard and flitted back and forth to put the final touches on it. She stretched and grinned.

This is a good sign. Good things will happen today. Good morning, world. Good morning, sunshine. Good morning, birds. Dear Lord, please be with me today and guide me through the day. I'm praying for the first time in a long time, and it feels soooo good.

She twirled around in front of the window, and felt the happiness flow through her veins. Her thoughts turned to her parents' visit.

She literally floated into the office, and decided nothing would get her down today. Except for Callie's dour face when she walked in the door, everything looked like sunshine and roses.

Mitch called around ten in the morning, and asked her to

stop by his office. He received some information from the BCA forensics department.

It's about time!

Her schedule on the computer showed no appointments for the remainder of the morning, so she left right away. She walked into the Law Enforcement Center and for the first time saw the inside of Mitch's office. Surprised to see how neat and tidy he kept his desk, she compared it to her organized disarray.

"Thanks for coming over, Steph." His first remark sounded very official. With a pile of papers on his desk, he looked concerned while he rubbed his right ear again.

I wonder if his earlobes are going to grow if he keeps pulling and rubbing on them.

"Sit down. Finally…some news."

Ecstatic with anticipation, she sat down and leaned forward. "What did you find out?"

"Okay, this is what the forensics team verified," he said, as he handed the file to her.

She scanned over the results and then haphazardly read them out loud, perplexed by what she first read.

"Okay, so the victims…two males in their early to mid-twenties, inconclusive on ethnicity of either male, running further tests, forthcoming within a few weeks, … buried before the final cement poured for the boiler room." She screwed up her nose in displeasure. "We already knew all this stuff. There's no more than that to go on?" she prodded.

"Well, yes, read on."

She continued, "A gunshot wound in victim one, but not victim two. Several buckshot pellets found on site came from a shotgun—not a handgun." She scanned farther down the papers. "The skull on victim two cracked so they determine a blow to the head. The clothing, or the remainder of the clothing, indicated they wore blue jeans and t-shirts, and a cross found on victim one with the initials JG inscribed on the back." She looked at Mitch, puzzled. "So what does that mean so far? Can you put this in perspective?"

"What I suspect the forensics team said—there's an official definite timeframe, which we already knew, and we can continue our investigation with that information. If you read further on, the gunshot did not kill victim one. Something else happened to cause both deaths. This late in the game it's going to be hard to determine, unless we find someone who knows what happened. Since it's been over forty years, it may never happen."

"Your job is more difficult right now. Will the BCA send any investigators, or is this all on your plate?" She gave him a weak smile, and felt remorse for all the work it involved. "Anything our agency can do to help."

He wrinkled his forehead and sensed a desperate need for answers. His call to his friend at the St. Paul Police Department gave him some guidelines to follow for unsolved cases.

"First, we need you to find all the records in storage in regard to the construction of the building, if any, to make sure we're on the right path. We know it was summer or fall by the clothes they wore, but if we can find the date the contractors poured the floor for the boiler room, we can narrow it down."

He stopped for a moment, and waited for her to put an obstacle in his way. Steph listened intently.

"Then we need to find the payroll for all employees who worked on the building, find who is still alive and still live in the area. Even those who aren't in the area, we can attempt to locate them for questioning. It'll be a lot of intense work." He drew a sigh of relief as he got all that out.

She wanted to help as much as possible. She leaned forward, clasped her hands together, and looked Mitch straight in the eyes. "I'm not sure we even have any of the records around. There is the storage room on the so-called fourteenth floor, the only place I think any of the records would be stored." She hesitated and shook her head. "I looked in there a few days after I started work and was shocked by the disarray. There are boxes piled up so high that it'll take a month of Sundays to get through everything."

"That's where we can help," he insisted. "We can use the volunteer Sheriff's Posse. You tell them what to look for, and they'll help go through the boxes."

Relief showed on her face. "Oh, thank you, Mitch. I never thought about them. That would be wonderful, and I'd be so grateful for the help."

"Oh, by the way," she added, "Mom and Dad are on their way here from Texas. They should be here by the end of the week or early next week."

"Driving or flying?" he asked.

"Driving, of course," she replied. "Mom always packs too much stuff to fly."

"Sounds like a plan," he smiled. "Let's get everything started. The sooner we move on this, the faster we can solve the case." He escorted her to the door. "How about dinner this evening? I can grill, and we can go over a game plan. I will notify the volunteers, and any spare deputies available will come tomorrow at nine."

"Dinner sounds fine. A bed is being delivered for Mom and Dad so I need to be there when they call for delivery. I can give you a call later today and let you know."

She hummed to herself as she left his office—a happy day

so far.

After she returned to the high rise office, Steph called another staff meeting for later in the afternoon. She hoped the furniture company delivery van would not interfere with the meeting.

She stopped at Karen's office and talked to her about the storage room. If anyone would know where to find the paperwork, Steph knew it would be her.

"As far as I know," she said, as she removed her glasses and rubbed her eyes, "there's never been any organization in the storage area. The maintenance people over the years stored our annual records up there. Who knows what other records could be up there? Even if we find the archived records, they may not be in very good condition. Forty years is a long time, and mice could have destroyed some or all of those records."

"I agree," Steph replied. "However, we need to start someplace. If they can't be found in storage upstairs, then we can check the city's storage facilities. I'll talk to the sheriff and ask him to contact the city to check their storage records dating back that far. Too bad we didn't use computers back then," she laughed, excited to get started. "It would make things a lot easier."

Karen nodded in agreement. "It'll be kinda fun going through all that old stuff, don't you think?"

Steph rolled her eyes at Karen's remark. "Wait 'til we're done, then make the same remark."

Finally, we might make some headway in the investigation. I hope the remainder of the staff finds fun going through all the boxes.

CHAPTER FIFTEEN

Before the staff meeting, Clarence Larsvig, the board chairman, walked into the office and briskly informed Steph that he requested an emergency board meeting.

He can't call an emergency board meeting unless it's an actual emergency. They need to be scheduled. What is he up to?

"For what reason?" she asked as she raised her eyebrows, ready to protest the emergency meeting.

"Because I just heard the Sheriff's Posse volunteered to come to the high rise tomorrow to help search through records," he stated gruffly, as he expanded his chest and stomped his cane on the floor. "I don't understand what is happening, but that information should all remain confidential. No one but the board and staff need access to those records."

"I'm sorry you feel that way, Clarence," said Steph, mystified why he was so upset. "This was requested by the sheriff's department to help further the investigation. I volunteered the records. I...I didn't think it would cause any trouble."

"We'll see about that," he exploded as spittle hit her in the face. "The other board members will be here shortly, and we'll need to discuss whether or not we will allow this. I'll see you in the boardroom." He walked briskly out of her office toward the meeting room. She noticed he did not need his cane as he exited the room. She plucked a tissue and blotted her face.

As soon as he left for the boardroom, she placed a phone call to the sheriff's office.

"Clarence found out about the Sheriff's Posse coming tomorrow morning, and he's furious. He called an emergency board meeting. Are you available to attend and explain the circumstances? I don't know how he found out so quickly. Do you have any idea?"

"No idea. Be there as soon as I can. I need to wrap up a few things here first."

Steph walked to the boardroom and sat at one end of the table. She asked Karen to be present to take notes because the by-laws of the agency did not allow for emergency meetings without prior notice, except for an actual emergency. She did not determine this situation as an emergency.

Collette and Wendy arrived first. Jake followed close behind them. They waited for Donald Hanson. Jake tapped his fingers on the table, which made Steph slightly nervous. According to Clarence, she may have committed an illegal act.

Collette and Wendy looked perplexed as to the reason for an emergency meeting. Wendy took out her nail file and started to file her nails. Collette gave her an exasperated look and started to tap her nails on the table.

Steph's nerves were on edge. She missed Mitch's presence.

Clarence, as board chair, in a dictatorial manner called the meeting to order without Donald Hanson. "We have a quorum, and that's all we need."

His face flushed from anger, he snapped, "The only thing on the agenda is the information passed on to me regarding the Sheriff's Posse arrival tomorrow to go through all the archived records in the storage room. I want an explanation? Why is this happening, and what is going on?" The tempo of his voice rose as he spoke.

The forensics report was still confidential information; and Steph did not know how to proceed with the meeting. She could not release any of the report unless the sheriff's department gave its stamp of approval. She waited and hoped Mitch would arrive soon.

She needed some stalling tactics. "Why don't we wait a few more minutes for Mr. Hanson to arrive?"

"No!" he said adamantly. "We will discuss this now. Hanson will be here shortly. He sent me a text from his cell phone a few minutes ago and said he was on his way."

Oh, great! Now how am I going to stall for time? Okay, here goes.

After she took a deep breath, she placed her hands deliberately on the boardroom table. She stood and looked at each one, let out a deep sigh, and started her stalling technique.

"First of all," she started slowly, "the sheriff requested we allow volunteers to attempt to find the construction records and reports and to get the payroll records previously submitted to the government so he can continue his investigation."

She continued to look at each one individually, scrutinized their body language for any indication of the same indignation Clarence Larsvig portrayed. Everyone else looked passive.

"I don't believe we are doing anything illegal or wrong here. Yes, we may find some things in the records that might

go against the Privacy Act, but at this point we need answers."
She could feel her temper rise as she spoke each word slowly
and deliberately. "By... not ... going ... through ... those
records ... it could take months ... if not years ... to try and
find out the names of the victims buried in the boiler room."

Wendy and Collette looked at each other, their faces
expressionless. Jake resorted to tap a pen on the table, which
irritated her. She pinched her fingers between her eyebrows to
avoid the start of a stress headache. Clarence sat stone faced,
and glared at her.

Jake finally cleared his throat. "I am concerned about the
privacy of former residents also, but I think most of them are
probably no longer with us. I don't see any problem as long as
there are employees from here who will work alongside the
posse volunteers."

*At last, someone who understands the importance of what
needs to be done.*

With a loud knock on the boardroom door, Mitch entered.
He commanded attention as he strutted toward the table with
his full-duty-belt hanging around his waist. Steph breathed a
sigh of relief and managed a shaky smile.

"I think I will turn the remainder of this meeting over to
the sheriff. I'm sure he'll explain the importance of what needs
to be done."

She motioned for him to sit in a vacant seat next to her. He
indicated he would stand as he placed his thumbs around his
belt. She sat down.

"I apologize for being late," he turned and grinned at the
board members, but there was no humor in his eyes. He
showed up to exercise his authority. "It's come to my attention
there is some contention to what I suggested to Ms. Runnell. I
would like to explain what we need, which might give you a

different perspective, and allow us to go through the business records."

Clarence opened his mouth, but before he could utter any expletives, Mitch raised his hand to stop him. "Let me continue," he asked. Clarence closed his mouth, but continued to glare. "We only want to look for the early construction records. I need the payroll records supplied by the contractor for at least the first half of the construction. We've recovered our records for missing persons during that time period from our archives, and our investigative team is going through them right now."

Clarence, finally able to speak, growled at Mitch, "I am concerned about the privacy of our former residents. By looking for that information, the posse may find private information such as social security numbers and so forth that concerns …" Don Hanson suddenly arrived and interrupted Clarence's train of thought, so he stopped in mid-sentence.

"Sorry I'm late," he puffed as he tried to catch his breath due to his heavy bulk. Steph noticed the bulge under his vest, and remembered he carried a gun. When he sat down, he asked to be updated. Clarence briefly filled him in.

Mitch continued to take command of the meeting. "I would like to continue and explain the plan. First, we will arrive early tomorrow morning. If any of you are available, we could use your help also. This will be an arduous task for all of us. There's over forty years of records up there, and it will be like finding a needle in a haystack. Of course," he rested his hand closer to his gun holster, glanced at Steph, and then back to the board members, "you can either agree to the arrangement, or I can get a court order. I'm sure I could still get one today to obtain access to the high rise's records."

Silence filled the room as the board members looked at

each other for support.

"I agree with what Jake said earlier," Wendy Benjamin squeaked in her shy voice. She looked at Clarence, and waited for him to explode again. With more confidence, she cleared her throat and continued. "Most of the residents or clients are probably long gone, and it should make no difference. There will be so many records to go through. I have never been up there. It should be interesting."

"Yes," agreed Collette, with a more aggressive voice. "The quicker we get this over with, the better for all concerned. Clarence, this was ridiculous to call this meeting. What were you thinking?" She continued to chastise Clarence, while she pointed her long, manicured finger at him. "You know Ms. Runnell is only trying to do what is necessary to get this investigation over with."

Clarence sat very still and did not respond. "Oh, very well, do what you want!" he spat. "But don't blame me if something happens."

He rose to leave, but Mitch walked to the closed door and stood in the way. He sullenly sat back down in the chair.

"I would really appreciate if all of you could take some time tomorrow morning to partner with one or two of the posse volunteers," Steph suggested. "This is one way you, as board members, can make sure no papers are removed from the building unless it's the information the sheriff needs."

Wendy and Collette wrinkled up their noses and looked at their manicured nails. Steph smiled as she thought what those nails would look like after tomorrow.

Jake raised his hand. "I'll volunteer."

Wendy and Collette reluctantly raised their hands simultaneously; both agreed to help.

Don Hanson and Clarence Larsvig grumbled, but

halfheartedly agreed to show up early in the morning.

The meeting adjourned. After everyone left, Steph walked over to Mitch and put her arms around his waist. "Thank you so much. I don't know what I would have done if you didn't show up and threaten a search warrant."

"No problem." He stretched his arms and engulfed her in a hug. "I think everything is under control for now. I don't need any more problems to deal with right now." He released her. "I need to get back to the office." A teasing smile crossed his face. "I knew you needed a hug."

Steph looked at him. A faint flush tinged her cheeks, and she bobbed her head in agreement.

"I'll see you tonight," he shot her a grin as he left the room.

Steph walked slowly back to the office and mulled over the reluctance of the board to help with the investigation.

Clarence had no legal right to call the emergency board meeting. If one of the board members filed a complaint with the city council, Clarence would be up for expulsion from the board.

When she walked into the main office, Miss Mattie sat in the waiting area. Callie did not seem too happy to see her there and gave Steph a cautious look. "Miss Mattie wants to see you," she grumbled.

Steph smiled sweetly at the older lady. "Hello, Miss Mattie. What can I help you with?" She bent over and patted her gently on the shoulder.

Miss Mattie moved her eyes toward Callie. "May I speak to you in private for a moment?"

"Sure thing. Come into my office." Miss Mattie hobbled

into Steph's office. She used a cane today and not her walker. Steph noted this change, and wondered how much Miss Mattie actually needed her walker.

"Now what can I do for you?"

Miss Mattie sat on the edge of the chair and rocked back and forth.

"Well, I want to report some mysterious goings on in this building late at night," she whispered, and looked around to make sure no one else could hear her. Miss Mattie looked skittish as if she would take flight.

Steph stood and walked over to shut her office door. She knew Miss Mattie's penchant for the dramatic. After she sat down again, she took out a writing pad to take notes.

"Okay, Miss Mattie, there is no one else who can hear you." Her face crinkled in confusion.

"Late at night I've heard footsteps in the apartment above me. It's all very mysterious because I don't hear it every night. I always thought it was ghosts of the people…you know…who lived and died here."

She lowered her voice to a loud whisper. Miss Mattie always enunciated her words slowly. "Last night I heard footsteps again, so I got out of bed and walked up the stairs to the floor above. Stood by the stair door, looked through the window, so I could see if anyone came out of that apartment—the apartment right by the stairway. My legs cramped. I didn't know if I could make it back down with my cane. I opened the stairway door to walk to the elevator when I heard the apartment door creak open. I hid back in the stairway. Ms. Runnell, Callie came out of the apartment with a man."

Steph looked at Miss Mattie, concern on her face, and did not know if she should believe this story, or if Miss Mattie hallucinated again.

"Do you know what time you started to hear the footsteps, and when you went back to your apartment?" she continued to interrogate the older lady.

"I looked at my digital alarm clock and it registered 12:24 a.m., and I waited a few minutes after hearing continuous movement up there before I left my apartment. My clock read 2 a.m. when I returned to my bedroom. I woke Maude this morning and told her what happened. She didn't want to believe me when I first told her about the ghosts, but I figured she would believe me now."

"Miss Mattie…you did a dangerous thing. First of all, to be on the stairs in your physical condition, and second, because it might have been someone who could hurt you."

"I know," she moved around, nervously twisted her hands, and stammered, "but the ghosts told me to go up there. I didn't have a choice."

"I thought the ghosts were upstairs. Now you're telling me there are other ghosts who talk to you?"

"That's right!" Miss Mattie whispered, her eyes wild. "They tell me about things going on in this building, bad things, but I keep most of it to myself because no one believes me when I tell them about the ghosts."

"Okay, Miss Mattie," Steph also lowered her voice to a whisper. "Why don't you let me handle this situation? You go back to your apartment, and no more night visits. Okay? Promise me no more night visits?"

Miss Mattie nodded her head and stood to leave. Steph opened the office door, and noticed Callie hurriedly sitting down at her desk.

Did she listen at the door?

She walked with Miss Mattie to the elevator to protect her

from Callie's glare.

Another fire to put out.

After she returned to the office, Callie's face was glued to the computer screen.

It doesn't pay to address this with her now. I'm not sure what Miss Mattie saw is true.

Karen sauntered into her office to remind her of the staff meeting at four. She looked at her watch.

Fifteen minutes to spare.

She checked the computer to see who rented the apartment above Miss Mattie on the thirteenth floor. Stunned to see no one had leased it for the past few months. Out of curiosity, she decided to take a quick tour of the apartment.

She stood outside the door of Apartment 1313, and used her master key to open it. The lock resisted as she twisted the key back and forth. The deadbolt finally clicked, and Steph stepped warily into the apartment.

Even though the air conditioner was set on low, the atmosphere sent an instant chill to her body. The apartment smelled of sulfur or rotten eggs. She pinched her nose, and tried to breathe through her mouth as she crossed her arms and hurried through every room. Only the low hum of the air conditioner could be heard.

She looked for evidence that someone occupied the apartment. Nothing. Satisfied, she reached for the doorknob to leave. She heard a whoosh and a cold tremor ran through her body. The chilled feeling startled her as she could not see anything that would cause it.

It reminded her of similar situations when renovations occurred. Steph remembered one building where they actually called in a local priest to exorcize and pray over the building before the workers would return. Her body chilled at the prospect of demons in this building. If they are in here, then they could be all over the building.

Frozen in place, it took all of her willpower to exit the apartment, and lock the door behind her. She started to hyperventilate, and her face turned as white as the wall she leaned against in the hallway.

She whispered, *"Dear Jesus, please help me."* Her breathing calmed instantly.

Miss Mattie might not be crazy after all. I didn't see any ghosts, but I felt evil lurking about the apartment.

She kept a tight-knuckled grip on the hand rails as she walked along one side of the hallway, until she reached the elevator. Even though she felt calm, the knowledge of what she witnessed remained with her. She pushed the button for the first floor and leaned against the elevator wall as she composed herself before the staff meeting.

Something was not right in that apartment. Worse than not all right, but who would believe me. What happened to my happy day?

CHAPTER SIXTEEN

Steph's luck changed when she arrived home to find the delivery van parked in her driveway with the bedroom set she'd ordered for her parents' stay. With the chaos of the day she forgot about the delivery. The delivery men set up the bed, dresser and nightstand in the spare room.

Azalea arrived to help decorate the room. They hung pictures and put sheets and a quilt on the bed. She looked at her watch, and realized Mitch would arrive within a half hour to pick her up for dinner.

"Gotta rush and take a quick shower. Can you let yourself out?"

"Sure. I'll come over tomorrow morning with fresh flowers," offered Azalea.

"I'll give you a key to the house. Keep it in case I ever get locked out."

"Let's hope that never happens."

"Thanks a bunch. I couldn't have done this without your help."

Mitch mentioned a barbeque, so she decided denim capris and sleeveless top would be appropriate. Her spirits lifted as she put on a pair of dangling earrings and thought about their dinner tonight.

Infatuated with Mitch since high school, she still felt a little tingle when he touched her. But then her new feelings for Rafe made her confused. She and Mitch shared an easy camaraderie, and she felt safe.

Rafe, on the other hand, stirred her emotions and made her think about her relationship with God. When she was with him she felt at peace, but he also made her feel excited to be alive again.

Her experience in the empty apartment did not enter her mind again.

The doorbell rang and pulled her out of her daydream. Her eyes popped to see Mitch out of uniform. He reminded her of the same teenage boy she knew years ago, only older and more mature. She expected to see Natalia stick her head around her dad's legs.

"No Natalia tonight?" she queried.

"Not tonight. Where we're going is not a place for little kids."

"Oh, my!" her eyes lit up with curiosity. "I looked forward to barbeque."

"We are."

Mitch drove out of town on a road familiar to Steph. She remembered several out-of-the-way restaurants and bars catering to the tourists during the summer months. Mitch pulled into the parking lot of The Last Stop—only the sign changed with the added words Barbeque Pit. Being both a bar and hamburger joint during her teen years, it looked remarkably the same on the outside. Pine trees still surrounded

131

the log building.

When she stepped out of Mitch's car, she detected the distinct odor of barbeque and not the greasy hamburger smell she expected. The mesquite barbeque and pine smell mingled together, and she could hear her stomach growl. Off to the side she noticed a covered area where smoke oozed out of a huge barbeque pit. The middle-aged man who attended it wore a white apron splattered with grease stains. His hair tied back in a ponytail stuck through the back of a baseball cap. He paused in the middle of turning some of the meat and saluted them as they walked closer to the restaurant. Mitch waved at him. She looked forward to some good old-fashioned smoked brisket.

As they entered the building a middle-aged woman, this time wearing a clean white apron over blue jeans and a red-and-white checkered shirt, recognized Mitch.

"Howdy, Sheriff. So nice of you to join us this evening."

"Hey, Tillie." He briefly put his arm around her shoulders and gave her a wide grin. At the same time she put her arm around his waist. "How about a nice table by a window?"

"Sure enough." She laughed and sauntered over to a table in the corner. She handed them menus, winked at Mitch, and then walked away. Steph could not help but smile.

"Someone you dated in the past?" she smirked after Tillie walked away.

"No. Just a high school classmate. You remember Tillie Jensen?" Steph shook her head. "Bill Jensen's daughter," he added. "She's his only child. He didn't marry until his forties. Her dad owned this place for many years." Steph shook her head again, baffled she could not remember who owned the place.

"He retired a few years back, and Tillie and her husband Jack moved back from Texas and turned it into a barbeque joint. It's made a big difference with the local crowd and the tourists. Jack retired from the service and then worked as a chef. It worked out perfect for them to take over. They cleaned the place up and don't allow riff raff in anymore. We hardly get any calls out this way."

She looked at the menu. "I can't wait to try their brisket." As she surveyed the room she remembered how dingy the place used to look. "They really did a nice job of redecorating." Thanks to a good scrubbing and oiling, the log walls gleamed. The animals' head mounts still hung in prominent places, but not as many as years ago. Checkered red-and-white tablecloths covered each table. Along with new lighting, it gave the place a retro look. They removed all the old booths. "Yes, this is definitely an improvement."

They both agreed not to talk business during the evening, even though originally Mitch mentioned going over a plan. It worked out fine until an elderly man stepped out of the kitchen area maneuvering a walker. He slowly made his way over to a couple at a table near the kitchen door.

"Mitch, is that Bill Jensen over there talking to that older couple?"

"Sure is," he replied, his mouth full of brisket. He swallowed and wiped his mouth with his napkin. "He must be close to eighty years old and still gets around. I've heard he comes out almost every night to visit with the customers. He's not in very good health right now."

Bill laboriously turned around with his walker and stretched his head towards their table. Even though his glasses looked thick, he seemed to recognize Mitch. He moved his walker in their direction, and hobbled over to their table.

"Well, Sheriff, it's about time we see you out here for pleasure instead of a call." He shakily extended his hand to

Mitch. "And who is this lovely young lady you brought along?"

"You remember Stephanie Thomas, Wayne and Anne Thomas's daughter?" He used her maiden name.

"Wayne and Anne. Hmmm..." He rubbed his jaw, and his bloodshot eyes through the thick glasses starred at Steph as he tried to pull some memory out of his brain. Then a smile formed on his face. "Haven't heard from them in years. How they doin'?"

Steph smiled politely even though she barely remembered Bill. "Well, they're on their way here from Texas for a visit."

Bill's withered face split into a wide grin and showed some missing teeth. He turned to sit in his walker as if he planned for a longer visit than just to say *hi*. "Certainly would like to see 'em when they get here. Bring 'em on out. I'm here just as much as me old body allows. Don't put in all the hours lately. You know that old 'ritis gang is gettin' to me, and I'm havin' a hard time movin' around."

"Sorry to hear that, Bill," Mitch replied. Then he looked at Steph as if apologizing for what he was about to do. "As long as we are out here, would you mind taking a few moments to answer a couple questions?"

"A couple questions. Well, my memory ain't so good anymore. But...I suppose my old memory is better than askin' me what I had for breakfast this mornin'," he whooped loudly and slapped his knee with his hand. "Go ahead, hit me with what you got." He leaned forward in his walker to hear Mitch.

"Okay," Mitch began hesitantly as he usually did this in the privacy of his office, not in a public place, but the opportunity seemed just right. "You remember when River View Towers was going up?

Bill scratched his head. "Yep."

"What do you remember? Anything strange or mysterious with any of the workers or anyone coming through during that time period that would make you suspicious?"

Bill looked down at his hands and tried hard to think back to over forty years ago.

"Maybe you saw some transients come through and not stay very long or people camped out, stopped by your bar for a few drinks with the locals? Anything you could remember would help."

"A long time ago, Sheriff. I'll think on it, and if I recall anything, I'll be gettin' in touch with you." He paused, then as an afterthought added, "'Bout the only thing I remember is them Mexican workers comin' to the bar, and I kept it open later than usual 'cause they wanted to come out and eat and drink during the week. Didn't like to drink in town. Got too much guff from the locals. I usually close down after Labor Day, but with the Mexicans wantin' to spend their money, I thought what the heck. If they want to spend it, I might as well take it. Made a pretty penny off those illegals too."

With a scoffing laugh he started to choke on his words, and his daughter rushed to his side. She grabbed a glass of water from the table, and gave her dad a few swallows while she rubbed his back.

"How do you know they were illegals?"

Bill continued to cough, his face contorted to a dull red.

"You okay, Pops" his daughter asked with concern.

Steph's jaw dropped by what she heard from Bill.

"I'm sorry," Tillie said, "but Pops needs to go lie down in the office right now. He gets these spells, and they lay him out for a while. The waitress will bring you some fresh water."

"I understand," said Mitch. "We'll stay in touch." Mitch stood and patted Bill on his back. Tillie led him slowly to the office.

After Tillie and Bill left their table, Steph looked at Mitch with concern in her eyes. "I think he knows more than what he's saying right now."

"I think you're right. I'm going to talk to him again. I need to apologize to you. I promised no business tonight, but I couldn't help myself."

"I guess a lawman is always a lawman," she chuckled. "Umm... This brisket is awesome." She picked at her brisket even though she no longer had an appetite. She did not want Mitch to know Bill made her feel ill at ease. "I'm definitely bringing my parents out here. They will be so surprised at the change in this place."

They ate the remainder of their meal in silence.

Tillie walked up to them as Mitch paid for their meal and apologized for her father's coughing spell.

"I'll touch base with him in a few days," Mitch promised.

"Dad is very sick, but doesn't want to admit it," her eyebrows pinched together in concern. "I don't want to discourage him from coming out here, but he should really stay home more. He comes out here every day, walks around and picks up garbage, helps Jack clean the barbeque pit, helps in the kitchen, and just doesn't realize he's retired."

"Be glad your dad is still alive. Both my parents died a few years back. Steph's parents are on their way here for a visit. Oh, by the way, I should introduce you two. Stephanie Runnell, this is Tillie Jensen. You remember Aaron Thomas from our class. This is his little sister."

"Yes, I recognized you from your picture in the paper," said Tillie. The man who tended the barbeque pit outside came in, put his arm around Tillie and smiled. She turned to him and returned the smile. "By the way, my last name is now

Culpepper, and this is my husband, Jack."

"Hello, Jack," Steph pasted on a smile toward the couple, and wished someone would look at her with similar love in his eyes. "You have a great restaurant here."

"Ya'll come back now, ya hear?" Jack added in his Texas accent. "Good to see ya'll again, Captain." He saluted Mitch as he walked out the door to check on his grills.

The ride home was very quiet with a few comments on the scenery. She felt the evening had been spoiled by Bill Jensen and his comments about the Mexicans. She thought he could provide more information than he let on.

A few minutes before ten Mitch arrived at her house.

"Would you like to come in for a few minutes?"

"I would like to, but I think I better get home and make sure Natalia is tucked in bed. Sometimes I wish I didn't have to go home, especially when I could spend more time with you." His face softened as he lifted her chin so he could look in her eyes.

His arms encircled her waist as his lips descended on hers. She wrapped her arms around his neck and leaned in for the kiss. She waited a long time. When it ended she felt somewhat satisfied but wanted more. Not perfect, but a beginning—if she wanted a beginning with Mitch. Not a decision she wanted to make yet. Just one kiss and he left—to go home to his daughter.

I love him as a friend, but my yearning from my high school days could easily take over. If he'd only give me a sign—a chaste kiss is not a sign. I want passion. I'm a grown-up girl now, and is this what I want in a relationship? I know his job always comes first—just like Azalea said. His daughter second. I'm not sure I want to settle for third place.

CHAPTER SEVENTEEN

Steph arrived early at the high rise in a cheerful mood, and found the board members at the front door ready to start the process of going through the old records in the storage area. Her euphoria left when she saw their dour faces.

The board members accompanied her in the elevator to the thirteenth floor. From there they walked up the flight of stairs to the storage area where they could discuss how to process the old boxes of records before the Sheriff's Posse volunteers arrived at nine o'clock. With the warm summer and no windows in the storeroom, they needed fans and lights. Derek and Darrin arrived early to set up the fans and quartz lights.

Once the other volunteers arrived, the five board members divided themselves up between eight Sheriff Posse volunteers and three off-duty deputies, who volunteered, as well as the office staff. This made over twenty people in the confines of a hot, stuffy storage room full of dust debris from some forty-odd years of inactivity. The board members showed up strictly to oversee that no personal information from former and current residents would be compromised. Steph noticed Eddie Barkley among the volunteers for the Sheriff's Posse.

Mitch showed up briefly before they started and explained their mission so everyone would be on the same page. During this time he looked at his phone and checked his watch every few minutes. Steph noticed his inattentiveness, but thought it best not to question him at that point.

She did not get a chance to talk to Mitch regarding Eddie Barkley, but Eddie came dressed in Posse uniform so she surmised him to be qualified to help. Just the same, she would keep an eye on him. After he clarified to the volunteers and staff what dates on the records they would need to look for and the information inside the boxes, Mitch left the building without an explanation to anyone—just said he would return shortly.

It soon became chaotic once the boxes were opened, dates observed, resealed and pushed around. The records kept being pulled open and looked at several times before Steph finally shouted, "Stop! Let's get some organization to this mess before we go any further."

The containers were not in any chronological order, so to locate the right ones would be like finding a needle in the haystack. No room to move around made organization of the boxes more difficult.

She asked everyone to move the records not pertinent to the dates needed by the door. The maintenance crew could then set them outside in the hallway and down the stairways.

Steph stubbed her toe on some old office equipment. She watched everyone's attempt to step around the same outdated equipment.

We need to get up here and haul this equipment to the junkyard.

After the first hour and a half it became evident that with all the bodies in the room, they started to suffer from heat exhaustion. Steph sent Karen to the community kitchen to gather bottled water for everyone, so they could take periodic breaks.

Steph kept a steady eye on Eddie Barkley. She still did not feel comfortable with him there, but he seemed to work as hard as the rest of them.

Shortly before noon, one of the Posse volunteers hollered, "I think I found the right year!" as he dragged out several boxes from the farthest back corner of the storage room.

Of course, those records would be in the farthest back corner since they were *probably the first records to be stored in here. Duh!*

The volunteer already opened the boxes, so he knew it held the employment records needed. Steph knelt down to confirm the records were intact and requested Darrin and Derek take them to her office for safekeeping.

Each of the volunteers looked relieved to get out of the storage room, and carefully maneuvered their way down the steps to the thirteenth floor.

She heard a few volunteers mumble something about bad luck to have only thirteen floors. Even though in reality the storage area counted as fourteen, they wanted to be done and gone. Their clothes bore the resemblance of a dunk in a lake as the sweat ran down their faces.

Wendy and Collette's nicely manicured nails broke as they moved boxes around. Their makeup smeared, and they used their shirts to wipe the sweat from their faces. Mascara dripped down their cheeks and made rings around their eyes. They looked a sight. Steph was surprised to see them work so hard alongside the other volunteers. She gave them a quick thumbs up as they walked out of the storeroom.

Even though their job was just to oversee, she noticed all the board members pitched in and moved boxes around.

Clarence Larsvig's shortness of breath and overweight status worried Steph as he sat down several times on top of boxes. His hands shook while he held his cane.

Jake wore a sleeveless muscle shirt that enhanced his pectoral muscles. It ended up soaked with sweat after he lifted and moved the records out the door toward the maintenance staff. "Good workout," he commented as he stepped past Steph to maneuver the crowded stairway. His body odor tempted Steph to hold her nose.

Donald's labored breathing also worried her as he walked out the door, but he drank water and not alcohol, which satisfied Steph. She noticed he did not carry his gun with him this time.

Mitch never did come back to oversee his volunteers in the storage room. Steph's concern turned to worry.

Why would he walk out on something that was his idea?

Steph stroked her fingers down her arm, and it left a streak of dark fingermarks on her skin. She shook her head. A light layer of dust covered her clothes, and her hair felt grimy from sweat.

The volunteers and board members left after Steph thanked them for their help.

She suggested the staff take an extra-long lunch break and go home to shower and change clothes. They readily agreed, while she volunteered to stay with Lola and keep the office open until their return. Even though she felt grimy, she secretly wanted to take a look in the boxes.

While the staff took their much-deserved lunch break, Steph opened the boxes and rummaged through the contractor's records. Of course, not much of it made sense to her, but forms and records looked quite different over forty years ago. She did, however, notice a few employees with Hispanic-sounding names. She also recognized her dad's name as well as several other names of local residents. This was Mitch's investigation. She had enough on her plate with the renovations right now, so she returned the papers to the boxes.

Reverend Rafe arrived as she started to close up the boxes. He talked to Lola for a moment before he walked into her office. Embarrassed for him to see her in her dirty state, she tried to run her fingers through her hair, but it didn't help her appearance.

"Hi! May I come in?" he requested, hands in his pockets, as he strolled in the room.

Rafe's eyes looked down and surveyed her soiled look. His lips turned up in a slow grin of amusement.

Her eyes lit up. "Hi, yourself," she replied.

"I heard through the grapevine there were some goings-on here this morning, and I should get over here."

"Who on earth told you that?" She lifted her eyebrows quizzically.

"One of the residents called me worried, as she put it, 'something was going down.' I think she's watched too many television shows." He grinned again as his eyes held hers.

"Yes, I think you're right. Sounds like something Mattie would do. But, on the other hand, we did find the past records."

"Records?" Reverend Rafe's eyebrows raised in interest.

"Yeah, the contractor's employee records from the original construction. It's just a theory, but maybe the missing men were one-time employees." She started to wrap packing tape on the first box. "If not, then maybe if there are any local people who worked on the project, they can also be questioned. There's got to be an explanation?"

"God knows," he replied, and got down on one knee to hold the box shut while she taped it. "He will let us know in His own good time. We need to give it up to Him, and pray He opens the right doors for us to give us the right answers."

On an eye-to-eye level on the floor, Steph could feel the butterflies in her stomach with the close contact to Rafe. She felt her face heat up, but did not dare touch her face with her dirty hands.

"You know, some of the residents established a prayer team to pray for you and the law enforcement officials to solve this puzzle." He added, "They pray morning and night. Sometimes down here in the community room and sometimes in each other's apartment. I've offered encouragement where I can, and I see more join in each day. Lola holds them together when I'm not around."

"Really? I knew they prayed down here, but I didn't know they also prayed in their apartments. Interesting." She looked upwards and silently prayed, *God, we need help right now.*

Rafe noticed her actions. "God works in mysterious ways. You never know who He's going to pick to join His team. Look at me." He pointed his finger at himself. "You never would think I would end up a minister, but for some reason the Lord brought me here."

"I'm sure glad He brought you here," she took a deep breath, not wanting to sound foolish. "But with you here in the building with the residents (*and with me,* she wanted to add) brings a sense of peace to everything going on around us. I appreciate you in more ways than you can imagine."

Definitely in more ways than you can imagine.

Reverend Rafe blushed and attempted to change the

subject. "Do you think there is a chance I could get a look at those records to see if there is any possibility my relatives worked on this project? It would mean a great deal to my family if we could track their whereabouts."

"I'm sorry, Rafe." She shook her head, conflicted that she wanted to allow him access to the records. "As of right now this information needs to remain confidential. Even though the records are over forty years old I would need permission from the sheriff and the government to release them. Perhaps we can talk to Mitch and arrange to have you act in some official capacity so you can gain access to the records."

His voice changed to frustration. "That may take some time!"

Thinking of Clarence's statement made the day before, she replied, "Yes, that's true. It's the only way I can think of right now to allow you to look at them. I can lose my job if I give you access to these records."

"I understand," he said somberly. "Don't worry about it. I will talk to the sheriff myself, and see what can be arranged. That way you won't be involved at all."

"I appreciate it," she replied, as she put the last piece of tape on the final box to secure it.

"Well, I guess I better go meet my prayer team in the community room." He cleared his throat as she looked up at him from the floor. "Could I possibly talk you into dinner one evening soon or even lunch? We need to quit meeting here at the high rise." He winked. "I'd sure like to get to know you a little better."

Now it was her turn to blush. "Yes, I would like that very much. Just to let you know, my parents will arrive soon. I'd like you to meet them."

"That would be my pleasure, and be sure to bring them to

church." He smiled and left the office whistling *Amazing Grace*. He recalled the smile on Steph's face when she attended church, and she allowed herself to finally see that Jesus loved her.

Karen arrived back at the office. Steph was glad to see her smiling face rather than Callie's dour frown.

Callie had been quiet earlier in the day while they went through the boxes. Steph did not understand her complexities. It seemed Callie always carried a chip on her shoulder and looked for someone to blame everything on, but today she remained calm. She noticed Callie also watched her dad as he worked.

Once the remainder of the staff returned, she asked Darrin and Derek to put the boxes in her vehicle, so she could deliver them personally to the Sheriff's Department. At this point in time she did not trust anyone else to do the job.

Mitch sat at his desk when she arrived at the Law Enforcement Center, but she noticed through the window in his closed office door that he was on the phone. Unable to talk to him, she dropped off the boxes, walked past his door and waved. He waved back and made a circular motion with his other hand that he would call her later. She nodded her head. She wanted a sandwich before she keeled over from hunger, so she did not want to stick around.

One thing about a small town is that wherever you wanted to go, it did not take long to get there and within a few minutes she arrived at her front door. Steph made a grilled cheese sandwich and opened a cold diet cola, and consumed it as she walked up the stairs to take a cold shower and change clothes. She had been so in tune with eating on the go that it came natural for her to walk and eat at the same time. She did not think to lock her door before she ambled up the stairs.

She tuned the radio to the local station for noise, and stepped into the shower.

Meanwhile, downstairs two elderly people rang the doorbell and knocked on the door.

"I can hear a radio going. I'm sure someone is home."

"Well, keep ringing the doorbell. I'm sure she'll hear it sooner or later."

"I'll try the door and see if it's open. Oh, my, the door is open. I guess we can just go in."

"I don't know if that's a good idea!"

As she stepped out of the shower, Steph thought she heard voices downstairs. She turned the volume on the radio down to make sure it was not the radio voices she heard. Someone invaded her house. She wrapped a large bath towel around her body, slipped across the hallway to her bedroom, grabbed her cell phone, and dialed 9-1-1. "There's someone in my house. I'm upstairs and they're downstairs."

The 9-1-1 operator said a squad car was on its way after she gave her address.

She grabbed a baseball bat from the bedroom closet and slowly descended the stairs. The sirens heard in the distance made her feel brave because the police were on their way, and she walked toward the noise in the kitchen. Steph raised the bat and turned the corner into the kitchen only to bump directly into her father.

"Stephanie Anne Runnell, are you trying to give me a heart attack?" her father exclaimed.

"Oh, Dad!" She felt relieved as she put the bat down and fell into her dad's arms. "I thought you were a burglar. In fact, I called the police from my cell phone while upstairs." She giggled, and clutched her bath towel tightly to herself, as the police car glided to a stop in front of her house. What an embarrassing time to explain her parents broke into her house. Well, not exactly broke in. She did forget to lock her door.

CHAPTER EIGHTEEN

Not even the middle of afternoon and Mitch's head spun with frazzled thoughts from all directions. His feelings for Steph collided with his duties as sheriff. Last night he continued to renew their friendship and started to enjoy their evening and conversation. That is, until Bill Jensen stopped at their table.

Of course, I just had to talk business, which I promised earlier not to do.

Bill's comments about the Mexicans who worked at the high rise bothered him throughout the night, and caused him to toss and turn.

Early in the morning Tillie Jensen called and said her dad wanted to talk. He decided to drive out to Bill's place today anyway to pursue further questioning.

When opportunity knocks—one of the few people still around during construction of the high rise, Bill may be able to give us a lead.

He first stopped at River View Towers. Mitch scheduled

the Sheriff's Posse and several off-duty officers to assist in the storage room to search for personnel records from the construction phase of the high rise. He wanted to stay and oversee the project, but Tillie sounded insistent he come right away. He needed to prioritize this investigation. He knew Steph could handle the storage room. He did not want to upset her, so he said nothing about his upcoming meeting, and left after he briefed all the volunteers.

After he arrived at the Jensen home, Tillie led Mitch to Bill's bedroom. Tillie explained Bill's attack last evening left him weak. She suggested he stay in bed for the day.

"Pops, Mitch is here." Bill attempted to sit up using his elbows, but Tillie pushed an extra pillow under his head and made him lie back down. "Stubborn old man," she complained. "Won't stay still for a minute."

"Sorry, daughter, just not used to all this fussin'." Tillie's eyes filled with worry as she turned to leave the room.

Bill looked as pale as the sheets surrounding him. Mitch pulled out a hand-held recorder just in case Bill said anything of significance. Tillie stood by the bedroom door to keep a watchful eye on her dad.

"I need to record our conversation today, Bill. Is that okay with you?" Mitch set the recorder on the bedside stand.

Bill nodded. Mitch flipped the switch for the recorder.

"Okay, we'll start. Will you state your name please?"

"Bill...Jensen...William," he stuttered.

"Okay, Bill, tell me whatever you can remember around the time the construction of the high rise. Any little thing, even if you think it's insignificant, still may be a clue to help us solve this mystery."

"Ain't got much to say 'cept I got to thinkin' about that time when all them Mexicans worked at the high rise, and then most of them left that quick," he attempted to snap his fingers, but his hand dropped back on the sheets.

"What do you mean most of them left that quick?" Mitch leaned in closer to Bill to hear his answer.

"Well, it had been a slow year for us at the bar," he shakily began his story. "New restaurants and bars opening up in town and all. Then the construction crews started comin' in for buildin' the high rise. The crew boss hired the Mexicans for cheap labor—you know, two for one. You hire one, but get two and only pay for one. Locals weren't too happy with that situation. It didn't affect me 'cept my business wasn't doing too well anyway. So I started comin' to town and bein', you know, friendly to the Mexicans. Told them about my bar. None of the business owners liked them Mexicans. I spoke a little of their language. Enough to get me by. Several could speak pretty good English, and soon they started comin' out to my bar." He stopped to catch his breath as it became more labored and his voice weakened.

"On weekends they knew I catered to tourists and weekenders so they didn't show up. On the weekdays I'd stay open later than usual just for them. Sometimes they got so drunk they would sleep in their pickup trucks in the parking lot. They didn't bother me, and I liked the extra cash I got off 'em. I didn't like them takin' jobs away from our locals, but I wanted to get married and needed money to buy a house." He paused with a faraway look in his eyes, and then tears flowed.

Mitch noticed him drifting off. "Are you okay, Bill?"

"Wa...ter," he squeaked out as he held his hand to his throat. Tillie started into the room and Mitch motioned her to stay. Mitch handed him the glass of water on the nightstand. He took a few sips from the straw and sighed. "Sorry, my throat gets dry when I talk too much."

"That's okay. Do you want to continue?"

"Sure. Where was I?"

"Mexicans would sleep in their pickups sometimes when they got too drunk to drive. Do you know where they stayed?"

"Sometimes at one of those cheap motels just comin' into town—dumps back then. I don't think they're even there anymore. Otherwise, they camped out wherever."

"I think they're all gone. I'll check that out. What else can you tell me?"

"I never really liked them Mex...icans." He started to cough again and took another sip of water. "But like I said, they never bothered me, but I remembered one night a bunch of them left the bar drunk, about five of them, past closing time. I locked up after they left, but I swear I saw some other pickups followin' them. I had a few snoots, too, and didn't think too much of it. But then those five never came back. I figured they just quit or got fired and moved on. Still a few other Mexicans would come out to the bar, but shortly after those five left I finally just closed the doors for the winter. Didn't think too much about it until the news about the bodies being found. It's bothered me ever since with those men leavin' so sudden."

"Is that it?" asked Mitch.

"That's about it, Sheriff. Like I said, it just bothered me and needed to get it off my chest. I know there ain't much time left for me, and didn't want to die with this hangin' over my shoulder."

"Now, Pops, just quit your talkin' that way. I don't want to hear it." Tillie came to his bedside and tried to soothe her dad as she rubbed his back. "You'll be with us for a long time yet." She fluffed his pillows again and put them back under his head.

"Just don't count on it, girlie." He attempted a phony hoarse laugh.

"Do you remember anything about the pickups following the Mexicans that night?"

Bill started to close his eyes, but Mitch needed more answers.

Bill slowly tried to focus. "Not really. Remember pickups." He hesitated. "Now that I think about it, I remember hearing dogs whine as they drove down the road. Funny... I've been layin' here tryin' to relive that night and first remembered the dogs. I thought at the time they were out huntin' 'coon and turned around in my parking lot."

He turned off the recorder. "Well, thank you. I'll get back to you if there are any more questions. You take care, Bill."

Tillie walked with him to the door.

"Thank you, Sheriff, for coming so quickly. The doctor already told us Pops only got weeks to several months left. I've been tryin' to just keep him comfortable. He doesn't know, but I think he suspects."

"I'm so sorry, Tillie."

"It would be nice to solve this before he passes on. I think he would feel more at peace to know what happened to those poor men."

"I'm sure he would. We all would." He shook his head, a worried frown creased his forehead.

Later in the afternoon as he re-wound the tape and started to review the conversation with Bill and take notes, the BCA agent, Norman Schmidt, assigned to the case called him. He was on the phone with Agent Schmidt when Steph walked by his office and waved. He wanted to apprise her of his conversation with Bill. He motioned with his free hand he would call her later. She nodded and smiled as she walked by.

Within minutes of her departure, Reverend Rafael stopped by the main desk, and asked Mitch's secretary, Sally, to make an appointment so he could speak to him. Mitch noticed the reverend at the desk, and turned the tape player off. Curious as to his reason for the visit, he walked out to greet Rafe.

"Good afternoon, Reverend." Mitch extended his hand. Rafe responded with a firm handshake. "What can I help you with today?"

"May I talk to you for a few minutes about the investigation at River View?"

Mitch hesitated, ready to deny him a few minutes, but then noticed the strong single-minded determination in the reverend's stance. "Well…I can listen, but I can't give out any information. Come back to my office anyway, and we can talk."

Not quite sure what Rafe could say to affect the investigation, Mitch closed the door so their conversation would be private. The police scanner could be heard in Mitch's office making background noises as officers talked back and forth to dispatch and to each other. Used to the chatter, Mitch ignored it, but the noise intrigued Rafe.

He cleared his throat. "Just came from meeting some residents who were concerned about the Sheriff's Posse volunteers and deputies there today. I also talked to Ms. Runnell. She mentioned the group found the construction records, and you would be going through them."

"How does this concern you?" Mitch looked quizzically at the Reverend.

"The reason I'm asking…and I've not shared this with anyone except for Ms. Runnell…is that I feel God placed me here in this community for a reason other than discipling my congregation. I've had that feeling for a long time." He paused and waited for a reaction from Mitch. "I wanted to wait to talk with you, but while at River View, I felt God put on my heart to get over here right away. I know it sounds odd, but I just got up from our prayer meeting and left to come here."

Mitch folded his arms and leaned back in his chair. "Okay, so continue. What's this got to do with my investigation?"

"My mother is Hispanic. My father is Irish-German descent. Her last name was Garcia. When she married my father, she took his last name of McGowan," he offered.

"Yes, I figured you had some Hispanic blood in your veins. We don't get many Hispanics in this area, but I did work for a few years in the Twin Cities area in a heavy Hispanic neighborhood." He cleared this throat. "So what's your story?"

"My mother's family emigrated here from Mexico," Rafe began hesitantly. "Several of my cousins and one of my uncles moved north back in the late 1960s, early 1970s to work construction. They kept in touch for a while, and then my grandmother said she heard nothing from any of them. My mother was young when José left. Her wish is to find out what happened to my uncle and cousins. She said the last letter the family received from her brother came from Minnesota back in the early 1970s. He would write at least once a month and send money. Then the letters stopped."

He took out his wallet and withdrew a worn and faded picture and handed it to Mitch. "My uncle is on the right and his two cousins on the left. The two in the middle are friends who left with them. I've searched to find traces of them on my days off. You know, going through old records in courthouses like marriage licenses, death certificates, and the like. Haven't come up with any clues so far." He ran his hands through his hair. "It's like they completely disappeared."

"Or moved on to another state or another part of the country," Mitch added.

Mitch squinted his eyes to look at the picture Rafe gave him. "What kind of help do you want from me?" He raised his eyebrows.

"I would like to get a look at the employee records to see if my uncle or his cousins were ever on the construction payroll."

"Oh…I get it." He nodded. "Would you mind if I took a copy of this picture? Not that I'll be able to help you find your uncle and cousins, but I could file it away for future reference. In fact, if I could enlarge this picture on the copy machine, we might be able to get a better view of the faces."

"Sure, but I need the picture back. It's the only one I have of my uncle and cousins before they left."

As Mitch left his office to give the picture to his secretary to enlarge, Rafe looked around the room and noticed the picture of Mitch's daughter on his desk. Several officers chattered with dispatch over the police scanner, and he listened as he drummed his fingers on the desk.

Mitch returned with the picture and several enlargements. "Yeah, you can see the faces a little more clearly in the larger picture even though they're still a bit grainy. I made an extra for you."

They examined the pictures together. Rafe wiped the tears from his eyes as he looked more closely at the larger picture and the smiling faces of his uncle and cousins. He turned one enlargement over and wrote down the names of his uncle and cousins—José Garcia (uncle), Fernando Osorio, Antonio Osorio (cousins), Roberto Morales, Hernando Valdez (friends) and handed it back to Mitch.

"I didn't know any of these men in the picture. Just what my grandma and mother told me. What concerns me is that we've heard nothing from any of them."

"A BCA agent will arrive with a small team to go through the records. I just now got off the phone with him. If any of those names show up on the employee records, I will get in touch with you."

"Thank you," replied Rafe, grateful for the small favor.

"Not that it will do a lot of good. I'm sure none of those men are in the area, but you know since we made the news, I hope that someone will come forward."

"What will the agent look for?" questioned Rafe, as he put the picture back in his wallet.

"First of all, we want to question any of the locals that worked on the project. Now we got access to the employee records, it'll be easier to track them down for questioning. Then those that aren't local, we'll be able to run a data base to find out their current whereabouts—whether they're dead or alive."

"Any leads?"

He hesitated, not sure how much information to reveal. "Well…not a lot at this point. However, I did do an interview this morning with a local person who verified that Mexicans did work on the high rise construction. We won't know their names until we look through the records. The director just brought those records over. I haven't even looked at them."

The 9-1-1 operator voice sounded over the police scanner, "Cars in the vicinity of 804 Oak Street, occupant reports a break-in currently in progress. Female in house by herself."

"We've got it," came another voice over the scanner from a squad car. "We're on our way…less than one mile away."

Mitch looked up, startled, "That's Steph's address!" he

exclaimed. "I think I'll follow up and check on this. I'm sorry, Reverend, but I need to take this call."

"May I accompany you as a ride along? I've done a ride along before and know the drill."

"Sure. Let's go."

CHAPTER NINETEEN

The sirens closed in, and Steph could hear the screech of the tires on the squad car as it stopped in front of her house. She looked at her parents as they stood in the kitchen with their mouths open and eyes wide, and she went into protective mode.

Mortified by her state of undress, she still needed to stop the police who might misinterpret the awkward situation. She ran to the door and opened it.

Two deputies walked cautiously up the sidewalk with their hands on their holsters ready to draw their guns at any time.

She stood nearly naked in the doorway and tried to shield her parents as they strained to look out the door behind her. Steph held on to her towel, but used her other hand to stop them from drawing their guns.

"It's okay, Officers. I am sooo sorry. It was a false alarm." She waved her one free hand. "Can you give me a moment to run upstairs and throw some clothes on and I'll explain?"

"Yes, ma'am," replied one of the officers. Grinning, he

added, "I sure do want to hear an explanation." As she turned to go upstairs she noticed her parents still behind her.

"Mom, Dad, I'll be right back. Give me a minute."

Before she could dash upstairs, another squad car pulled up behind the first. This time it said "Sheriff" on the side.

Oh, no, Mitch is here! Oh my goodness, so is Reverend Rafe! Oh dear, here I am...half-naked.

"Hi, Mitch. Hi Rafe." Her face turned a deep pink. She gingerly lifted her one hand to wave, while she attempted to hang on to her towel with both hands as they sprinted up the sidewalk to her house.

Steph needed to get out of there. "I'll be right back and will explain."

Up the stairs she ran, taking delicate steps, one at a time, so the towel would stay intact. In a few minutes she walked back downstairs, fully dressed in blue jeans and t-shirt. She did not want to take the time to dig out another outfit for work, so she grabbed whatever laid on her chair by the bed.

Mitch kept himself occupied and engaged her parents in conversation. He had his arm around her mother, and her mom snuggled against him. Steph did not see the first deputies on the scene.

Mitch noticed her confusion and gave her an amused smile. "I sent the other deputies back out on patrol. It didn't look like these were dangerous people who broke into your house."

His eyes danced with suppressed mirth as he spoke. Steph glared at him and did not think his statement humorous.

"I am so sorry, Mitch," she started to explain. "I was upstairs in the shower when I heard noises downstairs. I thought someone broke into the house and called 9-1-1. The squad car pulled up to the curb, and I needed to stop them

159

before they gave my dad a heart attack. I scared my folks enough just swinging a bat around."

Rafe, amused by the comical scene, stood in the doorway unnoticed. "Ahem," he cleared his throat. "It looks like y'all are okay?"

They all turned. Steph smiled, her eyes locked with his. She walked up to Rafe, put her arm through his, and maneuvered him toward her parents.

"Mom, Dad, I would like you to meet Reverend Rafael McGowan from the River Falls Christian Church." Her eyes softened as she introduced him. "Reverend, these are my parents, Wayne and Anne Thomas. Rafe's helped out at the high rise with the residents during the crisis...and we've become friends."

Rafe stepped forward and gave them a disarming smile. "It's nice to meet you even under these extraordinary circumstances." With a slight bow he formally shook their hands. Her parents looked from one to the other and then back at Mitch, who, with watchful eyes, observed the introduction. Mitch felt a stab of pain in his chest.

Could it be jealousy?

"I'm sorry, Steph." He seemed uneasy and gave a weak smile, as he realized new feelings of envy. "I should have introduced the reverend, but I guess the excitement to see your parents again, I actually forgot he rode along with me."

Anne Thomas responded to Rafe. "We are so glad you are a friend of our Stephanie's."

Well, maybe more than friends.

Steph tried to assume a professional face to dig her way out of an awkward situation.

"I rummaged through Steph's cabinets to find some tea. Can I offer you gentlemen a cup of tea in compensation for getting you over here under false pretenses?"

"I would love to stay and chat, but maybe some other time," replied Mitch. "The hazards of being the sheriff. More papers to shuffle than field work." He looked pointedly at Steph. "The BCA agent assigned to the high rise case will be here in the morning with several other agents to start going through the employee records. Would you be available in case they want to talk to you?"

"Sure, no problem," she replied.

"I guess I better go with the sheriff." Rafe gave her a crooked smile and raised his eyebrows. "He's my ride here."

"Nice to meet you, Reverend," Wayne Thomas patted Rafe on the back as they walked out the door. "Hope to see both of you soon." Both Anne and Wayne stood in the door and waved as they drove off.

"Well, Daughter, so glad to see you're dressed again," Wayne teased as he ran his hand through his thinning gray hair.

"Oh, Dad, why didn't you guys tell me that you would be arriving today? I wouldn't have made such a fool out of myself," she chided him.

"But, honey, we wanted to surprise you." Anne innocently grinned. "We didn't know when we'd arrive. In all honesty, it really did surprise you. Got my heart racing there for a bit. I'm just glad it didn't give your dad a heart attack, what with his heart condition and all."

She looked at her dad and broke into a short laugh. "I could have hurt you if I swung the bat. You're lucky it was during the day. At night I wouldn't be looking to see the perp. I would just start swinging."

"Oh, my," admonished her mother, purposely putting a hand to her chest. "You've become quite independent, haven't you?" Steph, familiar with her mother's dry sense of humor, took it in stride.

"Yes, Mother, I learned to take care of myself—not any choice in the matter," she sighed.

"Well, its tea time, and let's catch up for a few minutes before we settle in. I'd like to rest for a while before we unpack. What is this...calling your minister by his first name?" her mother teased as they eased themselves into the kitchen chairs for their chat.

"Right now, Mom, we're friends."

Steph seemed happy her parents finally arrived, but knew in her heart something else brought them to town. She worried about them, but they looked to be in good spirits even after the long drive. They drank their tea, teased her about Mitch and Rafe, talked about their few stops on the way up, and said nothing about the real reason they drove all the way up from Texas.

Her mother appreciated the small cozy room Steph and Azalea took such great care to decorate. Steph noticed Azalea added a bouquet of flowers from her garden.

After giving her parents a goodbye hug, she left them to unpack. She wore her blue jeans and t-shirt to the office. She wanted to make sure the maintenance crew put all the boxes back in the storeroom and secured the entrance to the stairs. She wanted to be back home within the hour, but it ended up more like two hours. Darrin and Derek attempted to put the boxes back in chronological order, and it took a little extra time.

She arrived back at home with plans to take her parents out to dinner, but was surprised her mom already made her special spaghetti recipe for supper. Steph regretted she never took the time to learn from her. Oh, yes, she could throw a meal together, but it would never taste as delicious as what her mother made.

"Let's eat out in the back yard," she suggested, as she smacked her lips in anticipation of her mom's spaghetti and garlic bread.

"I'm sorry I didn't take time to make a dessert, so I sent your dad to the store for some pie and ice cream and a few other supplies," she said contritely, as they carried the dishes out to the small patio table Steph purchased at a garage sale.

"Mom, I'm going gain twenty pounds while you are here," she chided, but smiled with a gleam in her eyes as they sat down to the feast.

"I hope we can have Mitch over for a meal one night," her dad piped in. "After seeing him, I get emotional just thinking of our past here, and then everything happening to you." His eyes misted, and he wiped them with a napkin.

"Are you thinking about Aaron?" she probed.

"Probably," he replied and lifted his eyes toward the sky. "I often wonder if we would have stayed here if it weren't for the accident."

"Dad, I know you and Mom are here to offer me support, but you didn't need to drive all the way up here just to do that. I'd like to know why you came back when you specifically told me you would never come back to this town again."

Her parents looked at each other as only couples do when they have been together for so long.

I know they're avoiding the subject of why they returned to River Falls. They're holding out on me—not telling me the entire truth.

"Honey, we want to be with you at this time." Her mom patted Steph's arm. "Maybe we can help in some way. We felt so helpless down there when we could be here. Besides it's so

163

humid back home right now."

"Okay, Mom," she gave in. "I guess I won't get it out of you just yet. I know you better than that, and I know you have more reasons other than to support me."

Her parents smiled, but she knew they were counterfeit smiles.

They're up to something. I'll eventually find out.

"Let me help you with the dishes," Steph offered.

"No, that's okay," replied her mom, as she picked up some of the plates to carry back into the house.

Steph carried her plate inside and scraped the leftovers into the garbage. As she pulled the trashcan out from under the sink, she noticed several different jars of ready-made spaghetti sauce.

Mom's special spaghetti recipe. Yeah, right!

She formed her hand into a fist and pulled it down to her side to show she discovered her mother's secret.

CHAPTER TWENTY

Steph slept peacefully, knowing her parents were safe in her house. In spite of their age and health issues, they lived as vital people.

Her dad played golf and liked to fish. He said he looked forward to fishing for catfish in the river again. Her mom stayed busy with her charity work, played tennis, and walked daily in their neighborhood.

They both complained of the humidity in Texas during the summer, and the evening before used the excuse to visit her as a chance to come up north to 'cool down'.

Her parents already up and dressed for the day prepared breakfast, so Steph, who normally relied on a muffin and coffee, ate with them.

She arrived at work earlier than the rest of the staff, and took a few minutes to relax at her desk. She checked the schedule on her calendar.

Meeting with contractor at nine, going over the progress of the renovations. Maybe I can catch up on some paperwork and be available to meet with the BCA investigator at Mitch's office.

Sighing with relief, she sat back in her chair and closed her eyes. Since she started to attend church again, she began her workday with a prayer.

Rafe's presence really influenced my life: prayer in the morning, and the Bible in the evening.

The drilling noises from the installation of the new indoor sprinkler system grated on her nerves, and she found it hard to concentrate on prayer. She knew once the hallways were done the new system would then be installed in all the apartments. That would muffle some sounds, but probably irritate the residents even more.

Karen arrived. She carried her satchel and heavy handbag. Steph could hear her labored breathing. Karen talked about losing weight all summer, but Steph noticed no progress in her diet.

Callie and Lola followed behind. They all seemed in better spirits today now that the dreaded storeroom issue was a thing of the past. Steph made a note on her desktop calendar to organize the storage area and remove the outdated office equipment when the weather turned cooler.

"I'll make the coffee this morning," Karen shouted, as she plunked her handbag in her desk drawer.

"I'm sorry," Steph shouted back toward Karen's office. "I didn't think about making coffee."

"No problem. I brought doughnuts from the bakery." She pulled out a bag from her briefcase.

"Sounds yummy," Steph rubbed her full stomach.

Not really.

She heard Karen rummage around in the break room and fill the coffee pot while she hummed to herself.

Karen opened the refrigerator located next to the window to reach the coffee creamers. As she closed the door she looked out the window. Something looked odd, a broken branch from the tree, and she moved closer to the window to get a better view. She let out a scream and dropped the creamers on the floor.

"Oh, my! Oh my!" she cried out.

Steph and Callie hurried into the break room. They believed Karen hurt herself. She stood by the window, and held her hands over her horror-stricken face.

"What is it?"

Spilled coffee creamers—not a disaster.

Karen, in shock, not able to say a word, looked out the window and pointed. Her body shook as she covered her face again.

Steph looked out the window. Electrical equipment and a large elm tree protected the view from the street. Right in front of the window lay a large broken tree branch that partially covered a body.

"Call 9-1-1 and an ambulance!" shouted Steph.

Lola, who stood by the counter, picked up the phone and placed the call with trembling hands.

Steph rushed out the door and around the corner of the building. Callie followed her.

Even though the body laid face down she recognized Eddie Barkley. He wore his Sheriff's Posse uniform from the day before. She observed how the body was twisted and contorted, and knew he did not walk out of the building on his own volition.

He did not just fall down and die, not with those broken branches under him.

She looked up toward the top of the building and noticed

an open window on the thirteenth floor. Steph closed her eyes and attempted to visualize the apartment with the open window. Trepidation filled her heart—Apartment 1313.

She knelt down and touched his neck to find a pulse. His body, cold to the touch, made her shiver.

No need to take a pulse.

His limbs stiff, rigor mortis already set in, she realized he died late last night.

Two squad cars arrived—no sirens. They did not want to frighten the elderly residents in the building. Those who lived in the apartments on the north side of the building could be seen as they gawked out their windows.

Lola and Karen, wide-eyed, anxiously watched from inside the building, afraid to leave the office window.

The sheriff's car arrived within seconds after the other squad cars. Steph's face was drawn and tense as Mitch exited his vehicle. He glanced at both her and Callie and then at the body. He approached the scene with the other officers and started to issue orders immediately.

"Call the coroner over here," he shouted to the two deputies. "Cover the body until the coroner arrives. Get the department photographer to take pictures. Pick up any evidence and bag whatever you think would be helpful. But do NOT touch the body," he emphasized.

Mitch held his cell phone and speed dialed the county investigator. "Steve, we have a death. Can you come to River View Towers right pronto? Possible homicide!"

Callie stood off to the side. She did not move or show any emotion.

"I'm sorry, Callie. This has got to be terrifying for you," Steph said, distressed that she could not do anything to help.

"Poor fool. I knew he would end up like this one day,"

Callie callously replied. Her body tense, she wrapped her arms around her chest.

I cannot believe she feels that way about her father. If it were my dad, I would be devastated.

Steph looked at her suspiciously. "Why don't you go back to the office, Callie? There's nothing you can do here... unless... " she added, "you know something about this."

Callie glared at her with narrowed eyes. "I prefer to wait here until they take him away."

"Are you sure?"

"Yes, I'm sure." Callie walked over to the side of building where she could not directly see the body. Her hands trembled as she removed a pack of cigarettes from her pants pockets, drew one out, and attempted to light it. Between her shaking hands and the wind, it took a few attempts before it lit. It seemed to calm her nerves as she leaned against the building and inhaled the aroma of the cigarette.

Steph focused her attention on Mitch after she made sure Callie would be okay.

"Okay, Steph, tell me about this?" Mitch asked. "We don't know yet if it's a crime scene or a suicide. We'll let the coroner make that decision."

"This is such a shock! I came in this morning, but didn't bother to go into the break room or look out the window. If I had, I would have noticed him sooner," Steph moaned.

"Just go over the details...if you can." Mitch said in a steady, low-pitched voice.

"Okay...okay. Let me think." She put her fingers to her temples. A headache started to form. "I came in a few minutes early this morning," she began, and explained all the details to Mitch in the order she remembered them.

Steph looked warily at him, put her finger to her lips and

lowered her voice. "Mitch, look up at the thirteenth floor window." She pointed. "It's open. I'm sure he fell out of that window."

He stretched his neck toward the window. "Good possibility," he agreed.

"The apartment is vacant," she whispered. "He had no business in that apartment. How did he even get in there?"

"This sounds more like a crime scene all the time."

"Miss Mattie came to see me several days ago. She thought ghosts were in 1313, but she also said some other disturbing things. I documented it, but put it out of my mind. With her mental condition, I didn't think too much about it."

I don't dare mention to Mitch my fear when I entered that apartment. He'd think I'm as crazy as Miss Mattie.

Their conversation was interrupted when the coroner and the ambulance arrived.

"Morning, Sheriff. Ms. Runnell," Dr. Sanderson, the coroner, gruffly greeted them, and put the emphasis on the word Ms. "It seems like this is going to be a busy place today. What do we have here?" He looked toward the covered body.

"Eddie Barkley, I'm afraid," replied Mitch, as he shook his head at the same time.

The coroner walked cautiously toward the body. The county investigator, Steve Bishop, arrived right behind the coroner with a camera around his neck. The BCA commissioned him to assist with the case of the remains found in the high rise, but Steph never had the opportunity to meet him.

Shorter than Mitch and stocky, his casual dress would never indicate he belonged with the county investigative team. His clothes looked like he slept in them. Steph immediately thought of a frumpy police lieutenant on an old TV show.

"I guess I'm also the photographer today. Update, Sheriff," he requested, as he held a pen and notebook in his hand.

Mitch informed Steve Bishop what he knew and what Steph relayed to him. After the briefing, he walked over to the coroner and observed as he examined the body. He started to snap pictures. After many camera clicks, the coroner, with the help of Detective Bishop, turned the body over. Steve Bishop wrote in his notebook as he watched the coroner continue his brief examination.

Mitch strolled over to observe the examination. Detective Bishop continued to snap additional pictures from every angle.

Steph stood on the sidelines, too ill at ease to look at the body again.

Dr. Sanderson and Mitch put their heads together for a brief moment and then sauntered toward Steph.

The investigator remained by the body and gave orders to the deputies on the scene.

"It looks like he's been dead at least six to eight hours," Dr. Sanderson confirmed. "There are bruises on his face and his knuckles. Those would not come from jumping out the window even if it was from the thirteenth floor. I think we can consider foul play here."

"I guessed as much. Can you give me any more details, Doc?" Mitch looked at Steph as she massaged her head.

"Well, I can tell you this much. Almost every bone is his body looks like it's broken. There's some debris under his fingernails I need to examine. Could be dried blood. It might yield some DNA. Looks like he struggled with someone. I'll have the body taken to the hospital where I can perform an autopsy. You can take it from there, Sheriff."

"Thanks, Doc. I appreciate your quick report on this." Dr. Sanderson gave a curt nod and walked back to his car. The ambulance personnel stood by and waited for Bishop to give the okay to take the body to the morgue at the hospital.

After Detective Bishop snapped enough pictures, he walked back to Mitch and Steph. "Can I get into that apartment?" He pointed to the thirteenth floor apartment.

"Sure," replied Steph. "I don't see how Eddie would be able to get into the apartment without a key…unless someone let him in or took him there."

Steph remembered her conversation with Mattie.

"By the way, I want to give you copies of some documentation I took from Mattie Turnborn several days ago. I don't know if there's any basis to it, but I'm concerned it affects one of our employees."

She turned her head toward Callie, who stood by the ambulance, as they loaded the body of her father.

Mitch and Steve accompanied Steph to her office. She closed the door so the office staff could not hear their conversation. She removed the file from the cabinet and handed it to Mitch.

"Let's call Callie in here and ask her about it," requested Mitch.

"Do you think it's necessary to do it right now? She just lost her father."

"Better to get it over with," commented Detective Bishop. "No time is really a good time, but I need to know if she had any idea why he would be in that apartment. I'll play the bad guy here."

Lola and Karen tried to comfort Callie, who finally broke down in tears. As soon as she saw Steph, the tears dried up.

She's put on a show for the rest of the staff? Earlier she showed no remorse.

Steph looked puzzled, and drew her eyebrows together.

"Callie, please come in my office." Callie hesitantly walked in. "Please sit down." Steph pointed to a chair.

"I'm Detective Bishop, Callie. I will be investigating the death of your father."

Callie nodded sullenly, not speaking.

"Do you know where your father was last evening?"

"No."

"Do you know why your father would be visiting the high rise?"

"No."

"Do you know if he had any friends here that he might want to visit in the building?"

"Nope," she volunteered. "I don't keep tabs on him."

"Okay, Callie, now I am going to get personal with you. I'm looking at a file that has an accusation of someone seeing you come out of an apartment on the thirteenth floor. Actually, it's the same apartment that has the window open right now and from where it's presumed your father fell to his death. What can you tell us?"

Callie opened her mouth and nothing came out as she stared at Mitch and Detective Bishop. "I...I can't tell you anything," she finally said.

"You have a master key, do you not?"

"Yes, sir."

"Where is it?"

"It's on my key ring." Callie looked at him with cold eyes.

"Okay, show me."

She jumped up from the chair and walked quickly to her computer station. Steven Bishop and Mitch followed her. She opened the desk drawer and pulled out her purse, fumbled around inside for her key ring. "Here it is!" she blurted out. "The key is here!" she repeated with a sigh of relief.

Steve looked at Mitch and raised his eyebrows. Mitch's nostrils flared, and he made a motion with his eyes that Steve understood.

"Okay, Callie. That's all for now. We'll be in contact."

Steven Bishop walked back into the director's office with Mitch and Steph. "I do need to get into the apartment and run some fingerprint tests to see if there is any evidence we can use."

"It's been vacant since I arrived here. There's no furniture in it. I checked it out myself after my little talk with Miss Mattie."

"All I need is your permission since it's vacant. I won't need a search warrant since Eddie was not found inside the apartment."

"Sure. You got it."

"Thanks. I'll get the county lab crime team over here and relieve you of this one."

"The saying goes that the thirteenth floor is a haunted floor. I guess I agree with the adage," quoted Steph.

"You don't really believe in superstitions, do you?" Mitch smirked. "I think I'll have a quick look at the apartment, too."

The three rode the elevator to the thirteenth floor. Steph stopped in front of the door to the apartment, afraid to use her master key.

What will we find when we enter?

The door lock did not give her a problem. The door stood partially open. Both Mitch and Steve looked at each other.

Steph dreaded to go into the apartment, even with Mitch and the detective. She did not like the feeling that crept into her body after her last visit. She hesitated and waited by the entrance while the other two checked it out. Her nose still detected a faint smell of rotten eggs in the apartment.

Detective Bishop and Mitch walked around and made sure not to touch anything—not even the light switches. The apartment had only three windows, and the living room, the largest, stood open. Detective Bishop looked out the window to view the outline of where the body had lain. He turned, looked at the floor, pushed something around with his foot, took a pair of tweezers out of his pocket, and used it to pick up a key from the carpet.

"Does this key match yours, Ms. Runnell?"

Now forced to walk into the room, Steph looked at the key, careful not to touch it, and compared it to the master she held in her hand. "It appears to be an exact match."

Detective Bishop reached in his pocket and withdrew a clear bag with a zippered top. Almost ready to drop it in the bag when Steph asked, "Please turn the key around so I can see both sides."

He flipped it back and forth while he held it with the tweezers.

"It looks like a match, but it doesn't have the master number engraved in it. All our keys are numbered. Each employee signs for the master key when they start work, and they're given one with a number stamped into it. This one does not have a number engraved on it." She showed him her key with the engraved number on it.

"Umm…that's interesting," Steve Bishop remarked, and shoved the key in his pocket. He continued to walk around the apartment with his eyes focused on the floor.

Steph did not want to get in their way, so she left while Mitch and Steve waited for the county crime lab team to arrive.

Another mystery to be solved. Another secret. Where did Eddie get a master key? Unless…oh my…unless he had a master key copied.

Callie remained despondent as Steph returned to the office.

"Why don't you go home for the remainder of the day?" offered Steph. "You need to make funeral arrangements for your father, and call your family and friends. Did you call your husband and son?"

"Thank you," Callie replied somberly, "and no I did not call them. I'm still in shock over all this."

"Please go home and do what you need to do."

Callie picked up her purse, and started to walk out the door in a slow-gaited pace.

"Callie, again, I am sorry about your father." Then added as afterthought, "What did your father do for work?"

"A locksmith…most of his life." She turned and looked at Steph. Her eyes looked empty and haunted. "In between his drinking and gambling he was a good locksmith, but lately I don't think he did much of anything."

"Oh, okay … just wondered."

The key…that's probably where the key came from. He got access to a master and made copies. Ah ha. The plot thickens.

Steph went to check on Karen. Her eyes stared blankly at the papers on her desk. She shuffled them back and forth into piles. Steph did not want Karen to become an emotional wreck. She needed her staff to stay strong.

Steph cleared her throat. Karen looked at her. "Are you going to be okay?"

"Oh, yes," replied Karen, as she reached for her coffee mug. Her hands shook as she took a sip of coffee. "You know, it's not the first time I found a body. With all the elderly in the building, it's not uncommon to find someone even after several days. Each time I get a little more calloused. It's just… it's just…this time was different: seeing a horrific, unnatural death."

"I understand how you feel," Steph commiserated. "I should explain to you what happened and ask your opinion."

She explained what the coroner said and revealed the information about the open window. The color drained from Karen's face, and she almost dropped her coffee mug. Steph reached over the desk and held Karen's shaking hands for a brief moment.

"We'll get through it as a team, and we'll be here for each other." She patted her hands and started to walk out of the door.

"By the way," she turned and raised her eyebrows," where is Lola?"

"She's in the community room. Some of the residents on that side of the building could see everything from their windows. They were upset that something else happened in the building and needed comfort. Lola's doing her best to calm them until Reverend Rafe gets here. I don't think he's arrived yet."

"Oh, all right. I wanted to make sure we account for everyone. Don't want anyone going off the deep end right now. We all need support."

Karen nodded. "I'll be okay."

"I'll talk to you when I find out more information."

The fingerprint team arrived during her meeting with the construction foreman. Karen let them in and escorted them to the apartment. The meeting lasted less than half an hour. Steph could not concentrate on the update, and felt relief when he finally left.

So many things she wanted to do. Her temples throbbed as her headache worsened.

"This is not going to be a good day," she grumbled to

herself.

She could not see anyone coming or going from her desk, so she did not know if the detective and crew were still in the building.

Short-handed in the office, Karen volunteered to sit at the reception desk.

Unable to concentrate, Steph decided to check on the detective and his crew.

Bishop's crew were busy dusting for fingerprints over every square inch of the empty apartment.

"Finding anything?" She stood in the doorway of the apartment, and did not want to disturb their work.

"Not much right now. Just don't touch anything, or we'll have to fingerprint you."

"FYI, my fingerprints are probably on the door knob already."

He sauntered over to the window and pointed. "There are some scratches on the window sill here." She gingerly walked over and looked at the marks. "Could be a sign of a struggle. Looks like fingernail scratches in the metal. We'll know more when the coroner gets done with the autopsy. We also found a small amount of blood in the carpet and took a sample of that."

"I think I need to tell you I talked to Callie about her father. He used to be a locksmith, and that's probably where the key came from."

"Interesting." He raised his eyebrows and jotted a few notes on his pad.

"Yes, isn't it though," she gave him a sidelong glance.

"We're still going through the apartment. I'll let you know if we find anything else."

Steph took that as her cue to leave them alone. After she rode the elevator down to main floor, she noticed Reverend

Rafe arrived and sat in the community room with at least a dozen residents.

Steph decided she needed to call her parents and inform them of what happened. Shocked by the news, they asked if she wanted them to come to the high rise and help. She discouraged them, and stated the investigator would probably be there all day.

As she looked out her office window she noticed a car drive by with a logo on it and recognized the local newspaper reporter with his camera.

"I gotta go, Mom," she cut the call short and hung up the phone. The TV station van also pulled up, and before she could even get out of the door to the building to stop them, the cameraman videotaped the scene. The deputies on the scene quickly blocked their view and entrance into the roped-off area.

Thank heavens, I don't have to deal with them again.

She turned around and walked back to the building, relieved she did not have to face reporters and TV cameras again.

Rafe came to her office about a half hour later. He strolled in solemnly and looked deep in thought. Steph did not want to interrupt his thoughts, and waited for him to speak.

"I'm sorry," he said. "I just asked God for wisdom, and the right words to comfort everyone."

"Rafe...," she hesitated, and looked at him with sympathy. "I know you will say what's in your heart, and it will be the right thing. I don't know of anyone with more understanding than you."

"Thank you. I appreciate your confidence in me, but comforting people can be a difficult task."

He continued, "I am concerned with Miss Mattie and

Maude. Mattie especially. Maude tried to calm her, but Mattie speaks incoherently, spouting innuendos about her former fiancé."

"Mitch mentioned her fiancé left town suddenly, and he was listed as a missing person in their files. I understand they closed the case and never re-opened it. Mitch thought he might be one of the bodies buried in the boiler room."

"Mattie's not making any sense. She said she felt her fiancé has tried to get in touch with her."

"In what way?" She leaned forward and looked at him curiously.

His eyes bored into hers. "Phone calls and no one on the other end."

Steph slapped her hand on her forehead.

Another mystery. Miss Mattie receiving anonymous phone calls? Why would anyone want to do this to her? Who would want to hurt her like this?

"Well, you know about Mattie's hallucinations, and her unusual behavior."

I don't want to call Mattie crazy, but it seems as though she's going down that road.

"I'm going to stop by the sheriff's office," Rafe abruptly stated. "I need to know if and when they find anything so I can help Mattie."

"Sounds like a good idea," Steph replied. "I think I will just stick around here until the investigator leaves with his crew."

"Can I call you later?"

"Sure. Call my cell phone if you don't mind."

"Okay."

Why are they taking so long in that apartment? There's not much square footage in those apartments. Maybe they found more evidence.

Within the next hour Detective Bishop, or Steve as he asked to be called, knocked on her door.

"We're done," he said as a matter of fact. "And we found some interesting tidbits." He grinned and held up three large gallon storage bags full of marijuana cigarettes, pills, and a powdery substance, all in small bags ready for street sales. He laid them on top of her desk so that she could get a good look.

"What did you say?" her eyes wide as she gazed at the bags full of drug paraphernalia. "Staff cleaned that apartment. I checked it myself several days ago."

"One of my men found this stuff doing a search for fingerprint evidence. The baseboard in the closet seemed to be loose. Curious, he removed it, and found a string tied to the floor joist. When he pulled the string, these bags came up out of the cavity in the wall."

"Wow!" she replied, stunned. "Does that mean there is definitely a possibility of foul play?"

"I would think so. I'm going to get this over to evidence and get it analyzed. We'll keep in touch with your agency."

Steph nodded. Steve and his crew packed their evidence into an unmarked squad car and drove away.

An older model Cadillac parked halfway down the street pulled out behind the unmarked car and followed it.

Jessie Maverick, a streetwise drug dealer, needed desperately to figure out a way to get those drugs back.

CHAPTER TWENTY-ONE

Mitch sat in his office and reviewed the pictures from the boiler room at River View, close ups of the skeletal remains found, the report from the coroner, and the forensics report from the BCA. He wanted to keep his mind off Eddie' death, and this helped to do it.

It's hard to let go. I need to delegate more to Steve as my investigator. He's always so thorough. I feel comfortable that he'll get the cases solved.

He looked up, noticed Reverend Rafe walk toward his office, and glanced toward Sally's desk.

Oh, no, not the reverend again. Sally's not at her desk either.

His lips pinched together in irritation. He rose out of respect, forced a smile and greeted him cordially even though he thought it an intrusion.

His door stood open. "Come on in," he waved to Rafe, and started to pick up the pictures.

"I stopped by to see if there's anything I can help with

concerning Eddie Barkley," Rafe tactfully asked, and hoped he could be of some comfort.

Out of the corner of his eye, he caught a glimpse of an object in one of the pictures. "Can I take a look at those pictures please?"

"These are from the boiler room so they're evidence. They're not for public viewing," Mitch scowled.

"But...I think I saw something I recognized," declared Rafe, as he anxiously leaned over the desk to get a better look at the pictures, and ignored Mitch's irritation. He was not about to let Mitch put those pictures away.

What on earth would the reverend recognize in those pictures? I suppose it doesn't hurt to show him. Any information gained would be helpful. He seems mighty interested in things going on at River View.

"Sure, take a look," he gave in. "It's not a nice scenario."

"I know," said Rafe, as he rifled through each picture. "This is what I wanted to see." He took out the picture of one of the skeletons where there were remains of a shirt and a necklace with a cross. "This cross... this cross," he said excitedly. "It's this cross. I've seen it before. It matches the one my mother always wore around her neck. She said she gave one like it to her brother before he left to come up north."

"What!" shouted Mitch, as he grabbed the picture to look at it again.

"Do you have the actual necklace?" Rafe held his breath for the answer he wanted to hear.

"It should be in the evidence room," Mitch bit down on a smile, and hoped there might be a break in the case.

"Could I see it?" His heart raced as he waited for Mitch to reply.

"Absolutely. Let's go down to the evidence room right

now. If it's what you think it is, maybe we can solve this well-kept secret."

"Do you remember the picture I gave you of my uncle, and you gave me some extra copies?"

"Yes, it's here on my desk." He dug through the pile. "Ah, here it is." He opened the file and took out the picture.

"That's my uncle, José." Rafe pointed to his uncle in the picture. "And that's the necklace my mother gave him. He wore it in the picture. If you blow up that part of the picture, you can make sure it's the same one."

Mitch, excited, asked his secretary, who just returned to her desk, to scan the picture and enlarge the part with the necklace.

"Let's go to the evidence room while she's messing with the picture," Mitch suggested, as he almost sprinted to the stairs.

Rafe apprehensively followed Mitch to the lower-level evidence room and prayed.

Dear God, am I finally going to get some answers for my family?

The deputy in charge of the evidence room asked Mitch to sign for the box that held what little remained of the clothing.

"It's only been a few days since we received these items from the State Forensic Unit," the deputy in charge reminded the sheriff.

Mitch, with slow motion, opened the box and retrieved the cross and chain. He gently placed it in Rafe's hands.

Rafe handled it with reverence as he turned it over and looked at the back. "You can barely see it, but there's my uncle's initials: J. G. You probably couldn't make them out unless you knew what to look for."

"Those initials were on the report we received back from

the BCA."

"This belonged to my uncle, José. I'm positive." He took the cross, held it to his chest, his lips quivered, and he started to weep. "Oh, Mama, maybe we finally found your brother." He looked upward. "Thank you, Heavenly Father, for giving us this sign."

Mitch looked stunned. "If this is true, then maybe we can get some answers about what happened, and why the makeshift grave."

"You still need to know the identity of the other person." He threw out the first thing to enter his mind. "I wonder if it's one of José's friends who went up north with him. I wrote the names on the back of the pictures. Could you somehow research the names to find them?"

"Sounds like a plan." He smiled with satisfaction to finally make some headway on the case.

"I will contact my mother and family and let them know the news. I will also ask if they could contact the families of these men to find their whereabouts. It's been so many years, and I'm not sure we can help you much in your investigation."

"Anything will help," replied Mitch. "And Rafe, thanks for your help. I'm sorry to hear it's a family member, but glad this case might move forward. We have the bullet found in the shoulder of your uncle. According to the forensics report he did not die from the bullet wound. There were some broken bones and skull fractures, so there still is a mystery to be solved."

"Thank you for allowing me to look at the pictures. I believe in my heart God is moving things along, and our prayers are being answered."

Mitch nodded in agreement, mad at himself for his grumpiness earlier.

The enlargement laid on Mitch's desk by the time they returned. Rafe still held the necklace in his hands. He carefully placed it by the enlargement of the cross. The picture remained grainy.

"This is the best we could do on short notice. It looks like a perfect match as far as I can see," stated Mitch.

"I agree. As a child I've looked at this cross so many times in my mom's jewelry box."

"Would you be willing to give up some of your DNA so that the BCA can test it for positive identification?"

"Sure, no problem. If this helps to seal the deal that it's my uncle, I'll do whatever you want."

"I'll call over to the hospital and talk to Dr. Sanderson. If you go there right now, I'm sure he'll get whatever DNA he needs. We'll overnight it to the BCA crime lab, so we can get the results right away. I'll call him and let him know you're on the way over."

"Thanks, Mitch. Will you let me know as soon as you get the results back?"

"Absolutely."

He handed the cross back to Mitch, who returned it to the evidence room.

Rafe left first to go to the hospital. Then he placed the call to his family. His mother cried after she heard the news, but gratefully thanked God to finally hear an answer to her prayers. She asked Rafe to pray for whoever put them in the makeshift grave. She agreed to attempt to find family members of the young men who went up north with José, even though she had not heard from anyone in years.

Mitch thought it appropriate to call Steph and tell her what he believed to be a partial answer to the mystery.

"No way!" The shock evident in her voice as he relayed the news to her over the phone. "Of all the people, I never thought it could be Rafe's relative."

"The reverend went to the hospital to give a DNA sample. We're sure it'll be a match, but want to overnight it and put a rush on the results."

"This all sounds like something you'd see in a movie or read in a book—it's unreal."

"Norman Schmidt, the BCA agent, started a name search for the others in the picture that Rafe showed me several weeks ago. If we can find any of them, maybe they will shed some light on the other victim." Mitch hesitated. "Steph, if we want this solved quickly, the BCA and our investigative team agree that we need to get national publicity."

"Are you saying there will be more reporters to interfere with the renovations and disturb the residents?"

She wanted to clarify that he was out of his mind, even though she knew they needed to do the press conference.

"Yes, I'm afraid so. I don't look forward to the publicity, but if we can get word out to the public we are searching for those particular names, maybe one or two will come forward."

"What about Eddie Barkley? His murder, or if you must call it an untimely death, at the apartments will spark additional interest." She stopped and thought for a moment. "I understand what you're saying. It's not up to me, so plan on a press conference or whatever is necessary to get things rolling."

"Thanks, Steph. I knew you would understand."

After she hung up the phone, Steph immediately thought of Rafe and what he must feel at this particular moment.

She closed the office and decided to take a detour to the

River Falls Christian Church to stop and pray—and hoped to find the reverend.

My life changed so much since I met Rafe. He's influenced me to start to pray again, and he makes me feel special again. As his friend I need to support him in this dark time.

She noticed his car in the parking lot, so she parked and walked to the doors of the church. The heavy door pulled hard, and it let out an irritating sound—*squeeeel.* Clunk, the door slammed shut.

Door needs some silicone spray and an adjustment. Get your mind off construction, Steph.

Steph slowly walked toward the front. The stained glass windows held the diffused light throughout the building, and she noticed Rafe in a pew toward the front. As she walked up to him, he turned, and his faint smile held a touch of sadness.

She sat down beside him. "I am so sorry to hear about your uncle."

"Well, yes, so am I," he nodded, "but at least we now know he's in God's hands."

In a sympathetic voice, she asked, "Is there anything I can do to help right now? Can I talk to your mother and give her my condolences?"

"That's very nice of you, but right now please sit here and pray with me." He reached for her hand.

She bowed her head, and with an impassioned voice he started to pray for peace of mind, for answers to find out what happened, for luck in the search for José's friends, who disappeared over forty years ago. The prayer only lasted a few minutes, and the final "amen" came much too early for her to release his hand.

They sat in quiet contemplation, and while their hands were still intertwined, Steph could feel her mind reach out to meet his, eager for the fusion.

After a few minutes she asked, "Why don't you come for dinner tonight? It's not good to be alone at a time like this."

"Thank you, but I'm afraid I'll need to decline. My youth group meets tonight, and I need to get ready for their arrival."

"But…"

"However, I will take a raincheck."

"You always think of others before yourself," she smiled, as she released his hand. "You need someone on your side right now. I'm here if you need to talk."

"Thank you. I want you to know I do think about myself once in a while."

His eyes focused on her lips. It took all of his restraint not to pull her against him and kiss her, but Rafe knew she was too vulnerable right now to take advantage of her. Instead he reached out to embrace her in a hug. She went willingly into his arms. He finally broke the embrace and could feel the flutter in his chest while his fingers lingered on her arms.

Steph's skin flushed, and her lips parted as she cherished Rafe's touch on her skin.

The sun shone through the church window and created a halo effect around Steph's head. She looked like an angel to him. He reached out to push a strand of her hair back in place and their eyes held. Steph could see the pain in his eyes.

CHAPTER TWENTY-TWO

Steph was busy gathering her thoughts on the computer in case she would be asked to comment when Mitch decided to hold the press conference he mentioned several days ago. Donald Hanson walked in with Clarence Larsvig at his heels. Donald wore a suit and tie, which looked unusual for the already hot morning, while Clarence looked like he had been pulled off the golf course in his shorts and golf shirt.

Callie did not show up for work, so no one greeted them at the front desk. Steph knew Callie would still be in shock over her father's death, but she never called and asked for time off. Because of the compromised master key, Steph seriously considered placing Callie on an indefinite leave of absence until the autopsy report came back and the investigation completed.

Right now she needed to find an out-of-town locksmith to re-key all the locks in the building—part of her agenda for the day.

"Hello, gentlemen," she greeted them with bland politeness.

"Ms. Runnell, may we have a word with you?" Donald Hanson spoke briskly.

His words made the hairs on the back of her neck bristle.

Something's wrong. I wonder what the problem is now!

"I've asked Mr. Larsvig to be here while I approach you on this since he is chairman of the board."

They both sat in the chairs across from her desk.

"I don't know how to begin," Donald Hanson's face looked stolid.

"Please, just get it over with so I can finish what I am doing," she saved her work on the computer, and turned her preoccupied attention to both men.

"We…or rather I received an anonymous call last evening. We know about Eddie Barkley's death, and I found out there were drugs found on the site. Is that true?"

"Yes. We're not trying to hide anything."

"Well, back to this anonymous call. I've been told that the apartment was vacant at the time."

"Yes, get to the point." Steph flinched.

"We… I … The anonymous caller said you sold drugs from your office," accused Donald Hanson.

"What!" she exclaimed, her eyes wide in disbelief.

"Would you please open your desk drawers for us?"

"Why?" Her lips tightened.

"Because we were informed you hide drugs in your drawer, and you use drugs as well as sell them to the residents."

"You've got to be crazy." Heat flushed through her body. "Why would I compromise my job doing something stupid like that?"

"I don't know," replied Clarence. "That's what we would like to know. Now will you please open your desk drawers?"

he demanded.

This is ridiculous. I've never taken drugs.

"Okay, you're welcome to go through my desk and see what you find," her anger rose as she held up her hands and moved away to the other side of her desk by Clarence and Donald. "I can assure you there are no drugs in my desk." She crossed her arms as she waited.

Donald Hanson extricated a pair of latex gloves from his pocket, pulled them over his chubby fingers, walked around the desk, opened each drawer, and shuffled items around. The fourth drawer was deep and toward the back was a divider. Steph's eyes grew wide as he reached behind the divider. She thought he would find her candy stash. After he shuffled a few things, he pulled out a handful of small plastic bags, some with pills and others with a tannish brown powder and another she recognized as crystal meth because of its sugar candy form.

"I can assure you gentlemen that…that I have no idea who put them in the drawer…or how they even got there," she stammered, shocked to see what looked like similar bags the investigator found behind the baseboard the day before.

"I've called the sheriff's office," Donald Hanson admitted. "This needs to be investigated. In the meantime, there will be a board meeting to see what we are going to do with you."

"What do you mean?" she probed, and could not believe what just happened.

"Your job is on the line here, and there may be criminal charges against you," Donald's eyes glared at her.

At that moment Mitch walked into the office.

"What's going on here, gentlemen?" he demanded.

Donald Hanson explained about the anonymous phone call, and the drugs they found in Steph's desk.

"Now, gentlemen, can you honestly believe that Ms.

Runnell is involved in drug trafficking…in this building?" He hooked his thumbs in his belt loops and looked from Donald to Clarence.

"We don't have any other choice but to believe the caller as we did find the evidence," replied Clarence looking sheepish. Mitch could see he did not believe Steph would be involved, but Donald held the evidence in his hand.

"There will be a special board meeting called to see if Ms. Runnell is still fit to be the ED and complete the renovations," Donald Hanson brusquely replied. Clarence reluctantly nodded his agreement.

Steph stood there with her mouth agape and eyes wide as Mitch continued to question the two men. They were adamant the special board meeting would be held.

Not another emergency board meeting. Ugh.

"We request you go home and come back this afternoon at two o'clock," Donald declared. "We're meeting at one-thirty and will listen to your explanation after our meeting."

Her face red and on the verge of tears, she protested, "I will do no such thing. You know yourselves that this is a setup, and someone put those drugs in my desk to incriminate me."

"Okay, gentlemen, that's enough." Mitch held up his hand. "Steph, I think you should do what they suggest." He walked over to stand in front of her and said in a low undertone. "I will get our fingerprint expert to see if there are any prints on the bags that can be identified. In the meanwhile, they have every legal right to ask you to leave because of the drugs found in your desk."

She could see Mitch was upset; his nostrils flared.

"All right. I'll go, but under protest," her voice sharp as she glared at both men and at Mitch. "I'll leave instructions with Karen regarding what needs to be done until I can return."

Steph, her voice quivered as she explained to Karen what happened, ashamed to even admit she probably allowed it to happen. Not sure she could fully trust Karen, but she knew she did not have much choice.

Callie might be the culprit—or Karen—actually, any of the employees. My office is always open during the day. Only my key opens the door. So someone snuck into my office during the day—or used a key. All the more reason to re-key everything.

She looked solemn faced at Karen, "I'll be back this afternoon."

Mitch followed her out of the building.

"How could you allow this to happen to me, Mitch?" Steph tried to hold back the tears as they ran down her cheeks, but they started to flow. She opened her purse and took out some tissues. "Haven't I been through enough this past year? I should never have come here," she sniffed.

"Steph, I didn't have any control over what happened in there. For some reason, someone is out to get you in trouble. We need to figure things out." Mitch put his arm around her shoulders and walked her to the car. "Will you be okay?" he asked, conflicted, caught between his duty and his belief that Steph was set up.

Steph continued to wipe the tears from her eyes. "Right now I feel so degraded...so vulnerable. I know you couldn't control what happened in there. I'll go home and wait until this afternoon to see what happens."

CHAPTER TWENTY-THREE

Her parents, surprised to see her home, turned to shock as she relayed the story of the drugs found in her desk. She tried to remain calm as she told it. After she released all those tears in front of Mitch, she did not want to repeat it in front of her parents.

"I can't believe it. Wayne, what are we going to do about this?"

Her dad looked perplexed and shook his head. "There's nothing we can do, Annie. At least not right now. We need to be here for our daughter."

Anne's sympathetic eyes turned toward her daughter. "Would you like us to come with you to the board meeting?"

"No, Mom." Steph clenched her jaw, and prayed for release of the pain inside her. "There's nothing you can do. I just hope Mitch is able to find some evidence to vindicate me. There's so much going on right now with the skeletons found, and now we know one of them belongs to Rafe's uncle. Then there's Eddie's death and the drugs found in the apartment.

Now this!" she wailed out of frustration, and threw her hands up.

Even though the day was hot, her parents opened the front door with only the wooden screen door to keep out the bugs. Used to Texas weather, the warmth in the room did not seem to bother them. Steph felt clammy from the humidity and walked over to shut the door. A slight breeze swept by, so she stood in the doorway to let it cool and calm her body.

A car screeched to a stop in front of her house. Rafe exited and ran up the sidewalk.

Even though he was in good shape from weight lifting and his daily runs, he seemed out of breath by the time he stopped in front of the open door. "I stopped at River View...and Lola told me what happened. What a shock! ...So I drove here immediately...to see how I can help."

Steph was on the edge of tears, and they gushed again as Rafe opened the screen door, and she stepped outside. Unaware of her emotional state, all he could see were her weepy eyes as he wrapped his arms around her. He let her cry until no more tears flowed. For the moment she felt safe and secure in his arms. When she finally stopped, she noticed his damp shirt from her tears.

"Sorry," she said, and attempted to brush away the tear stains on his shirt. "Such a frustrating morning."

He led her into the house and over to the couch as her parents stood in the kitchen and looked at each other. They suspected Rafe loved their daughter. Because he was a minister, they questioned whether he comforted her as a minister...or a man.

Her mom walked over and handed her the tissue box. She withdrew several more tissues.

"Let's start from the beginning and tell me what happened.

Lola was so upset. I'm not sure I got the entire story right."

As she told the story again, both her parents and Rafe listened intently. After she finished, she added between sobs, "I should not have taken this job…"—*sniff, sniff*—"…don't think I was cut out to be Executive Director of anything."

"That's silly," replied Rafe. "You've held your cool through everything that happened in the last couple months." He shook her gently by her arms, then put his hands on both sides of her head, and forced her to look into his eyes. "No one could do a better job. You've been sympathetic with the residents. You've dealt patiently with all the complaints and setbacks. Even I don't think I could have done your job as well. The board should be glad to have you."

"Thanks, Rafe. I needed that. Mitch isn't going to be able to find out anything today. It takes time to run fingerprints…if they even find any. My meeting with the board this afternoon may mean the final straw for me."

"Whatever happens, we'll deal with it," Rafe said with unequivocal conviction.

Rafe stayed with Steph and her parents until the time came for her to leave for the board meeting. He asked her parents to pray with him and Steph before they left.

"Father, in the name of Jesus, it is written in Your Word to call on You, and You will answer us and show great and mighty things. Keep our sister steadfast, give her strength, and guarantee her vindication. Father, I say no weapon formed against her shall prosper, and any tongue that rises against her in judgment I shall show to be in the wrong. As a child of the light, I enforce the triumphant victory of my Lord Jesus Christ knowing that all of heaven is backing her. Praise the Lord!

Amen."

"Oh, Reverend Rafe, that is a beautiful prayer. I'm sure the Lord heard," Anne Thomas replied. "I feel so full of hope for Stephanie."

"The Lord has His plan. We just don't know what it is. Sometimes we need to be patient."

"Steph told us about your uncle. I am so glad you're getting closure even under such an unfortunate situation."

"Thank you," he replied. "We need more information. It's taken years to find the little bit we now know, so a little more time won't matter."

"We're praying for you and your family," added Anne Thomas.

Rafe nodded. "I will be back at the church office if you need me. I'll stop by a little later to see how things turned out." He hugged Steph again and whispered "good luck" in her ear as he left.

Full of anxious uncertainty she drove to River View Towers, and timidly knocked on the board room door before she entered.

All the board members sat around the table. Clarence requested her to join them.

"We've gone over all the information we received from Donald Hanson so far. As I explained to the other board members I was with Don when we found the drugs in your drawer. However, as I relayed to the board your shock at us finding the drugs leads me to believe your story of being set up. We're waiting to hear an explanation from you."

Clarence paused, folded his arms over his large stomach, and waited for an answer from her. She looked at each board member and wanted to see something in their eyes or their posture that would give away their thoughts.

Donald Hanson copied Clarence with his arms folded across his chest. He changed into pants, a shirt, and his typical vest where he carried his gun.

Why does he need his gun? What does he think I'm going to do?

Jake Leddering leaned back in his chair, and his eyes bored into Steph. His eyes gave no indication of how he felt. Both Collette and Wendy looked down at the papers before them and did not want to make eye contact.

Steph looked up and prayed, *Lord, please give me the right words to say. Give me the strength to answer their questions with the truth.*

She began, "I'm not sure what exactly was said during your meeting. I would like to go over what you discussed."

Clarence did not seem to be in full charge of the meeting as Donald Hanson piped up, "We want to hear your side of the story."

"I don't know what my side of the story should be when I'm not sure what I'm even being accused of," she inquired.

"Selling drugs in a federal building is a criminal act. I told you this morning we are seriously considering firing you as Executive Director."

Steph steeled all her strength together and hoped what she was about to say would make a difference. "First of all, I have never done drugs in my life. The only thing I've taken even close to what you consider drugs are antidepressants. Thankfully, I am no longer on any medication," she paused and then took a large breath. "It surprised and shocked me this morning to see drugs in my desk drawer. I don't know how the drugs got there. I don't even know what drugs were found. All

I know is the bags looked similar to the ones found in the vacant apartment on the thirteenth floor. I told all of this to the sheriff, Mr. Hanson and Mr. Larsvig. I don't know what other information to give you."

"Hmmm," Clarence murmured as he looked around the room. "Anyone else have questions for Ms. Runnell?"

I need to start defending myself. I should have some rights. She struggled for the right words.

"I guess I would like to add a few more things…before you ask any more questions and make a decision." She gulped, bowed her head for a moment in prayer, and then looked up at them. "Callie did not show up for work today. I understand the the trauma she felt in the death of her father, but she did not even bother to call. I certainly would give her time off, but her impertinence over the past few months and then the suspicious death of her father bothered me to the point of possibly giving her a leave of absence."

She continued, "The master key for the entire building has been compromised. A copy was found in apartment 1313 after Eddie Barkley's death."

The two ladies on the board let out gasps. "Oh, my!" they said in unison.

"It's not one of the originals distributed to the staff. One of my jobs today was to call in an out-of-town locksmith to re-key all the door locks and make a new master key. This is going to be costly, but the safety of our residents needs to come first."

She stopped and her eyes looked directly at each one before she continued. "If you have any idea I am involved in any of this, you are sadly mistaken. You need to look at the staff right now as they are only ones with access to the master key besides myself; and I know my key never left my side."

"This gives us something more to think about," lamented Clarence, who hoped to get out of the meeting so he could play another round of golf. "I think we need to take a vote and get this over with. All in favor of firing Ms. Runnell say 'aye'."

Two *ayes* were heard from Donald Hanson and Clarence Larsvig. "Okay, those opposed say 'nay.'" Two nays were heard from Jake Leddering and Wendy Benjamin. Steph smiled. One abstention.

"Finegan, you did not vote," Clarence Larsvig gave her an austere look.

Collette looked at Donald and Clarence and shook her head. "You are foolish to vote to dismiss Ms. Runnell. First of all, if you dismiss her, who will take over and finish the renovations. Second, how do you know she is even involved in any drug trafficking? An anonymous tip called in, and you found some drugs in her desk. Any of the employees could have access to her desk. Yes, I think Ms. Runnell should lock her desk every night, but it's not a crime. I think we need to reconsider and come up with an alternative."

Steph sat stone-faced and tried not to act surprised by Collette's speech. Usually she and Wendy would agree with whatever motion brought before the board. This was the first time Steph heard her stand up for herself.

"I agree," piped Wendy. "I think we need an alternative."

"Ms. Runnell," Clarence addressed. "Would you please excuse us for a few minutes while we discuss this among ourselves?"

Steph stood and left the room. She held her breath until the door shut behind her and then exhaled. Disappointed that several of the board members did not support her, Steph knew this job would not to work for her.

I should hand in my resignation and let them figure things out for themselves. But…but then it would put a stain on my reputation for any future employment. I need employment, but after today I don't want to stay in this town.

She paced back and forth outside the boardroom, and ran ideas through her head about what she should do. She could hear muffled discussions going back and forth inside the room.

His face red and flushed, Clarence opened the door. "Ms. Runnell, please step back in the boardroom."

"Thank you for waiting outside. We've come to an agreement, an alternative to propose to you," stated Donald Hanson with no enthusiasm.

"Okay, I'm listening."

Clarence cleared his throat, "Mr. Hanson, I am chairman of the board, please allow me to speak and make the final decision."

"Umm…go ahead then," Donald acquiesced.

"This is what we agreed. We will put you on paid leave until the sheriff gives us a final report on the drugs found in your desk. No charges will be filed against you and no further action taken until we hear from the sheriff." His face now changed to a lighter shade of pink. "Is this agreeable?"

"Agreeable. Hardly." She said aghast. "If that's your decision, then there's no other choice." She stood to leave. "I will gather a few things from my office. All work will need to stop on the project until you receive the report from the sheriff. You can't continue the project without supervision."

Jake spoke up, "I've agreed to act as temporary supervisor."

"Really! Then gentlemen and ladies of the board, I want to inform you I am sure to be cleared of any wrongdoing. However, once this project is finished, I will not continue with the renovations for the other buildings, and you'll receive my resignation. I don't want to work for a board of directors who don't support their ED." She turned and walked out of the room. There remained dead silence in the boardroom after her final statement.

As the board members attempted to leave, Collette made a final statement. "I think we made a big mistake in what we just did. Not supporting our own ED is the biggest error we could possibly make, and I'm sure we'll regret it once she leaves." She glared at the two older men, held her head high, and walked briskly out the door.

Steph gathered a few files and some personal items from her office. She secretly planned to continue work from her home—just not come to the office.

Jake thinks he can handle supervising the renovations. I doubt it. If he had the capability in the first place, why didn't they hire him instead of me? I can pass orders on through Karen, if she'll agree.

While Steph was at the board meeting, Rafe decided to stop by the sheriff's office instead of going back to his church office.

"Sheriff, please tell me you believe Steph's been set up."

"Of course, I've known Steph and her family for years. I've talked with her extensively since her return, and there is no way she could be involved with drugs."

"If I may ask," Rafe inquired, "what type of drugs were found in her desk drawer, and what type of drugs found in the empty thirteenth floor apartment?"

Mitch looked on his computer and scrolled down the list. "There was heroin, crystal meth, red meth, mushrooms, and a new drug out there called Fentanyl that's used like morphine and sold as pain killers. Also, some marijuana cigarettes. All of this was already packaged for street sale in similar bags found in Steph's drawer," he replied shaking his head. "I'm still waiting on the fingerprint lab for information."

"According to Steph there were only a few bags found in her drawer."

"Correct. We found some Fentanyl, which looks a lot like cocaine but it's cheaper. Cocaine is too expensive for this community, and we don't see a lot of it around here. Also several packages of heroin and crystal meth."

"Thanks for the information. I'm going over to her house right now. The meeting with the board is probably over. She's worried they will dismiss her."

"Foolish board if they do."

"I agree," Rafe added adamantly.

"What I don't understand is how did this particular board get so much power that they can start to declare emergency board meetings, go into Steph's desk on an anonymous tip without a search warrant, and attempt to fire her without a fair hearing? It doesn't seem right. Sounds awful fishy to me."

"You got a point there. One reason I stay out of politics."

"We scheduled a press conference today," Mitch declared, "but I canceled because of this development. Steph was to be at the conference. It's going to put a chink in our plans, so we're going to wait until tomorrow morning to put everything out over the airwaves." He paused and took a deep breath. "Just so you know since you're already involved, we hope someone will come forward with information as to the whereabouts of the four missing men, plus Miss Mattie's fiancé, or should I say ex, since he hasn't been around for over forty years. He's still reported as missing."

"Yes, Miss Mattie and Maude mentioned him to me. In fact, I wondered if one of the skeletal remains found could be him," Rafe inquired.

Mitch lifted his eyebrows and pulled on his ear. "That would be interesting. In fact, it would really make the case... verrry...in-teresssting." He dragged those last two words out as he nodded in agreement.

Rafe arrived at Steph's home earlier than planned. He sat fidgeting in the living room while he talked to her parents. Happily surprised that her parents prayed and read the Bible every day, he invited them to a Bible study for seniors at his church. Delighted to hear about the senior Bible study, they accepted and made plans to attend.

Steph attempted to smile as she walked in, but was unsuccessful. Her demure manner and beaten look spoke volumes. No words were needed. She felt embarrassed, angry, sad, and demoralized.

She explained the board's decision to put her on leave until the sheriff's department ran the fingerprint check on the drugs found in her desk. Rafe took her hands in his. Comforted by the warmth, she could feel his heartbeat in his hands.

"I need to apologize to both of you for all the trouble since you arrived," she articulated to her parents. "You came to help me, and now I'm officially out of work."

"Steph, you need to talk to your father." Anne Thomas nodded her head toward Wayne.

"Anne, I don't think this is quite the time for a talk, but, honey," he looked at Steph, "we will talk later. I've got some serious thinking to do."

"Oh, Dad, don't worry about me. I told the board I would hand in my resignation once the project is done on the River View Towers. If they can't stand behind me over something like this, then I don't need to be there anymore," her voice emphatic as she looked at everyone in the room.

"I need to leave for a while and see about something," her father picked up his cap and walked out the door.

"Why don't I make you both some iced tea and bring it out to the back yard?" offered Anne. She wanted to be kept busy, and not think about the drama in the town she wanted to escape from almost twenty years ago.

"Sure, Mom," Steph agreed. The large tree in the backyard gave them good shade toward late afternoon.

"I love this little garden space," she said for lack of anything else to say.

"Yes, it's so peaceful back here. I can see how much you enjoy it out here."

"I'll be getting lots of time out here now that I'm on administrative leave." Tears started to flow again, but this time she caught them, sniffed and wiped them away.

"A time for forgiveness." Rafe's eyes lit up. "I think I will talk about forgiveness for my sermon this Sunday. I need to forgive those who put my uncle in an unmarked grave, and you need to forgive those who attempted to hurt you."

Steph shook her head, "I'm not sure I can right now, but… I will try."

Rafe attempted to change the subject. Steph listened absently, her mind still on the board's decision.

"I stopped by the sheriff's office, and he told me they delayed the press conference until tomorrow morning. He's hoping they find some matching fingerprints on the drug bags from your desk and the ones found in the apartment."

Her mother interrupted with the iced tea, so Steph did not comment on his last remark.

"What really upsets me is I thought about dismissing Callie

because of the master key fiasco. Now she has the run of the building, and no one is there to stop her…if she's involved in all of this."

"I just don't understand why she would be involved with her father's death," Rafe inquired.

"I don't know if she is, but how else could Eddie get a master key to copy. Sure hope Mitch can find out more information. She can pull the wool over his eyes if he tries to question her. I've never seen anyone so adept at deceit." She relayed to Rafe her encounter in the park as she watched Callie talk to her father and later act as if nothing happened.

"Let's not talk anymore on the subject." He leaned closer to her. Rafe could smell the soft residue of her cologne. "I know this probably isn't the right time, but…" he set down his glass of tea and put his index finger under her jaw as they locked eyes. "I've wanted to do this for a while."

He bent his head to kiss her. Steph went willingly into his arms, and their lips met. Her heart thumped, and a quiver ran through her body. She leaned in, put her arms around him, and pressed closer.

"Boy, does that take my mind off my problems," she admitted when the kiss ended. Still with their arms entwined, he did not want to appear too sappy, but wanted his intentions known upfront.

"I know it's so soon, but I really do care for you, and it's not as your minister."

"Oh, Rafe, what a wonderful thing to say," she sighed, and then moaned. "Just…it's bad timing."

He gently took her hands and kissed each one. "We'll work it out. I want to know up front how you feel about Mitch. Are you two involved romantically? If so, I need to know the competition." He waited for her answer.

I really don't know how I feel about Mitch anymore. He's never made any romantic advances toward me except for that one kiss. I'm still attracted to him, but I'm more attracted to Rafe. I've never felt this fluttering in my stomach before with any man...not even with Larry. But I can't get involved with anyone with my future so unpredictable.

"Rafe...right now I can't make any commitments to anyone. I care for you, too...and not as my minister. Please give me some space, so we can see what happens with all of this," she pleaded.

Rafe lowered his eyes to conceal his pain. "Don't worry. I won't rush you. I'll be here for you as you need me."

"I've never met anyone as tolerant as you." She attempted a wan smile.

"This whole situation will go away as quickly as it came. My faith is strong, and soon we'll talk about our future."

"I'm so glad you have enough faith for both of us," she said, enthusiastic he even wanted her in his life.

Anne Thomas stood watch at the kitchen window. She smiled and thanked God her daughter found someone who would appreciate her as a caring and compassionate woman. With Larry out of her life, and Anne never did reveal to Steph how she truly felt about her ex.

CHAPTER TWENTY-FOUR

The press conference took place early the following morning. Television cameras from Minneapolis and St. Paul stations, the local cable TV station, as well as newspaper reporters from all over the state were present.

Along with Mitch, the BCA assigned agent, Norman Schmidt, would officiate as the central figure at the press conference. Mitch wanted very little attention given to himself, so he willingly turned most of it over to Norman. Agent Schmidt had been in the background throughout the investigation and was familiar with all aspects of the case.

Mitch stood on the platform in nervous anticipation behind the microphones with Norman next to him. Steve Bishop stood in the background.

"May I have your attention please," he cleared his throat. "I would like to start this press conference in regard to the skeletal remains found on site at River View Towers in June of this year. We now discovered one of the remains was a young Mexican, José Garcia. Records show his name on the payroll during the early construction phrase at River View Towers. Identification was made from a necklace found on his remains given to him by a family member and also by a DNA sample from the victim. We will continue to investigate the identity of the other person. I will now turn the remainder of the press conference over to the BCA agent, Norman Schmidt."

Norman moved to the microphones. He appeared unbothered by the news media, while Mitch moved to the background to stand close to Steve. Norman began to speak in an easygoing manner as he looked at the reporters, "The BCA and sheriff's department need the assistance of the media to help find five men who may know more information about the unidentified individual. Since so many years have passed, these individuals may or may not be alive...or even living in the United States."

He removed the picture Rafe gave the sheriff and showed it briefly to the media. The TV cameras continued to roll. "We've made copies of the pictures and will hand them out at the end of the press conference. The names we are in search of are Fernando Osorio, Antonio Osorio, Roberto Morales, and Hernando Valdez. These were friends and relatives of the deceased, and they could provide additional information to help us solve this case."

Norman continued as he reached for another picture. "We are also looking for a George Walters, who disappeared during the same timeframe." He held up a blown-up version, but grainy picture, of George taken shortly before he disappeared. "This picture is over forty years old. This new artist's sketch is what he would probably look like today." He held up a hand-drawn sketch. "I want to reiterate that these men are wanted for questioning only. We hope they would have knowledge of the second victim and can supply additional information or evidence." He ended with, "This is all the information we can release at the present time. With your assistance we can get these pictures out to the public. We hope someone will see it and come forward."

One television reporter asked if they could ask questions. Norman looked at Mitch, and they both nodded their consent. Mitch stepped up to microphone again. They needed the help of the media to get the word out, and to not cooperte with them would hinder their investigation.

The television reporter from St. Paul spoke up. "Is Eddie Barkley's death considered a homicide or suicide, and could it be connected in any way to the identity of the remains found?"

Mitch allowed Norman to answer the question.

"As of this time," he replied, "there's no indication that Mr. Barkley's death is connected in any way to the remains found. It is still a new and ongoing investigation conducted by the county investigator, Steve Bishop. I'm unable to say anything else at this time."

Another reporter, who identified himself from a Minneapolis newspaper, spoke up as Mitch and Norman turned away from the microphones. "Is it true the Executive Director at River View has been released from her duties because your department is investigating her involvement in the death of Eddie Barkley?"

Mitch's temper rose as his nostrils flared, and with anger in his eyes, he glared at the reporter.

Boy oh boy, they sure can get things mixed up. Word travels fast with fake news.

Norman put his hand on Mitch's arm to warn him not to lose his temper.

Mitch took a deep breath and spoke into the microphone, "The Executive Director is not under any suspicion in the investigation around Eddie Barkley." He balled his hands up into a fist and crumpled the papers he carried.

"Any more questions?" Norman asked. No other reporters made inquiries. The press conference ended.

Mitch gave a sigh of relief. "Thanks, Norman, for handling most of the press conference."

"No problem," he replied as he patted Mitch on the back. "All part of the job. You need to keep your cool. Those reporters are trained to extract as much information as possible."

Mitch tried to straighten out the papers he held in his hands.

Now I can get back to work, and help Steph out of her predicament.

Karen took temporary charge during Steph's suspension from work. She called early in the morning, and Steph gave her instructions for the day. Karen did not have any idea how to manage a renovation project, and Steph was reluctant to suspend work to avoid being behind schedule. They agreed to keep this knowledge from the board.

"I don't want you to get into trouble and lose your job, so make sure none of the employees overhear any of our conversations."

"Don't worry. I'll only call early in the morning or if there is an emergency with the renovations."

"Watch for Jake at the building. He might try to override any orders you give the contractor."

"He's already been here, but didn't stay very long. I think he saw them at work, and there's nothing he could do but stand around," Karen giggled. "The men don't like his superior attitude and won't say much to him."

"And that does not surprise me," snarked Steph.

Callie continued her absence from work, and Karen voiced a legitimate concern for Callie's mental health.

"Why don't you call Reverend Rafe and ask him to drive over to Callie's home to make sure she's okay," suggested Steph.

"I'll ask him if he stops by today. With you gone, we may not see too much of him."

"What!"

"You know…it's very obvious," Karen admitted.

Steph's face turned red and was glad Karen could not see her through the phone. "Hum, can't say too much there. He's just a friend."

"Yeah, okay."

Steph enjoyed the time with her mother during the morning. Anne insisted she help her bake cookies to keep her mind off work, especially during the press conference.

Her dad conveniently made himself scarce, and drove to the golf club to tee off with several former friends. Wayne had been a building contractor before retirement, and acquired many contacts and friends during his years in business. Through his business and conscientious investments, he and Anne retired early.

Anne made them a light salad for lunch to follow all the cookies they consumed. Steph wanted to make sure to catch the noon news to see if the press conference made the airwaves yet. They watched together as Mitch and the BCA agent gave their commentary. The enlarged picture Rafe offered to Mitch showed on the screen along with the picture of George

Walters. The news clip cut off at the end of the question in regards to Eddie Barkley. They did not show the question in regard to the Executive Director, so Steph was left in the dark. Her sympathetic thoughts went out to Miss Mattie.

After lunch Steph decided to relax in the backyard and catch up on a book she started several weeks ago. A few minutes later her mom called out, "Dear, Azalea is here to see you."

Azalea did not stand on ceremony and walked out back after she gave Anne a one-armed hug and welcomed her back to River Falls.

"Your mom hasn't changed a bit." Azalea handed Steph a bouquet of mixed flowers from her garden.

"These are beautiful," replied Steph, as she sniffed the fragrant flowers.

"My roses are doing well, and the zinnias and salvia are so colorful this year with all the rain. My flower beds are just oozing with color right now."

"I'm sorry I haven't visited you lately," Steph contritely responded, and knew full well she neglected Azalea and Becca. "You should start your own flower shop. Your gardens are beautiful."

"It's a labor of love, and I also do it as a stress reliever. I'm so glad God gave me the ability of a green thumb. I love to watch things grow and mature."

She stopped for a moment as she remembered why she started to work in the garden.

"I guess it all started when Jake would come home drunk and started his abuse. It started with just words. When I didn't react, then he decided to hit me. I would go out and work off my frustrations in the garden."

She took her hand and pretended to shovel with a hand

spade, "Every time I shoveled or dug out a weed, I would say to myself, 'take that Jake' or 'this one's for you, Jake.' It made me feel better until I got the gumption to file for divorce."

"I'm so sorry you went through that abuse," commiserated Steph. In her heart she knew similar pain.

Larry never hit me, but cheated on me and made me feel insecure and unwanted.

Her cell phone rang. When she pushed the button to answer, caller ID showed it was her ex-husband.

Speak of the devil. I wonder what he wants!

"Hello…Larry." They were the first words she said to her ex-husband in months. "What do you want?" Her voice held a sharp edge.

"Well, hello yourself. I heard you took a position back in your hometown." His cheery demeanor made it sound as if he was an old friend.

"Yes." She clenched her jaw. "Why are you calling?"

After twelve years of marriage, I know he wouldn't call me without a reason.

"I heard you were in trouble up there finding bones buried, and then a man falling from the thirteenth floor. You know thirteen is an unlucky number," he mocked. "Why on earth would someone put up a building with a thirteenth floor? Didn't they know about bad luck?"

"Larry, if that's all you have to say, I don't need to talk to you any further." She started to hang up, but he continued.

"I called because I saw a newscast. It's gone viral. I understand the press conference was only this morning, and it already made the Chicago news."

"Then you didn't see the same newscast I saw. They never mentioned the building being thirteen floors."

"I did a little further investigating to see what you got

yourself into," he snickered.

"Oh, really. That's good news. If that's all you called about, then thank you for calling and goodbye."

"Don't hang up on me yet. I have a proposition for you."

"A what?"

"A proposition."

"Not interested." She reached with her finger to push the button and disconnect him.

"Listen to me first," he started to plead. She moved the phone back to her ear. "I signed a contract on a new building going up in Minneapolis. I need a project manager. I could use your expertise."

This could get me out of my current predicament. What in the world am I thinking?

"Are you kidding me?" she shouted into the phone. "After the way you treated me during our divorce, you have…the nerve…to call…and offer me a job." Her entire body shook as she moved the phone away from her ear and stared at it.

How dare he ask such a thing!

"Stephie, Stephie, are you still there?"

She put the phone back to her ear. "Yes, I'm still here. And my name is Stephanie…not Stephie. I can tell you right now that my answer is NO with a capital 'N'." She pushed the button to disconnect.

I am so over him. He is pure evil. Calm yourself, Steph. Don't let him get to you.

She looked at Azalea and laughed with irony in her voice. "The nerve of the guy. After cheating on me with another woman, getting her pregnant, putting our assets in her name, and giving me hardly anything from the divorce, he expects me to go back to work for him."

"You're kidding." Azalea raised her eyebrows. "He really

thought you would go back and work with him?"

"I know how Larry operates. I know the tone of his voice when he's in trouble. He bit off more than he can chew. He never could manage more than one project at a time. If he's taking on more than one project, I bet he's in financial trouble." She smiled at the thought.

"Good that you stood up to him. I think we should have a glass of wine and toast to your good fortune," she said, as she pulled out a bottle of wine from the large tote bag she carried.

"It's a little early in the day, but sounds good to me. I'll find some glasses."

"Ask your mom to join us."

After Steph relayed the conversation with Larry to her mom, Anne readily agreed to a glass of wine in the middle of the day.

"I need to leave and pick Becca up from school soon, but I wanted to talk to you about a business venture." Azalea's eyes glowed with mischief as she took a sip of wine. "That's why I brought the bottle of wine."

"Business venture!" both Anne and Steph shrieked together ready to hear more.

"Yes, you know my aunt Aggie and her friend, Donna." Both nodded their heads. "Well…they're ready to retire from their flower shop. I talked to them the other day. I can't afford to buy them outright, so we worked out a deal." Steph and Anne were all ears. "All I need is to come up with the money for the inventory. They would reduce the inventory as low as possible. Aunt Aggie agreed to carry the note for the building on a contract for deed."

She looked at both of them and waited for a reaction. Anne and Steph sat with their mouths agape. "I actually went and asked Jake for his opinion. Since he's in real estate, I thought he would give me an honest answer. I invested the money from my divorce and did pretty well with it. It should cover most, if not all, the inventory." Anne and Steph looked at each other and then back to Azalea. "Well, what do you think?"

"Azalea, I think that's wonderful. You'll do great." Steph reached out to give her a hug with one arm as she held the glass of wine in her opposite hand.

"I agree," added Anne.

"Let's drink to that," Steph said as they clinked their glasses and toasted Azalea's good fortune.

Anne looked pensively at Azalea. "How did Jake respond when you asked him about the investment?"

"It surprised me that he agreed to support my decision. He did mention the competition from other florists in town, but with Aunt Aggie and Donna's steady customer base, I'm not too worried. With God's help all will work out."

Anne smiled, "With an attitude like that you'll have angels at your back."

Azalea looked at her watch. "Sorry, I can't stay, but Becca needs to be picked up—dentist appointment at four."

Steph gave Azalea another hug as she walked her to the door. "Good luck. Let me know if I can help in any way. You helped me when I came to town. I can at least return the favor."

Azalea nodded as her body moved in a constant motion of nervousness. "I'm so excited. I want to run, jump, scream and whoop it up all at the same time. Can't wait to take over. I planned some renovations already to update the shop."

Steph watched as she skipped out the door. Azalea left most of her wine in the glass.

"Well, Mom, let's get rid of the rest of this wine." She poured them another glass.

CHAPTER TWENTY-FIVE

There had been no word from Mitch or the BCA in regard to the fingerprints found in the apartment where Eddie Barkley fell to his death or the drugs found in her desk. Every day since Steph left her job, she made a point to stop at the Law Enforcement Center to check in with Mitch.

"I check every day, and the BCA, which handles the fingerprint identifications, is backed up," Mitch advised her.

"I know it's only been a few days, Mitch, but I'm antsy staying home. You can only do so much shopping."

"I pulled some strings and hope to hear something by next week," he assured her. "We also received numerous leads for the missing men from all the media coverage. Agent Schmidt asked for additional help from the main office in tracking down those leads."

"Rafe says patience is a virtue, but hard to maintain."

"Sometimes it's a slow process to get things done right, so patience is necessary."

"If patience is a virtue, I'm short on it right now," she said in a strained voice.

"I appointed Steve Bishop to spend his time investigating Eddie Barkley's death. I think between the BCA and Steve Bishop, they should be able to solve these cases in a timely fashion.

Steph left Mitch's office with a positive attitude all of this would be over soon.

The same day she conned her dad to go with her to buy a used car. She still did not know her future, so she wanted something reasonable with good gas mileage in case she needed to cut back on expenses. Even though Mitch offered, she did not want to bother him anymore. She preferred he spend his time to clear her name.

They found a white two-year-old smaller SUV on the lot. The salesman said it belonged to a little old lady who only drove it to church on Sundays and to buy groceries. Her dad looked at her and rolled his eyes.

"It looks like a family car," Steph remarked.

It'll be great for hauling boxes, groceries, or anything else," her dad sweet-talked her, and hinted she may need to move.

Steph used a good portion of her divorce settlement to pay for it, and proudly drove it home to show her mom. The salesman promised to return her other vehicle to the dealership where she originally leased it.

Rafe stopped after they arrived home. Her eyes glowed with excitement to show him her so-called new used vehicle.

"I finally own a car of my very own."

Rafe looked at it, and repeated, "Sure looks more like a family car than a car for single person."

"The salesman said a little old lady only drove it to church on Sundays and to buy groceries. The mileage is low, and I can haul stuff," she snickered, as she recalled how her dad rolled his eyes at the salesman.

"It's good to see you laugh again," he said softly as he winked at her.

She playfully hit his shoulder as they walked back to the house.

"I need to move some boxes in the garage. It's a little larger than my leased car and doesn't quite fit in the space."

"I'll help you."

Her parents tried to stay out of their way, and made up excuses to leave when Rafe arrived.

They made a pact to not talk about any of the continued investigations, but stick to neutral subjects as they sat under the large tree in her backyard. However, Steph, still concerned about Callie, broke the pact when she asked Rafe if he paid her a visit?

"She's a tough cookie. I didn't get much out of her except she didn't care much for her father. His death did not devastate her as she led us to believe. I think she's concerned more about the master key business and embarrassed to face others at work. She feels you think she's to blame for the entire building being re-keyed."

How did Callie know we re-keyed the entire apartment building? Interesting tidbit.

Her mind, hard at work, attempted to figure out what role Callie played in any of this.

"We don't know if she was involved in the master key fiasco, but it looked suspicious her own father had a key. I hope Mitch and Steve will find out more with their investigation…and soon. I enjoy the time with my parents, but

I need to get back to work."

"Understandable. I don't know what I would do without my church."

Steph prayed more than she ever did before in her life. Rafe inspired her, and gave her hope to leave it all in God's hands. Steph, when alone, talked constantly to God: sometimes in her head, and other times she would talk out loud as if He sat right there beside her. The talks gave her inner peace. She knew God walked in the same steps.

Steph was excited to see her parents attend church service with her. She wanted them to get to know Rafe, and what better way than to listen to one of his sermons?

Rafe stood at the church door and welcomed the congregation. This was not his normal routine as there were official greeters, but today he knew Steph would bring her parents. He wanted to be at his best even though his body spoke of nervous energy. The most revealing sermon of his career was about to take place.

Anne and Wayne Thomas knew many of the older people, and they greeted everyone with smiles as if it were a family reunion.

As they stood outside Steph noticed Jake Leddering with his parents. His father's health had deteriorated, and he looked gaunter than the last time she saw them. He now used a walker. Jake helped to steady his father as they sat in the back of the church.

The worship team, with the help of guitars, drums, and keyboard, sang *Here For You* and *Exalted Over All* and stirred Steph's heart with their music. Steph's soul leaped for joy as she joined in the singing. She recognized *Amazing Grace* and

How Great Thou Art as favorites of her parents. She looked at them during the service, and saw the beauty of loving God in their faces. With communion served and donations collected, Rafe stood to give his message.

"Dear friends, I want to begin my message today with one word—forgiveness." He nervously cleared his throat. "I want to tell you my story."

The sermon started with the story of his family: how his mother's side of the family immigrated to the United States, how they struggled, the closeness of the family even though they were poor immigrants.

The congregation could visualize everything as he eloquently spoke about his family. He explained his father was a career soldier on leave when his parents met, and married before his leave was over. The love story of his mother and father, and how they fell in love at first sight had everyone saying "ahhh" as if they had been right there for that special moment.

As a final point to his story, he reminisced about when his mother, as a teenager, said goodbye to her older brother, several cousins, and friends as they left for the North to find work. They wrote letters for a while. They found work as laborers in the building industry, and sent money back to the families. Then the letters stopped. They were never heard from again.

When he mentioned their disappearance, no one made a sound. The congregation again held spellbound with his words.

"I promised my mother I would search for them when I accepted the position of your minister. The end of the story is that we finally found my uncle after searching many years. He and several others were on the employee roster during the construction of River View Towers." Rafe stopped and choked back tears. It was hard for him to continue. "He…he was one of the men buried in the boiler room at River View Towers."

The reaction from the congregation could be heard throughout the church. "Oh, no", "It can't be true", "I can't believe it" were some of the words spoken.

He continued, as he needed to get it out or break down. He raised his voice to a higher level, "Now I ask you, should I hate those people who buried him there?"

He could see several people nod their heads in agreement as he looked out at the faces he loved so dearly. He tried to keep focused on his congregation and not Steph and her parents.

"I should really turn away and blame God for what happened to my uncle. But God didn't kill my uncle. We still don't know what happened, but there are those who do know. It is on his…or their hearts…what sin they committed. It's not up to me to judge them, because I know God will judge them in the end. But I do ask for them to be forgiven, as I will have to forgive them for the sin they committed."

He stopped for a moment, and his voice became softer. "God sent his only son, Jesus, to save us from our sins. Jesus gave up His life so we might live in grace. Grace is the one thing God gave us, and only grace will save us from our sins. I can't bring my uncle back, but I can show mercy and forgiveness to those who put him in that grave."

"There are several simple questions I would like to ask that person…or persons. Did you even know my uncle's name…or the name of the other man buried with him? How sad if you didn't. However, all will be answered in Heaven when it's our time to leave this world. Forgiving is easier said than done. Only God's power can bring us to a place of being willing to forgive. In the meantime, if I can forgive what happened to my family, I think those of you who hold grudges, however minor, whether family or friend, it's time for you to forgive. Bitterness is the poison you drink and hope the other dies. Bitterness will completely destroy you if you allow it. If you can't forgive, then the other person wins."

"Let's pray and ask God into our hearts, and to forgive those who have trespassed against us. Let us recite The Lord's Prayer as we start the new week with forgiveness in our hearts."

By the end of The Lord's Prayer, there were very few dry eyes in the church. Rafe slid out the side entrance. His body trembled and tears flowed as he stood in the side vestibule.

Am I able to go out and face my congregation now? My hands still shake. Heavenly Father, please show me what to do next. I cannot do this without your help.

As he stood there, a small voice whispered, "Go and see how your congregation reacted to your message." He turned to look at the person who spoke, but there was empty space. He felt in his heart God spoke to him.

I am your servant, Lord, please guide my words and actions today. Praise be to you, O Lord.

As he turned and walked out to talk to his congregation as he usually did after a service, he was surprised to see so many stood both inside and outside the church. Many of his congregation walked up to him and told him what a wonderful sermon he gave, and offered their condolences.

Her acute perception made Steph aware of Rafe's emotional reaction at the end of the service; but his complete turnaround surprised her as he smiled and thanked everyone for their thoughtfulness.

She saw Jake drive up close to the church and rush his dad

into his vehicle. His mom sat in the backseat and waved to Steph and her parents. Jake looked up and observed Steph stood a short distance from her parents—alone. He walked up to her and put his hands on each side of her arms. "Dad is not feeling well, and I need to drive him home. I came here today because my mother requested help. So glad I did. Who would have known that the minister was related to one of them?"

One of them!

Steph gave him a distinct frown. She knew Rafe's service today said to forgive, but it proved to be a hard move for her. Even though Jake voted on her side, he agreed with the board to the suspension from her job. She did not want Jake to touch her no matter how innocent it seemed.

Rafe watched from the side ready to take action if Jake did not take his hands off Steph.

"Jake..." she began as she backed out of the hold. "I'm sorry about your dad. He does not look well right now. You need to get him home."

"Yes, I know, but I want to explain to you, away from the board room..." She held up her hand in protest.

"Jake, don't bother. I know I didn't do anything wrong. I've got faith in God that whatever happens, I will accept."

Jake nodded. "Yes, I know you are a *strong* woman."

With his head hung low, he walked slowly back to his vehicle. After he drove off, Azalea and Becca walked over to Steph.

"He hasn't been to church in a long time. I think his mom and dad insisted he attend today," Azalea commented.

"Hmm...his dad was sick and his mom asked for help, so he left right away."

"Grandpa sick! Mom, we need to go see Grandpa again," Becca pleaded.

"I'll ask your dad to take you one day next week after school."

"Can we go today, Mom? Pleeeeasse," she begged again.

"Now you see how my little one demands things," she laughed. "Sure, honey, I'll drop you off on the way home. You can have lunch with your dad and ask him drive you home."

"Thanks, Mom," she said, as she skipped away to visit with her friend, Katy.

"Reverend Rafe's sermon stirred my heart today. I noticed several times he got choked up, and I thought he would lose it."

"Yes, I know. I worried he would break down. It was a big thing for him to reveal so much of himself to everyone today," Steph replied, and felt proud of Rafe's candid sermon. "It took a lot out of him. He looks exhausted right now, but happy."

"I agree. You didn't say one word to me about this," scolded Azalea, "and I'm your best friend."

"I wish I could spill the beans," Steph replied wistfully. "It would have made my life a lot easier, but because of the investigation everything needed to be kept hush hush until Mitch held his press conference."

"Well, anyway, it's now out. I wonder about the other person?"

Hopefully, we'll find out soon," she replied.

"I better get Becca over to her grandparents. See ya later." She waved goodbye as she walked away to find her daughter.

Most of the congregation went home, but Rafe still visited with several who stood around and continued to ask him questions. Steph decided to interrupt him and pull him away from what she considered nosy members of the church.

Anne already invited Rafe to lunch. It was an unobtrusive dinner with mostly polite conversation. Wayne stayed quiet throughout the meal, and only answered questions when they were directed to him.

"Dad, how come you're so quiet today?"

"Got a lot on my mind, sweetie. I got to do something tomorrow that I dreaded for years."

Steph put down her fork. "Dad, you want to tell us about it?"

Wayne looked at his wife. Anne nodded her agreement. "Steph, I think you and Rafe should accompany us to the Law Enforcement Center tomorrow morning. I've got something to say and both of you should know about it. I don't want to discuss it now, but you'll find out tomorrow." Wayne stood up and walked outside to the backyard.

"Mom, what's going on?"

"Stephie," she used her daughter's pet name as a child, "I can't tell you right now. It's up to your dad. It's not for me to say anything." She stood up from the table and with nervous energy started to clear the dishes. "Why don't you and Rafe go into the living room while I do the dishes," she suggested. "Leave your dad alone with his thoughts right now."

"Thank you for lunch, but I think I should leave. I still have hospital visits to make today," said Rafe. He wanted to give Steph time to talk to her mother.

Steph walked with him to his vehicle. "You know you don't need to leave. I don't know what's going on with Dad, but I'm worried he knows something about your uncle or at least thinks he does." He wrapped his arms around her, and she laid her head on his shoulder.

"Steph, things will work out. Keep your faith." She nodded as he held her. He pulled her away to arm's length, and their eyes locked. "My uncle's remains will be returned to my family shortly. I want to bring them down to Texas where

Mom plans to bury him on their ranch. Would you accompany me and meet my family?"

"Rafe, I would love to go with you, but I told you before I don't want to make any commitments with all the things hanging over my head. If everything were normal, I would go in a heartbeat."

His disappointment showed, but he took it in stride. "I don't know how long I will be gone. I'll call every day."

"I'll miss you. How soon 'till you go?"

"I'm not sure. Might not be for a few weeks yet."

"I forgot to tell you how much I enjoyed your sermon today. Your parents sound like wonderful people."

"They are. In fact, I think I fell for you as quickly as my dad did for my mother. It must run in the family. I guess I never thought about it until I mentioned it this morning. My mother talks about their whirlwind romance, and my father laughs because, as he explains, it took him almost his full two-week leave to convince her that he was serious."

"How romantic. Just like the movies."

"You said you liked my sermon today."

She nodded. He put his hands on each side of her face and looked at her with a sense of calmness.

"What I'm trying to say is you need to forgive your ex-husband before you can move on with your own life. Forgiveness is not always easy, but if you can't forgive, then that person still has a hold on you. We can't move on with our own lives until you can forgive those who hurt you."

She felt bereft and tears formed on the edge of her eyes. She wiped them with the back of her hand.

He doesn't believe I can forgive Larry. I don't know if I can.

Even though they stood outside in the daylight, Rafe took

her in his arms. His lips felt warm and sweet on hers. Steph did not want the kiss to end, but when it did, her eyes took in his square jaw, deep-set eyes, and the dimple in his chin as he smiled as though she were memorizing them for the future.

"I am serious, Steph," he repeated. She felt at a loss for words and could only nod. "Jesus knows what's in your heart was part of my sermon. I can't read your mind, but Jesus can."

"I'll try."

Yes, I really will try. If I want his love, then I need to do this.

She reached for her phone in her pocket, and asked if they could do a selfie. They posed together. She noticed as she looked at the result that Rafe was just slightly taller than her. Her slim figure and his muscular body made her look more petite as she stood beside him.

"Okay, Mom, what's going on?" she asked as soon as she walked back in the house.

"I'm sorry, but I don't want to go against your father's wishes. He just wants to get some stuff off his chest. I think it will make him feel better."

"Do you think Dad will talk to me about it this afternoon?"

"No," she answered firmly. "Don't even consider asking him."

Her mother turned away toward the sink. Steph pouted for a moment, disappointed her parents would not share their secret with her. Her mom was not going to talk about it, so she decided to change the subject.

Even though Anne was almost done with the dishes, Steph grabbed a dish towel and started to dry and put everything away.

"Mom, you know Rafe's sermon this morning really got me to think about Larry. I was so furious with him when he cheated and then took all our assets and hid them throughout the divorce. I wanted to get even with him. Sometimes when I think about it, I get so angry. If I had a gun handy, I would have shot the guy."

"Good thing you didn't," her mother smirked, then frowned. "Anger just causes more problems."

"Now I feel nothing for him, but I've never really forgiven him," she sighed as she finished the last of the dishes. "I thought about it during lunch, and Rafe mentioned it to me before he drove off."

"That's why you're so quiet," her mother chided. "Did you talk to Rafe about your animosity toward Larry?"

"No, I haven't. Rafe has an uncanny sense, and I think he knows what's in my heart. I guess I was afraid to go too deep with my hatred... afraid Rafe would think different of me. Now after hearing his sermon today, I can be more forthright and honest on how I perceive Larry. I actually feel sorry for him. I believe he's in financial difficulty. Otherwise, why did he call me? I need to forgive him and move on with my life."

"Steph, Jesus knows what's in your heart."

"Rafe just said the same thing to me."

"Well, he's a smart man. Even if you can't get the words to your lips right now to forgive Larry, think about forgiveness in your heart. You are too needy if you can't forgive, and then the other person wins."

"Oh, Mom, you're so right." Steph and Anne embraced. Wayne walked into the kitchen and looked at the two women.

"Can I get in on this family hug, too?" he asked.

"Sure, Dad." They stood in a circle for a few minutes, each prayed silently. Steph prayed for her heart to forgive her ex-husband. Anne and Wayne prayed for God to give Wayne the courage to do what he needed to do the next day.

CHAPTER TWENTY-SIX

"I called the Law Enforcement Center, and Mitch would be available around ten," Wayne announced as they ate breakfast. Steph, an early riser, thought breakfast at eight was the same as being on vacation.

"Would you call Reverend Rafe and ask him to meet us there?"

"Sure," mumbled Steph through bites of her mother's egg bake.

Morbid thoughts ran through her head as she watched her parents, and yearned for some reaction from them as to why her dad wanted to meet with Mitch. She knew her father worked on the construction crew of River View Towers as a teenager for the summer, but he only as a laborer and gofer. What information could he possibly give the sheriff? She could never believe her father, always a loving and religious man, a good father and husband, would do anything wrong or illegal.

"I'll call right away." She went to her bedroom to get

dressed and call Rafe.

The Law Enforcement Center buzzed with activity as they arrived. Rafe drove his car right behind where Steph and her parents parked. They waited for him and walked into the building together.

Mitch watched the arrival of the group from his office. Wayne's phone call to him that morning sent out antennas of curiosity and apprehension. He did not know Reverend Rafe and Steph would be present. Mitch wanted to talk to Steph anyway. They received the report back on the drugs found at River View Towers, and it would be an opportune time to talk to her.

"Hi, Wayne and Anne. Steph. Reverend Rafe. It's so good to see you again," he greeted them cordially. "There's not enough room in my office for all of you, so why don't we go to the first conference room on your right."

Anne and Wayne took the lead, and Mitch followed. He turned to give an animated wide-eyed questioning look to Steph and Rafe. Steph shrugged her shoulders to indicate she had no idea why they were there.

After they seated themselves around the table, Mitch asked, "Okay, Wayne, this sounded important when you called this morning. What's on your mind?"

"Well…" began Wayne and hesitated. Anne leaned over and held his hand for support. "I want to tell you a story, and you can make what you want of it. It's bothered me for over forty years now."

"Okay, start at the beginning," offered Mitch, as he attempted to make Wayne feel more comfortable.

Steph sat next to Rafe, and they both looked at her dad in anticipation of something unpleasant coming from him.

"At seventeen I got my first car," he began. "Like any

other seventeen-year-old, I would party and then drive. I was always careful though, and took the back roads home so I wouldn't get stopped." He paused and swallowed.

"One Friday night in October I was on my way home from a beer party. I wasn't feeling well and stopped my sports car near the river. I could hear dogs bark toward the river. It was a full moon, and I could see a path through the woods, so out of curiosity I decided to follow it. When I got close to the falls, I saw several men with bandanas over their faces. One had a gun pointed at two other men who I recognized as Mexicans. The Mexicans tried to talk in broken English and Spanish to the other men, but I couldn't hear everything they said." Wayne stopped and put his head down and covered his arms on the table. When he looked up tears shone in his eyes.

"Are you okay to continue?" asked Mitch, who tried to hold back his eagerness and what he imagined could be another breakthrough.

"Yes, I need to get this off my chest. I…I couldn't understand what was going on. All of a sudden one of the Mexicans reached into his boot and drew out a knife and someone fired a gun."

His voice became frenzied, and he started to move his arms using frantic gestures.

"The Mexican with the knife fell into the river and started to drift toward the falls. The other Mexican shouted," he looked over at Rafe, "and jumped in the river to save him. He grabbed hold of him and tried to swim to shore."

His voice slowed down to a more even tone. "Two more men showed up with bandanas over their faces. One of the men hollered to help the two in the river. They ran down the side of the hill to help, but the strong current dragged the two over the falls. Then the dogs saw me and started to bark. One of the men shouted to check on the dogs."

"I…I got scared and ran back to my car, and didn't dare turn on the lights until I made sure they couldn't see me anymore. One of them tried to follow me, but I hid behind a cabin near the road. I drove home and wanted to call the cops, but then I thought what would happen to me when my dad found out I had been drinking and driving. I decided to wait to hear if there was any scuttlebutt in town. I heard nothing said around town, or even around the construction site. I figured they were rescued, and there was really nothing to report until news of the excavation of the remains reached us. I knew then the possibility what I thought I witnessed actually happened."

"Wow! That is some story." Mitch shook his head. "I need you to make an official statement, Wayne. I don't know what to say. You may have helped solve a forty-year-old case."

Wayne nodded, "I know I'll have to make a statement, but I want to say that as a kid I thought nothing was wrong. After a while I honestly believed it was a bad nightmare because I wasn't used to drinking…or maybe somebody even put a mickey finn in my drink to give me hallucinations. All these years…the same nightmare over and over again…and it turned out to be real."

"Can you, by any chance, give us a description of the men wearing masks or even of the two Mexicans?"

"The Mexican shot had the knife. The other one wore a red shirt as I could see it clearly in the moonlight when he dove into the river to rescue his friend."

"What about the masked men? How many were there?"

"Four that I saw."

"Any identification? Height? What they wore? Breed of hunting dogs? Anything at all will help," Mitch probed, with the hope to get more information.

"I keep seeing the scene in my head when I close my eyes," said Wayne, "but over forty years dulls a memory. I remember a tall, thin man and a short stocky man, who held the dogs. The other two I don't think I even heard them talk." Wayne hesitated and thought. "You know, I remember one with a husky, deep voice."

"The more information you can remember would help us tremendously. Do you realize we still don't know the identity of the second victim? At least now we know it belongs to one of the Mexicans."

Mitch looked at Rafe, who had his head bowed. "I'm so sorry, Reverend, but I'm glad Wayne asked you to be here. I had no idea where we were going with this meeting, but I'm pleased we have this information." He looked toward Wayne. "Can you stay and give your official statement to the BCA agent? Norman's around here someplace, and I think he'll be happy to hear we finally got a break in the case."

"I'm at your disposal, Sheriff. I want to do what's right. I wasn't sure if it was a dream because of my drinking, or if it was real. If I keep racking my brain, maybe I will come up with some more details."

"I'll stay with your dad," Anne whispered, as she continued to hold Wayne's hand. "You youngsters go back to the house. Maybe prayer will help your dad remember more details."

Wayne rose and walked to where Rafe and Steph stood by the door. "Reverend, I wanted to say something yesterday, but I just couldn't. I prayed all night for the courage to talk about it without a breakdown. I almost changed my mind, but I hope you can forgive me that I didn't come forward earlier? I still can't believe it was real."

"Of course." Rafe put his hands on Wayne's shoulders. "I

forgive you, and I am also grateful to know what happened. Jesus knows what's in your heart. So willing is Jesus to forgive…and so am I."

"Dad, I am so sorry you kept this memory secret for so long. I suppose this the real reason you came back and not just to support me?" Steph asked suspiciously, but wanted it to be for both reasons.

"Stephie, you know our allegiance is to you no matter what; but when I told your mom about my memory, she agreed we needed to be here, and I needed to find the right time to tell my story."

"I love you, Dad." She hugged her father.

"I love you, too. Just don't be too angry at me for being a foolish teenager."

She nodded and smiled at her dad. Wayne walked back to his wife, and they waited for Agent Schmidt.

"This is so unreal," she said to Rafe as they left the conference room and past the reception desk.

"I know. Everything's happened so fast. It's hard to gather your thoughts and put it all in perspective. We know now that one of the Mexicans with my uncle also died. But I wonder about the entire circumstances—if the other masked men tried to help them. Then again, what happened to the other Mexicans? I think we need more information."

"I agree," she stated.

"I've got to get back for a wedding consultation, so I'll talk to you later." He gave her a kiss on the cheek. Mitch noticed the kiss as he walked out his office door. He wanted to talk to Steph about the drug and fingerprint report returned to him. His heart stirred a little as he watched the two together. A little jealousy ran through his bloodstream, and he could feel the heat in his face.

"Steph," he shouted from his office, "Will you stop by my office before you leave?"

"Sure thing," she said, elated that perhaps Mitch had some good news for her. She waved goodbye to Rafe and almost skipped to Mitch's office.

"I have some news for you."

"Oh, yeah, let's have it!"

"Well...the good news is your fingerprints are not on any of the bags of drugs found in your desk. As far as I'm concerned, you're cleared of any wrongdoing. I will contact Clarence Larsvig this morning. In fact, while Norman is obtaining a witness statement from your father, I will call Clarence. My hope is that the board will reinstate you immediately."

"Sounds wonderful! However, you said good news. Is there bad news in there somewhere I need to know about?" She eyed him with curiosity.

"I can't say a whole lot right now, but they found some identifying fingerprints. There will be an investigation. This is strictly on the QT, and no one can know about it as it could compromise the case. All I'm going to tell Clarence is your fingerprints were not on any of the bags confiscated, and you are not under any suspicion."

He hesitated and looked directly at her. "But, Steph, someone is out to get you in trouble. They may even want to physically harm you, so be very careful about where you go and who you talk to. Keep your eyes and ears open and report anything suspicious to me. There may be a leak in our department. I need to be extra careful...just in case."

Steph looked wide-eyed at Mitch in disbelief. "This is scary. It never occurred to me someone would want to harm me. I've never done anything to anyone in this town."

"Whoever did this to you probably thinks of you as a threat right now," he offered. "I don't want you to get hurt. I do want to ask you a question, and I want an honest answer." Steph looked at Mitch and waited.

"What is your relationship with Reverend Rafe?"

Steph stared at him, thunderstruck. "I'm…I'm not sure what you mean."

"I'm asking for your own protection. Are you involved with the reverend? Can he be trusted?"

"Of course, he can be trusted. Look what he's been through already. He's been my rock through this entire crisis. I guess I have more faith in him than I realized."

I'm not sure this is the answer Mitch wants. My heart is filled with love for Rafe. I realize now Mitch will always be a friend, but I'm not in love with him. He's married to his job, and his job would always come first.

Mitch pulled on his ear and struggled to find the right words. He had a sinking feeling in his stomach.

"I hoped we could get together as a couple. I knew I could trust you, but I kept seeing Aaron's little sister instead of a grown-up woman. I care for you, Steph." He finally admitted his feelings, but he knew it would be too late.

Steph needed to verbalize her inner conflict. "Mitch, I wanted a relationship with you when I arrived back here. But I want someone who'll put me first in their life, and look at me with love in his eyes—like Tillie and Jack. Your job will always come first with you, and I don't want to be second or third in your life. I love you, Mitch, but only as a friend. I hope you understand.

"I will have to accept it." He cleared his throat. "I would have fought for you if I knew I had a chance. I've been told this once before and lost a possible relationship at that time. I guess I am married to my job—at least for right now.

I wonder if he's talking about Azalea.

"You'll find someone, Mitch. You're a wonderful father, but you need to change your priorities. Rafe made me see that I need to forgive those who hurt me—especially my ex-husband, if I'm going to move on with my life. I found that my relationship with God is so important in my life right now... and forever. I hope you will see the need for God in your life, too."

"My life's been a mess for a while. I know I need to get it back on track. Natalia needs a woman in her life, but she'll have to settle for me."

"Natalia's a sweet girl."

"She's my life now." He leaned back in his chair and attempted a weak smile. "Back to your situation. Don't trust anyone too much, because right now we have an idea who planted those drugs, but still need to investigate."

"I take it you don't want to share any of this information with me," she pried, and hoped he would spill a little more information.

"No, Steph, for your own safety, I don't want you involved in any of this."

"Okay. I think I'll go home and wait for Mom and Dad to come back. Thank you so much for what you've done to help my dad. I thought you might be furious with him when he came forward so late with this information."

"To be honest it upset me at first, but then when I thought about it, I'm glad to find we're uncovering some leads—any kind of leads. I took a statement from Bill Jensen that corroborates your dad's story. Old Bill was not involved but remembers around that time period a group of Mexicans patronized his business, but then all of a sudden a bunch of them disappeared. I have the list of the men who came up here with José Garcia from the reverend. We are attempting to track them down. Do you realize how many people there are with the same Mexican first and last names?"

"No, but I'm sure you're willing to tell me," she giggled.

"Hundreds," he rolled his eyes. "Even with the computers we have available, it's going to take time. In the meantime, please be careful. I will have extra squad cars drive by your house periodically during the day and night just to be on the safe side."

"Thank you again, Mitch. I'll be careful."

CHAPTER TWENTY-SEVEN

larence Larsvig cleared his throat before he called the special board meeting to order. Even though it was the middle of a work day, it brought all the board members together. As the workers continued to drill holes for the indoor sprinkler system, the sounds echoed from a few floors above the board room. Clarence needed to raise his voice to a higher octave.

Steph sat quietly at the table while Clarence explained to the board the findings from the sheriff's department. Donald Hanson's frown evident as Clarence continued, "So, as board chairman, I recommend we reinstate Stephanie Runnell as director, and let her get on with the renovations and the management of this agency. All in favor say 'aye'."

Four 'ayes' were heard. "Any against reinstating Ms. Runnell say 'nay'."

Donald Hanson clearly stated, "Nay."

"For what reason?" quizzed Clarence.

"I guess I am not entirely convinced of her innocence."

"Well, you're outvoted, but your 'nay' noted in the records. Ms. Runnell will return to work immediately."

Stephanie wanted to jump up and shout from the rooftops, but Donald Hanson's nay put a slight damper on her joy at reinstatement. She needed to make a quick decision, and hoped she made the right one.

"Thank you," she began. "I will start to catch up on my work immediately. Because of the delays this past week, we are behind schedule."

She knew they were actually close to being on schedule, but did not want to admit this to the board. Karen cooperated with her orders, and had everything under control without the board's knowledge. Even with Jake's attempts to give orders and take over the renovations, his orders never got very far. She wanted the board to squirm a little, and led them to believe the project was now behind schedule.

"However, I am disappointed I did not receive the full support of the board on my reinstatement." She looked directly at Donald Hanson, whose face turned red, as he slumped down in his chair. "My statement to you at our last meeting will stand. I will not continue as the director after the renovations on River View are completed."

"Ms. Runnell," piped Wendy Benjamin as she glared at Donald Hanson, "we want you to know not all of us feel the same as Mr. Hanson. I personally would like to see you continue as director."

"I agree with Wendy," offered Jake. "I think you handled all the crises very well and deserve respect for how you kept things under control." He looked over at Donald Hanson. "Isn't your term up soon? Maybe we need reconstruction within this board."

"My sentiments exactly," offered Collette Finegan.

Donald fumed and glared at the other board members, his anger rising. "Ump...you guys think you know everything. Just you wait and see." He belligerently crossed his arms and continued to glare at them.

Steph could feel the heat rise in her face embarrassed to be the cause of dissention among the board. "Thank you again, but my promise stands." In a flat voice she continued, "Now if you will excuse me, I need to check on things in the office, and schedule a meeting with the contractor." She stood, her back rigid, and walked out of the meeting.

Agitated, Jake said, "Could we please adjourn this meeting? My father is not doing very well right now. I need to be with my mother."

"Meeting adjourned," Clarence announced.

Steph stepped into the office area to find Lola behind the counter. Lola rushed to her and gave Steph a bear hug around her waist. "It's so nice to see you back again," she babbled.

Steph's surprise by Lola's embrace brought her close to tears. "Thank you." She patted Lola on her shoulders.

She looked around the office. "I see Callie's not returned to work," she remarked.

Karen came out of her small office. "No, still no call from her." Displeasure showed on her face. "I stopped by the funeral home during my lunch break, and found out there was not going to be a funeral. I just don't understand her."

"Well, let's not worry about it now. We have work to catch up on."

Steph and Karen huddled in the director's office. They sent Lola on an errand, so they could talk freely. Karen caught Steph up on construction progress as well as other issues in the building. Karen handed Steph the new master key and a new key for her office before she left for the day.

"Callie still has the old master key, so she's unable to enter the building. I also changed the master code for the manual entry," she informed Steph as she handed her the new code.

"You are a gem," Steph complimented Karen, who gushed and seemed embarrassed by the remark.

"Thank...you. No one's ever complimented me on my job here," she said in a weakened voice.

"Well, now it's your turn."

Steph stayed at the office later than anyone else did. The sun began to set and dusk slowly maneuvered its way into night.

What did Mitch say? Oh, yes, do not stay by yourself, watch everyone, and watch where you go.

She felt anxious with the groans and banging noises, and people going in and out of the building. Each groan and bang she heard heightened her edginess.

Am I really in someone's way that they would do me harm?

She walked to the office door to make sure Karen locked it on her way out. She still felt uneasy as she sat in front of her computer. Her nerves felt raw. She jumped as her cell phone rang. Her heart started to pound, until she saw the caller ID.

"Oh, Azalea," Steph gasped. "When the phone rang I panicked."

"What... Where are you?"

"Still at work."

"They reinstated you. How wonderful. Praise the Lord," she said excitedly. Then her voice turned somber. "You shouldn't be there by yourself."

"I know. Mitch warned me that someone might try to harm me by doing something more than hide drugs in my desk. I think I'll lock up and go home. Is that why you called? Are you checking up on me?"

"Steph, I called to tell you that Charles Leddering passed away earlier this evening."

"I'm so sorry, Azalea. How is Becca taking it?"

"Not too well right now. She's in her room crying. I promised to take her over to Jake's so she could spend time with him and Grandma Beth."

"If there's anything I can do, please let me know. I'll tell my parents. I'm sure they'll want to attend the funeral."

"Okay, thanks Steph. I gotta go. Talk with you tomorrow when I know more about the arrangements."

"Bye," both said simultaneously.

CHAPTER TWENTY-EIGHT

Rafe stared at the blank screen on his computer. He tried last evening and into the mid-morning to contrive a new perspective on a sermon for the coming Sunday. He started many times, then deleted and started again. It would be more difficult to prepare one after this past Sunday's sermon when he revealed so much to his congregation. His cell phone rang. He uttered a silent *thank you* to God.

"Reverend, this is Sally, Sheriff Mitchell DeVries' secretary. The sheriff requested I call and ask if you could come to the station?"

"How soon?" he replied, curious as to why his secretary called him instead of Mitch.

"As soon as possible," she replied.

"On my way." He leaned back in his chair and felt relief he did not have to stare at the computer for another hour.

He arrived at the station within minutes. When he walked in, he noticed Mitch was not in his office. Normally he could be seen through the glass in the door.

"Reverend Rafe," Sally called from behind the counter. "The sheriff is waiting for you in the conference room, first door on your right."

"Thanks." He smiled at her as he turned down the hallway.

They might as well put a sign up and give me my own office. I've been a regular figure around here lately, and everyone seems to know my face.

As he walked into the conference room, Mitch confronted him, gently pushed him out the door, and shut it behind him. While they stood in the hallway Mitch explained, "There are two older Mexicans in the conference room. They drove here from California because they heard on national news about the remains found in the high rise. According to them, they know the buried men and were witnesses."

Rafe looked confused. "I don't understand why you called me? I don't know those men."

"You gave me the picture to identify the young men who came up here with your uncle. I showed them the picture you gave me, and they correctly identified each man."

"Are you serious?"

Mitch nodded and grinned.

"This is awesome!" said Rafe, elated by the news. "Can I meet them? Are they my mother's cousins?"

"That's the sad part. When I talked to them to make sure they were legitimate and not some grandstanders, I found out one of your cousins was buried along with your uncle. Your other cousin died a short time later in a car accident. These two are the friends who came up from Texas with your uncle and his cousins. I thought you would want to meet and talk to them."

"I sure would," he did not hesitate. "Did you take their statements yet?"

"Agent Schmidt is ready to take their statements, but I thought you might want to see them first. They seem awfully nervous and afraid."

"Afraid?" he queried.

"Yes, they're both afraid the men are still around who hurt their friends."

"Hurt." Rafe's eyebrows narrowed.

"Yes, they said they did not know your uncle and his cousin were dead when they fled the area. They were being chased... Oh, well, I better let them tell you their version."

Rafe could feel his heart race as he and Mitch re-entered the room. Both older men wore leathery complexions with deep wrinkles in their faces.

They look about the right age. I don't know how much to believe, but Mitch seems satisfied with their story. After all these years...it's too good to be true.

"Reverend Rafael McGowan, I would like you to meet Roberto Morales and Hernando Valdez."

"Gentlemen, it's nice to meet you. I carried a picture of you in my billfold for many years, but never really knew anything about you." Rafe smiled.

As he shook their hands, he noticed both men's hands were calloused, and probably still did manual labor.

"Gracias," replied the one named Roberto. Slightly taller than Hernando and heavier, he smiled and showed a few missing teeth. "Is good to meet a relative of José Garcia."

Hernando stood in the background and twisted his hat in a nervous gesture. His thin figure emphasized the deep crevices in his face.

"I think we better get started so Agent Schmidt can take your official statement. I asked the reverend here so he could hear your side of the story."

"Sí. Sí. Is good to tell what we know to the reverend," said Hernando.

Hernando looked hesitant, and Roberto nodded for him to go ahead. "Please, let's sit." They all sat around the table. "We tell the sheriff everything we know. It's hard to remember so many years ago." Hernando cleared his throat. "Five of us go from Brownsville, Texas, up north to work." His English was not grammatically correct. "We found work in Chicago, but not like big cities so looked for work in small towns. José, Fernando, Antonio, Roberto, and me find work here on big government building. Men in this town call us names and..." he looked at Roberto as he tried to think of the right word.

"Harassed," Roberto added.

"Yes, harassed us. Most of us hide and only eat at places not in town, or we cook over open fire. Sometimes we even sleep in pickup, so we can send money back to our family. We think we leave soon, because no one like us and it get cold. One night we drink *cervezas*—beers—at bar. Drink too many. It late and we start to drive to woods to camp for night. I am driver, and don't see two pickups following us." He held up two fingers. "They have no lights. José notice and yell. We are followed. I turn to look, and pickup ran in ditch. I cannot back up, so we all run different ways." He flayed his arms to indicate the chaos. "Roberto, Fernando and me go left, and José and Antonio run to the river. We hear dogs bark, and we scared." He held up two fingers again. "Two men followed us. Dogs and other two men chased José and Antonio." Hernando shook his head, unable to continue as tears filled his eyes. Roberto picked up the conversation in a deep, low voice.

"We hear gunshot. Men stop following us. They turn and run across the road toward the river. We turn around too, but stay back so they no see us." His voice changed to a slightly higher, excited pitch. "We see Jose and Antonio in the river, go over falls. We hear men who chase us say they go help Jose and Antonio. We not know Jose shot. Too afraid for our lives, we go back to truck and push it out of ditch and drive away. We keep driving until we are out of state."

"Fernando wanted to go back for his brother, but we said go back later, but too afraid same men come after us," said Hernando.

"Why didn't you contact the families? Or go back and try to find Jose and Antonio?"

Roberto and Hernando looked sheepishly at each other.

"We no tell others we have fake green cards. Truck get in accident soon after, and we go to hospital. Fernando, he die. Police find out we not legal, so Immigration Services send us back to Mexico. With Fernando gone, we don't know where family moved to. It take us five years before we get legal green cards to come back to America. Mexican families move mucho, so we no find families to tell about Fernando. We believe Jose and Antonio okay and moved on. We legal now and citizens of USA," said Roberto as he puffed out his chest, proud of his American citizenship. He pulled out his wallet and smiled. "See I have own driver license."

Rafe glanced at the California state drivers' license. "We both legal now and our families legal too," added Roberto.

"You men speak good English. How long have you been in the States?" Rafe asked out of curiosity.

Hernando and Roberto looked at each other. Roberto counted on his fingers.

"Over thirty-five years now. We both married and children grow up. We retired, but still work sometime. Hernando and I start own house painting business once we citizens of USA twenty years ago. Our children take over business and do well,

251

but we help."

"And you never once thought to look up my uncle and his cousin?" Rafe inquired, anguished and frustrated.

"No. We believed they okay," Hernando piped up. "It took us long time to get legal papers to come back. We no want to do anything illegal to be sent back to Mexico. Immigration Services show our records we come over once illegally, so we no want to cause any problems. We make good living here. Back there, not so good."

Agent Schmidt knocked on the door and stuck his head in. "I'm ready to take the witness statements whenever you are." He carried a tape recorder and his computer under his arm.

Mitch motioned for him to enter.

"I'm sorry, Reverend," Mitch stood and waited for Norman to deposit everything on the table, "but we need to get their statements and put these men in a safe place for several days while we check out their story."

"Thank you, gentlemen, for sharing this with me. I am so glad you made the decision to come back here and give us this information. It's a big relief to finally know what happened to my uncle. My mother's cousin, Fernando, died in what city?"

"We drive in Colorado," declared Roberto. "Not remember name of the city anymore. I think is D something."

"Do you mean Denver?"

"Sí, I think that is right. Big city. Is so long ago. I remember real clear the accident but no city. Just drive through it and want to get back south."

"Gracias again." Rafe used a little of his Hispanic language. "I will tell my family. It'll be good to know where he is buried."

As Mitch and Rafe exited the room, Rafe looked back at the two men who sat solemnly across the table from the

Norman. "Do you believe their story?" he asked Mitch.

"Well, it's worth checking out, and it matches Wayne Thomas' statement," said Mitch as he fiddled with his ear. "I don't want to make any mistakes on this case, and everything needs to be verified. I should be able to find out if your mother's cousin did indeed die in the vehicle accident they mentioned."

"God bless you," said Rafe with relief. "I wouldn't know how to begin to research an accident from over forty years ago."

"It may take some digging, but the BCA can get their hands on many kinds of records and a lot quicker than we can. I'll make sure we follow up on it."

Rafe looked back in the room again, and with a concerned look asked Mitch, "What's going to happen to these men?"

"Oh, we'll put them up in a motel somewhere with a police guard. They're our only witnesses right now, and I don't want anything to happen to them," he vowed.

"Me either."

"By the way, I want to keep all this on the QT. I don't want the press to get hold of any of this information. I believe there's an informant in the department."

"What about Steph? She needs to know."

"I'll talk to her…unless you planned to stop at River View."

"Since my sermon last Sunday, I've run into a mind block for this Sunday. Plus, Charles Leddering's funeral is tomorrow. I need a break, so I'll make a trip over there."

"I heard about your sermon last Sunday. Sorry I missed it," said Mitch, ashamed to admit the length of time since he attended any church. "My secretary attended and told me all about it."

Rafe blushed. "I needed to release my frustration after years of listening to my mother talk about her missing family. Now that they're found, I can put it to rest and start the forgiveness process. What about you?"

"What about me?"

"Steph told me a little of your history with your ex-wife. Have you forgiven her?"

Mitch looked surprised, and felt a bitter taste in his mouth. "I don't think about it. She's gone and out of our lives forever...I hope."

"But she still needs forgiveness before you can heal and move on. You can't keep carrying the bitterness in your heart. Your little girl will grow up and hate her mother. She's too young to learn to hate. If you forgive, then she will follow."

"I'll think about it."

"Please do," said Rafe, as he turned to walk out of the building. Mitch stared after him as if in a trance.

How does he do it? How does he know what I'm feeling? He's good!

CHAPTER TWENTY-NINE

Steph watched from the open doorway to the community room as Lola worked her magic on the group of residents gathered to pray. She could hear Lola pray for Reverend Rafe and his family to be healed and to find forgiveness for the tragedy with his uncle. Sounds could be heard from Mattie and Maude saying "Yes, Lord. Yes, Lord," and "Amen," several different times as they prayed.

It felt good to hear prayer in the building. Her opinion of prayer and God took a dramatic turnaround. She barely recognized herself as the same person who arrived in River Falls with hatred and animosity in her heart several months ago. Her thoughts rotated to Miss Mattie and Maude.

Miss Mattie and Maude should be able to live on their own without subsidized house. I remembered Karen made a statement earlier about Mattie and Maude's brother.

She turned to go back to the office and ask Karen what she knew about them when she bumped into a firm chest, then arms engulfed her as she lost her balance, and let out a little yelp.

"Oh…Rafe!" she looked surprised and then smiled.

"You seem to be in deep contemplation, and didn't even notice when I walked in," he smirked, his dimple in his chin more prominent. "I came to talk to you, but I see our little group's grown a few at a time. I should probably make an appearance."

"My mind is elsewhere." He still held her close in his arms.

"Only good thoughts, I hope." Their eyes met in silent communication.

She turned to see if anyone else watched as Rafe held her close. "See you later," she whispered.

Before she forgot, she stopped by Karen's office.

"Karen, you mentioned once before about Mattie's and Maude's brother. Where is he?"

"He's in a nursing home in Minneapolis," she replied.

"I'm curious. Why are Mattie and Maude living here of all places? Their retirement alone should give them financial security."

"You're right," Karen said, and closed the file on her desk. "Both Mattie and Maude give most of their income away for their brother's keep at the nursing home. From what Maude tells me, it's over $6,000 a month. They exhausted their savings. They couldn't afford to keep their townhouse, and help out their brother at the same time. Now there's nothing left for them. Mattie is going downhill because she forgets to take her medications. Sometimes she still lives in the past, and talks about her fiancé as if he is away on a vacation."

"Now I understand. It's bothered me for some time, but I've never followed up on it."

Do I dare trust Karen further?

She took a chance. "Did Miss Mattie ever say anything to you about ghosts in the building?"

Karen looked surprised. "No, but she made comments to me about the noise in the apartment above her. Since it's not occupied, I ignored her complaint."

"How come it's not rented when there's a waiting list?"

Karen shook her head. "We've tried, but every time I show the apartment, they change their minds and make an excuse." She mimicked what others said. "I want to be on a lower floor. Don't like the long walk to the elevator. I want to face another direction." She threw her hands up in the air in frustration. "Being on the north side of the building, it feels cold every time I show it. I think I've heard the same excuses over and over again."

"Might be superstition. Did you ever think to change the number on the apartment?"

"I suggested it several different times, but then someone comes along, and it doesn't seem to bother them. Now it's vacant for more than several months. So far we're still within our three percent vacancy range with HUD, so I'm not too concerned right now. Several tenants gave their notices, and it could hurt us with a higher vacancy rate."

"HUD will allow us a dispensation because of the renovations, so I don't think we need to be in a big hurry to lease it. Besides, we'll need more vacancies when we start remodeling apartments." she said.

Karen nodded her agreement. "I'll hold off on the wait list then."

"Reverend Rafe is here and wants to talk to me. I don't know how long he'll be in the dining room with his group. I'm going up to see the sprinkler system supervisor. Ask the reverend to call me on my cell, and I'll tell him which floor

I'm on."

After Steph checked on the progress with the sprinkler crew, she decided not to wait for Rafe znc pushed the elevator button on the eleventh floor. She watched the numbers climb from the first floor. The elevator door opened, and Rafe leaned against the wall with his arms crossed. Each time she looked at him, her heart leaped in anticipation of his closeness. She knew they needed to be careful with their relationship because of their positions in the community.

Gossip goes fast through a small town.

"Hi there," she replied as she stepped into the elevator.

The door closed, and Rafe pushed the button to lock the elevator. "I wanted to talk to you where I knew no one else could see or hear us."

Confused, Steph tilted her head, "Okay, what's happening?"

"I just returned from the sheriff's department, and Mitch had two older Hispanic men in one of the meeting rooms. He asked me to talk with them. They claim to be the missing men in the picture I gave him earlier."

"Oh, Rafe!" Her mind wanted to ask so many questions. "Did you talk to them? What did they say? Are they really your uncle's friends?"

"Hold on!" He raised his hand to stop her. "Yes, I think they're for real. Mitch will check out their story through the BCA. Apparently, the other person buried with my uncle was my cousin, Antonio Osorio." He continued to supply the same story told to him earlier.

"So what you're telling me is what my father believed he witnessed actually happened, and the two remaining survivors showed up here on their own volition to be witnesses."

"Yep."

"So why are we locked in this elevator?"

"Because Mitch wants this all kept hushed for now. No one can know except for you and me and a few trusty officers. They plan to guard the witnesses for several days, or until their story gets checked out."

"Understand. However, I wonder about all this secrecy. It seems no matter what you try to keep secret in this town, word somehow gets out."

"That's what Mitch is concerned about right now. He's worried about a leak in the department."

"You got my word," and she pulled an invisible zipper across her lips. He smiled as he kissed her zipped lips.

Rafe unlocked the elevator door and pushed the first floor button. "Will you be at Charles Leddering's funeral tomorrow?"

"Yes, I plan on it with my parents."

"I've got to work on my Sunday sermon, plus talk to the family about what they would like me to share about Charles. Beth and Charles weren't regular attendees until his illness. I did visit him a few times in the hospital, and know he was well liked in the community."

"I remember Charles as a kind person who loved animals and hunting. He was injured in the Vietnam War. While he recovered from his injury in Germany, he met his wife. He worked for my dad at his construction company. When my dad retired, I don't know what he did afterwards."

"I think I'll sit down with the family before visitation today. God will put the rest in place."

The door of the elevator opened, and Steph followed Rafe out the door of the building toward his car. "Before you leave would you please answer a question for me?" He turned, arched his eyebrows, and waited for her question. "Do you believe evil forces can enter a building and hold it captive?"

Rafe thought for a moment. "There are evil forces out there. You know, Satan and all his dominions. Are you talking about this building? His eyes scanned the area suspiciously.

"Possibly. I'm not sure." She shrugged her shoulders.

"If there is evil in the building, I think our small prayer group has hindered them."

She let out a sigh of relief. "You're an angel."

"No, just a minister who believes prayers are heard."

"Yes, I believe you are right," she agreed. "See you tomorrow." She waved goodbye and walked back to the office.

She did not realize someone sat in a car farther down the street and watched her.

Rafe, back at the church office, turned his computer on, and again stared at the blank screen. His mind turned in a whirlwind of emotions as he catapulted from one feeling to another. Most of his emotion had to do with his uncle and now his mother's cousins. His anger, already built up inside him, was ready to explode.

What did he say to Steph? Prayers are heard. I truly believe prayers are heard, but the hurt and anger I feel now is pulling on my insides.

He pushed his keyboard aside, put his arms on the desk, and laid his head down and burst into a flood of tears for those lives lost. He let them flow until he could not release any more.

"There," a voice said. *"Are you feeling better? Let it all out and turn around and forgive."*

Rafe looked up, but the room was empty. He glanced toward the window, and could see in the rays of sunlight that

God was there to give him the comfort he needed. He did not have to see God there in person, but to know He showed up in whatever form was enough for him.

The church filled to capacity for Charles Leddering's funeral. Rafe gave a sermon where he portrayed Charles as an honest, hardworking man, who loved his family, and how he wanted to stay at home with his family until the end.

Jake took his turn at the pulpit to talk about how much his dad loved his family, and he would remember all the times they hunted and fished together. One of Jake's sisters talked about their dad's early childhood days, and how their parents met.

Steph kept several tissues handy in her pocket just in case it got too emotional for her.

I hate to think of doing this for my parents. I am the only child left. It would be up to me to make all the decisions. I need to talk to them to find out if they've made any plans for burial. It seems morbid to think about it at this time, but it just occurred to me, life is so frail.

CHAPTER THIRTY

He watched, hunched down in the car, as Callie's husband left for work. Her son followed a few minutes later. He wondered if the son worked, or if he left to find another fix. He cut him off after Callie quit her generosity with cash to her son.

He slid out of his car, sauntered up to the door, and pounded with his fist.

She peeked through the curtained window. "What do you want, Jessie?" shouted Callie through the door.

"Now, come on, sweetie, open the door. I want to talk to you." He gave her a phony smile and showed his yellowed, deteriorating teeth.

She knew he meant business, and she slowly opened the door. His roughened hand pushed the door open, and he strolled in as if he owned the place. He grabbed her and attempted a kiss. She turned her face away, and his lips landed on her neck.

"Is that any way to treat a friend?" he laughed at her

refusal.

"Just leave."

"Just leave...what," he sneered.

"Just leave, please," she pleaded.

He walked around the kitchen and hissed. "I missed you... and our times together."

"You don't miss me. You just wanted to steal from me. How could you do this?"

"Oh, now, honey, I wanted more than that from you." He grabbed her roughly and kissed her again. He wiped his mouth after the kiss and tried to spit. "You stink after cigarettes," he spouted.

She chain-smoked since her decision not to return to work.

"What do you care? I can't go back to my job after I figured out how you got hold of the master key and duplicated it. I thought you cared about me. Fool me once, but not twice."

"Well, sweetie, I need the new key to get into the building to get the stash the cops didn't find yet."

"I can't go back. I'm sure they guessed already how the key got duplicated. It didn't take me long to figure it out."

"As far as I know from my informant, they don't know anything for sure. They're just speculating. If you go back, they'll think you're innocent."

"No!" She shouted, as she pounded on his shoulders with her fists. "Now get out of here!"

He grabbed her, pressed her up against the kitchen wall and pulled her ponytail back so she looked directly into his eyes. "Listen here, sweetie," he sneered. "You get me those keys or something might happen to your husband...or to your son. You know...your son...one of my customers."

"No...you can't."

I know he'll do it. Why, oh why, did I get involved with

him?

Her father murdered. She could not even cry as she spread his ashes. There was no money to pay for a funeral.

I know Jessie had something to do with Father's death... but how to prove it?

Callie put herself in a predicament of her own making, and now she had to pay.

"I'll see what I can do," she said, defeated.

"You will do it. I'm watching you," he sneered. "Just so you don't forget." He slapped her across the face with the back of his hand. "No one runs out on Jessie Maverick. Just remember that."

Callie put her hand to the heated flesh on her face. "Yes, Jessie."

He angrily slammed the door, walked out to his souped-up Cadillac. His tires squealed as he sped down the road.

She remembered the first time she met Jessie at the Corner Bar where she purchased pull-tabs. Jessie, a smooth talker, looked a bit rough around the edges, but he made her feel like a woman again.

She brought him to the empty apartment on the thirteenth floor. Throughout the past months, they met several times a week and used River View Towers as their hideaway. He picked her up outside the bar and always gave her a joint to smoke in the car. It made her forget about her empty life at home. She even tried some of the "hard stuff", as he called it, while at the apartment. She worried they would be found out and made sure to cover her tracks.

Too bad Miss Mattie had to snoop around. Maybe she needed to have an accident.

CHAPTER THIRTY-ONE

Callie stood near the front door of River View Towers. It was after office hours. She knew Steph attended Charles Leddering's funeral and would work late to make up time. A large bush by the ED's office partially covered a portion of the window, so no one could see her from the street.

The light was on, and the blinds stood open in Steph's office as she peered through the window. The sun moved downward as Callie leaned against the building and tried to get up enough nerve to face Steph before she shut down her computer and went home. The cool night air made her shiver.

With caution, she moved back to the front entrance and tried to ignore her increased panic.

I need a smoke. A smoke would calm me. She has to let me in.

Callie pressed the button on the intercom. She knew Steph could see her from the camera at the front counter. The main door unlocked, and Callie guardedly entered. Steph unlocked the office door to allow Callie entrance. She waited by the counter, arms crossed, and her expression suspicious.

Jessie stood outside the building. He did not trust Callie to do as he asked, so he followed her. He would wait and bide his time. If she did not return soon, he would find a way to get in.

He was in desperate need of those drugs he hid in the storage room after the Sheriff's Posse and staff assisted in the recovery of the old records. What a perfect hiding place. He figured no one would want to go back in there for a while. The street sales would be enough to pay his suppliers, or he would be in big trouble.

"Well, Callie, I'm surprised to see you here." Steph crossed her arms over her rigid body. She was not going to make this easy.

Callie's eyes darted around the room and her hands clenched into fists.

"I'd like to talk to you, Ms. Runnell."

"Sure. Let's talk." Callie followed Steph into her office. "You know you've been gone quite a long time, and never once called. I even asked Reverend Rafe to stop by to see you."

Callie sat with her head down, afraid to look directly at Steph. "While at home I went through a lot of self-contemplation. I alienated my husband and son, and refused a funeral for my father. I spread his ashes in the Minnesota River. I couldn't deal with his drunkenness and behavior over the past few years."

"I'm sorry. I didn't know your father, and I only saw him a few times. He seemed fine the day he worked with the

Sheriff's Posse, and helped in the storage room."

"One of his better days." Callie gave a low sarcastic laugh.

"Reverend Rafe says we all need to forgive those who wrong us before we can move on with our lives. I hope someday you can forgive your dad."

Steph did not see any remorse in Callie's eyes.

"Don't count on it. I'm here because I want to come back to work."

Callie fidgeted in her chair, her eyes refused to look at Steph.

"You do realize you should have called us. We've had a lot going on here including drugs found in my desk. You don't happen to know anything about that, do you?" Steph boldly asked.

"No, ma'am, I don't." Callie's face reddened.

I'm sure Jessie had something to do with drugs found in the desk—but how to prove it?

Steph nodded, not sure she believed Callie. She reached for her cell phone and put it on the desk in front of her.

Several years ago she installed the 9-1-1 phone number as an app on the front of her phone for easy access. Steph never needed to use it, but while she lived in Chicago it made her feel safe. Now, it could be her safety line.

Callie noticed the move, and Steph knew she would be angry with her next remark.

"I'm not here to cause any trouble. I just want to come back to work."

"Callie," Steph cleared her throat, "I can't give you back your job."

Callie acted way too nervous. It sent triggers down her spine, and made her wary.

"I must get my job back," her voice raised as her fist hit

the arm on the chair.

I've read too many stories of violence in the workplace. I'm the only one here, and no back up in case Callie gets violent. Lola's already in her apartment.

Every fiber in her body became taut, but she coolly replied, "I'm sorry, Callie, but the employee handbook clearly states three days of absence without at least a phone call constitutes your resignation. Since it's more than three days, we assumed you resigned and would not return. We care about you, but right now, as Director, I cannot give you back your job."

Rafe drove to Steph's home. It had been an emotional day for many after the funeral. He knew Steph's parents were friends of the Ledderings many years ago, and maybe Steph needed a little cheer.

"Steph decided to work late tonight since she took time off for the funeral," Anne Thomas informed him.

With an uneasy feeling in his gut, he replied, "I think I'll drop by her office and make sure everything is okay."

"We'd appreciate it. We don't like the idea of her working so late."

Jessie made the decision he waited long enough and needed entrance to the building. Sooner or later one of the residents would either return or leave. He would grab the door before it locked behind them and sneak in. He patted his 9mm pistol loaded in his pocket, just in case. He did not expect any trouble with either of the two women, but you never know.

Callie placed her hands on the desk with a desperate look in her eyes. She pleaded, "I have to get my job back. I need a key. You just don't understand."

"Understand what?" Steph stood up from behind her desk and reached for her phone.

Rafe drove slowly by the high rise and looked for a place to park. He found a spot where he could see into Steph's office. With the light still on, he noticed she had someone with her. Who? He squinted his eyes. It looked like Callie.

Steph stood behind her desk and appeared to be in an argument with Callie. This did not look right. There was no way to get in the office without causing suspicion from Callie.

He noticed a tough-looking man with greasy hair stood outside the building and paced back and forth in a circle. Someone just walked out. The man grabbed the door handle before it closed and ran in.

Rafe reached for his cell phone and dialed Mitch's private number.

"Hey, Mitch."

"Hey yourself, Reverend."

"I'm sitting outside River View Towers. Something suspicious is going on there. Steph was supposed to work late, but I see Callie in her office, and now a man just walked into the building without a key."

"You're concerned about this? Why?" He thought Rafe a little overly solicitous.

"Now I see this man in Steph's office. She didn't lock the office door." Rafe's eye widened with fear. "Mitch, he's got a gun. I can see it through the window."

"I'm on my way," Mitch growled into the phone. Rafe heard, "Natalia, go over to the neighbors right now," as he hung up the phone.

Rafe left his car and ran to the front door.

How to get in without causing any attention? How? Think, man! Yes! Dial Lola's apartment number. She can let me in through the intercom.

He pressed the buttons for Lola's apartment. She answered, "Yes, who is it?"

"Lola," he whispered. "This is Reverend Rafael McGowan. Could you let me in? It's an emergency."

"Sure, Reverend. Anything I can help you with?"

"No! Stay where you are."

The door buzzed as it unlocked. He opened it slowly and looked for anyone else on the main floor. No one. The man must be alone.

Steph stood by her desk paralyzed with fear as Jessie pointed the gun at her and then at Callie.

"Jessie, put the gun down. You don't need to do this," begged Callie.

"I told you before I'm an impatient man. I waited out there too long. Now I'm forced to take things in my own hands."

Steph saw the fear in Callie's eyes as her head moved back and forth between her and the man with the gun.

"I'm sorry, Ms. Runnell. Jessie said if I didn't get the new key for him that he would hurt my husband or son. I had to come here tonight."

"Who are you…and what do you want?" Steph spoke up.

Before Jessie walked into the office she already reached for her cell phone to dial 9-1-1. She put her hands behind her so he could not see the phone.

Maybe if I sat down I could dial 9-1-1 from under the desk.

She sat down in her chair. Jessie followed her move with the gun.

His eyes appeared glassy and his hands twitched as he

pointed the pistol. "You don't need to know who I am," he exclaimed, as he moved the pistol back and forth between the two women. "Grab your key, Miss Director. You need to open some doors for me."

From behind her desk, she discreetly slipped the phone in her loose fitting suit pocket.

Steph opened the desk drawer and reached for the master key. "What do you want from us?"

She tried to stall for time so she could secretly use her phone. His eyes followed her, and she was afraid he would fire the gun if she tried any obvious moves.

"Just move," he said, as he waved the gun toward the door. "We're going up to the thirteenth floor in the elevator. You better hope no one sees us, or I'll have to use this."

He held up the gun and kept his finger on the trigger. Steph worried about the way he fidgeted. It could accidentally fire.

Rafe, about to walk through the door, saw shadows from Steph's office move toward the reception area. He backed off as Callie and then Steph slowly walked out of her office toward the door that led to the community room and elevator. Rafe opened the stairway door next to the elevator to hide, but kept the door cracked open.

He watched the man point the gun at Callie, and demanded she press the elevator button. Steph stood off to the side. He could almost reach out and touch her, but afraid if he tried anything, either one of the women would get hurt or even himself. He needed to bide his time. The pistol shook in the man's hand, and Rafe knew the man, probably high on some drug, would get violent if he tried to stop him.

The elevator door opened, and he pushed Callie into the elevator. Steph did not want him to touch her, and she walked in silently and stood in the corner with her arms wrapped around her body. The door closed, and Rafe stepped out from behind the door and watched as it went to each floor. Finally, it stopped on the thirteenth floor.

Where is Mitch? He said he'd be here in a few minutes.

Time stood still as he waited and paced, because he did not know how to help the two women.

It seemed like hours, but only several minutes, when Mitch arrived with two deputies. No lights, no sirens. Rafe opened the door.

"They're up on the thirteenth floor," he whispered, even though no one but Mitch and the deputies could hear him. "He's got a pistol on both Callie and Steph. We don't dare use the elevator."

"No, you're right," agreed Mitch. "Let's take the stairs."

"All thirteen floors," the two deputies said in unison and groaned.

"Yep," Mitch replied.

As the four men started up the stairs, Rafe raced ahead and took two steps at a time.

Good thing I run five miles a day.

The other men, even though all in good shape, could not keep the pace. Rafe waited impatiently at the top of the thirteenth floor.

Dear Lord, please send your angels to protect Steph and Callie.

"Rafe, you don't have a weapon. You better leave this to us," Mitch ordered, as he reached the top floor. They stopped for a moment to catch their breath. Mitch put his ear to the door. Nothing.

He drew his gun, removed the safety, slowly opened the stairway door, and cautiously peeked his head out the door. No one in sight.

He pointed to his two deputies to draw their guns and start down the hallway. He motioned for Rafe to stay behind him. He preferred the minister stay behind altogether. As a civilian the liability for his safety was Mitch's, but he knew Rafe would not listen even if he tried to make the suggestion.

They inched their way around the circular hallway, but did not hear any voices except for television sets from a few apartments. They noticed the storage room door slightly ajar. Mitch slowly opened the door that led to the stairway for the storage room and the roof. He heard Steph's voice.

"Why don't you take what you came for and leave?"

"Well, girlie, I will do just that. But I need to take care of you first."

"What…what do you mean?" Callie's voice quivered.

Mitch used caution to open the door wider and motioned the deputies to join him. Rafe stayed behind the men.

"Well, I need to take care of you just like I took care of your old man."

"I knew you had something to do with my father's death. How could you be so cruel to an old man? What did he do to make you want to throw him out the window?"

Steph looked at Callie, and realized she attempted to stall for time. Jessie pointed the gun at them as he walked around the room and searched for his stash. She cautiously backed up as far from him as possible. He took his eyes off them for a moment. Steph put her hand in her pocket and pushed the mute button on the side of her phone so he could not hear or see her push the 9-1-1 app.

Steph talked loud to cover up for the 9-1-1 operator's voice. "Why do you want to hurt us? We haven't done anything to you. All you have to do is take your drug stash and leave us. You can lock us up here in the storage room at River

View, and have plenty of time to get away."

"I don't think so. Eddie was a liability. It was easy to get the keys from Callie as she was so out of it. She didn't even know I took it from her." Jessie laughed cynically. "I paid Eddie a lot of moola to make those keys for me. He didn't know what they were for. He followed me here that night when I came to pick up part of my stash. He threatened to turn me in. I told him you gave me the keys to duplicate, and if he turned me in, you would go to jail. He jumped me and tried to fight. After I knocked him out, it was easy to open the window, push the screen out, and get rid of him."

"You're nasty!" spat Callie. "You're scum! I wish I never laid eyes on you."

"Well, sweetie, you won't have to worry about it too much longer. You both go down the stairs first and no funny business."

He grabbed his hidden backpack from behind a pile of boxes and slung it over his shoulder. Callie's body shook, and she started to sniffle.

"Shut up!" he growled through clenched teeth. "I'm tired of your whimpering."

Mitch and the deputies quietly exited the door at the bottom of the stairs and closed it to where it was still slightly ajar. The door would hide them temporarily as it opened outward and gave them the advantage.

Steph was first to step through the door as they walked out on the thirteenth floor. Out of the corner of her eye she saw Mitch and several deputies behind the door. She wanted to get out of the way as fast as possible. Callie was right behind her. Steph turned to reach out and grab Callie's arm and pull her off to the side as Mitch and the two deputies rushed around the door.

"Drop your weapon," Mitch demanded. All three pistols pointed at Jessie. He turned to run back up the stairs with his heavy backpack, but the youngest deputy tackled him to the floor before he could get past the third step. His gun flew to the floor, and the other deputy reached for it. Before he knew it, he was handcuffed and searched.

"Steph, are you okay?" shouted Rafe as he came around the corner.

Steph did not see him at first as she only noticed Mitch and the two deputies. She ran into his arms and sobbed. He crushed her to him, and held her so tight she could hardly breathe.

"It's all right. I saw him through your office window and called Mitch. We had you covered. God was on our side on this one."

"Praise the Lord," Steph cried out. "I prayed for someone to save us. I've never been so scared in my entire life." She looked up at Rafe and smiled through her tears. "I'm so glad He had our safety in His hands."

"So am I. So am I. I prayed the entire time I saw him holding the gun on you." He turned to Mitch. "Who is this guy anyway?"

"Let me introduce you to Jessie Maverick, one of the biggest drug dealers in town. We tried to get something on him for quite a while. Even our undercover agent couldn't get anything positive against him. Now he walked right into our hands. He's going to be charged with the murder of Eddie Barkley, aggravated assault, and possession of drugs. It's going to be a long time before he gets out."

The two deputies gripped Jessie on both sides of his arms and dragged him toward the elevator. A few apartment doors opened while they escorted Jessie to the elevator, but the deputies told the residents that all was fine and close their doors for safety.

"This time we're taking the elevator down," mocked one of the deputies. The other deputy laughed as they entered the elevator, relieved the standoff was over

"Can I get both of you to come to the station and give us a statement?"

Steph glanced at Callie. Her entire body shook as she leaned against the wall. As they watched, she slumped to the floor and covered her face with her hands. Rafe walked over to her, and Steph followed. They sat down beside her, one on each side.

"You're safe now, Callie," Steph said, as she handed her a tissue from her pocket. She reached up and handed the phone to Mitch. "9-1-1 is still on the phone. Maybe you need to confirm with them all is well."

Mitch grasped the phone, relayed their safety and hung up. "Smart move," he commented, as he handed the phone back. "The operator is sure she got most of the conversation recorded."

Steph wanly smiled, her face still pale. She touched Callie's arm.

"Callie, did you hear what Jessie said about your dad? He tried to save your life and get you out of trouble. Your father loved you as your Father in Heaven loves you. He saved your life and gave up his life for yours, just like Jesus did for all of us."

Rafe watched Steph deliver her speech to Callie. He was astonished to hear such encouragement come from her. Only a few months ago, she would not even talk about God. Now she became a disciple of Jesus to bring the good news to Callie. He could not have been more proud of her.

Callie's sobs continued. Steph put her arm around her.

"I did my father an injustice," she moaned in between her sobs. "He did love me...and I turned away from him. I... I... am...so ashamed."

Rafe intervened, "Callie, you need to forgive your father for his past and move on. Have you ever read the Bible?"

"No," then added, "sometimes as a little girl," and looked at Rafe, "one my mom...gave me, but never look at it."

"In Mark Chapter Eleven, verses twenty-five and twenty-six it says 'And whenever I stand praying, if I have anything against anyone, I forgive him and let it drop, in order that my Father Who is in Heaven may also forgive me my failings and shortcomings and let them drop. But if I do not forgive, neither will my Father in Heaven forgive my failings and shortcomings.'"

She put her head on her folded arms and between sobs lamented, "Father, forgive me for I have sinned. I forgive my own father. I realize now he tried to protect me. I didn't know it, and resented he died so violently and put this burden on me."

Mitch listened to Steph and Rafe talk to Callie. It stirred his heart to hear above love and forgiveness. He needed to make a move in that direction with his ex-wife. He hoped he could make that move soon, but not yet.

"I am sorry to interrupt," he interjected with a lump in his throat, "but could we please drive to the Law Enforcement Center, so I can get your statements? We can then go home for a good night's sleep."

Steph smiled. She knew Mitch was affected by what they said to Callie, but it was something she could talk to him about later.

"Sure, Mitch, we'll meet you there. Callie, do you have your own car or do you want to ride with us?"

Callie nodded. Her crying stopped. "I can drive. I feel much better. Thank you, Reverend McGowan and Ms. Runnell."

"Leave your car here," he said to Steph. "I'll bring you back to pick up your car afterwards."

"Thanks," she replied, her face pale from exhaustion.

CHAPTER THIRTY-TWO

There were only a few hours until daylight when Rafe drove her back to the high rise to pick up her car. He followed her home.

Her parents, filled with worry, paced the floor at the house. When they saw both cars, Anne and Wayne rushed outside and threw their arms around their daughter. They refused go to bed without an explanation.

"I've tea brewing on the stove, chamomile to relax you," Anne said as they sat around the kitchen table.

"Thanks, Mom." Steph held out her hand to her mother. There were tears in her mother's eyes as they shared a smile with each other. Anne stood and poured each one a mug of tea.

"Thank you, Mrs. Thomas. Hopefully, we can get a few winks of sleep after everything," Rafe yawned and took a sip from the steaming mug.

"Young man, I'm so grateful to you for helping our daughter tonight. I don't know how to repay you," sniffed Wayne, who did not show his emotions easily. Steph was precious to him, and he felt emotionally drained when she arrived back home.

Together they explained the details of the assault at gunpoint.

When Rafe decided to leave, Steph pulled him aside and said, "I knew everything was in God's hands, and I would accept what He had planned."

"Now you understand what's it's like to know the love of Jesus." His whole face spread into a radiant smile.

Right at that moment Steph wished her parents were not in the house. She wanted to embrace him, feel his solid and strong arms around her, and never let him go.

Steph went to bed exhausted and woke up still fatigued. She decided several cups of coffee would give her the caffeine kick to stay alert along with a piece of toast.

When she arrived at the office the employees surprised her—double chocolate chip muffins and more coffee.

"Why the special treatment?"

Darrin pushed his glasses back up his nose. "We heard about the stand-off with Jessie Maverick, and we're so glad you're okay. We're just sorry to hear about Callie."

"How did you hear about it so fast?"

"It's a small town," he replied, and added with a smirk, "plus several residents who live on the thirteenth floor made sure they came down for coffee early and start to inform everyone what happened last night."

"Yeah," replied Derek. "We didn't want to lose you again. Give us the full details. We've been in suspense."

The four employees stood around the reception counter.

This feels like a family that can work together.

They ate their muffins and drank coffee together while she relayed the entire story.

"What's going to happen to Callie?" asked Karen.

"Well, Callie will not return to work. Our employee manual strictly states that over three days of absenteeism without at least a phone call constitutes a voluntary resignation. She also put our organization in jeopardy by allowing the master key to be stolen from her. The cost to re-key the entire building will need to come out of our budget."

She added a little more coffee to her mug to warm it up. "By the way, I think we will change the locks on the outside entrance to an electronic fob system so keys won't be needed to get in the building. We can also monitor the coming and going of our residents. Karen, would you get me a list of several security companies in town?"

"Sure thing," she replied. "How soon will this happen?"

"I think with what happened last evening the board will approve this new security measure immediately. I've worked with those systems before and know the drill. Now I just need prices," she interjected. "Oh, also, Lola, I'll prepare an ad for a new office person to replace Callie. If you would take care of inserting it in the newspaper and call the Job Center to put it on their website. We need to find someone soon. If you can work a few more hours until we find someone, it would be appreciated."

"Will do, Ms. Runnell," Lola replied, and waved her hand in a half salute. They all laughed. "Is it all right to continue with my prayer group meeting every day?"

"Thank you, Lola. I think a prayer group is definitely needed," she said with tears in her eyes and her voice started to crack as she looked at each one of her employees. "Thank you again everyone for caring about what happens here. We all have been through a lot these past few months. Now it's time to get back to work."

Their little celebration disbanded, Steph decided to continue business as usual even though she was weary from lack of sleep.

"I need to check on the progress of the sprinkler system if anyone is looking for me," she said to no one in particular and walked out the door. Pleased with the subcontractor's progress, the supervisor assured her they would be done within a week. Then the final inspection.

Things are finally coming together. Thank you, Lord, for being here with us.

Back at her desk, she diligently went over the job requirements for Callie's former position. The ad was ready before noon. Exhausted from only a few hours of sleep, she laid her head down on her desk, closed her eyes, when Rafe called her cell phone.

"Can I take you to lunch?"

"Oh, yes," she replied as she fairly skipped out of the office to meet him at The Nest. Her fatigue forgotten.

Rafe already reserved a table and waved as she entered the small restaurant. Steph glanced at the menu, and they placed their orders with the waitress.

"Did you get any sleep at all last night?" he asked, concerned as he noticed the dark circles under her eyes.

"Totally exhausted after you left. Went to sleep immediately, but I think I dreamt all night. When I woke up I felt just as tired as when I went to bed. I just don't remember any dreams... but I know I relived last night over and over again."

"Are you going to be okay?"

"Yes, I will go home early and probably crawl into bed."

"Have you heard anymore from the sheriff's office?"

"No," she replied, "but I think Mitch tried to keep things from getting out of hand with whoever is leaking information within the department."

Rafe nodded his agreement.

"I want you to know Callie and her husband visited me this morning. It surprised me, yet made me happy and hopeful that what we said to her last night sunk in. They asked for help. I suggested counseling, and gave them names of Christian marriage counselors. I didn't see her husband last night, but apparently Callie called him from the center, and he came to be with her."

"Yeah, I don't remember seeing Callie after we gave our statements. Since they kept us apart, I didn't know what happened to her. You know, I've never met her husband, but I'm so glad they stopped to see you."

"Mitch did not file any charges against her...yet. She swears she didn't know Jessie had duplicate keys made."

"After what Jessie said while he held us captive, I would tend to believe Callie had no involvement with selling drugs."

"Her son is a user. He needs help, too. He needs to voluntarily want to quit. All we can do is pray for him to turn his life around."

"He bled her dry for money—a two-way train wreck waiting to happen. She was involved with the person selling her son drugs, and didn't even realize she also supported Jessie, plus gave him a place to hide his stash. Her two lives finally collided when he threatened her husband and son."

The middle-aged waitress came with their meal. "I am so sorry for the delay," she apologized as she put the two plates in front of them. "Busy day," she said, as she blew a strand of hair away from her face.

Rafe smiled at her, "That's okay. I know you're swamped."

"Oh, but you two are special today. Your meal is on the house. They just had the news on the radio about the drug dealer who held you hostage last night, and my boss says you deserve a free meal."

Rafe chuckled. "In that case I should order lobster."

"Yeah, right," the waitress laughed and tapped him lightly on the shoulder. "I'm so glad you are both okay and no one got hurt."

"Thank you for your concern and also for the meal," said Steph, as the waitress walked back to the kitchen.

"Word sure gets out fast. I'm surprised the newspaper hasn't called for a statement. I suppose they can get all they need off the sheriff's report. I always say 'no comment', so they probably think I'll do the same thing."

"I'm meeting with Lola's prayer group right after lunch today. I think Lola is doing an outstanding job with her group of residents to pray and read from the Bible each day."

"Lola will work a few extra hours now until we hire someone for Callie's position. It'll be tough to find a qualified person."

"Well, let's pray before we eat, and ask the Lord for help to find someone suitable."

Rafe bowed his head, folded his hands together, and in a low voice shared a short prayer to ask God to bless their food and to praise God for the safe end to the previous night; then added a prayer to send the right employee for the housing authority.

Steph never prayed in public before today, but followed

Rafe's example and bowed her head. She noticed people stare at them, but really did not care as it instilled a special feeling in her heart to be able to praise God and ask His blessing.

"I never mentioned to you..." she gulped and swallowed hard. The memory engulfed her. "But Jessie planned to take us to the empty apartment on the thirteenth floor where he pushed Eddie Barkley from the window. If you, Mitch, and the deputies had not arrived when you did, I don't know what would have happened to us. It frightened me that he would push us off the roof, but, no, he insisted we go to 1313."

"I believe angels sent me to the building, and knew you needed to be rescued. After I left your house I thought I would go home, but got this uneasy feeling after I talked to your mother. A little voice kept saying to drive by. I could see you through your office window even with the bush in front of it, and by the way, you should really close the blinds when you work late."

"If it weren't for the open blinds, you might not have seen us."

"Yes, true, but for security, your blinds should be shut in the evening hours."

"Yes, boss," mimicked Steph, and gave him a sassy grin as she took another bite of her sandwich.

"I'm sorry. Didn't mean to boss you around. Just wanted to make sure you're safe."

"I know." She put her sandwich down and looked seriously at Rafe. "Do you believe in demons? I know as a Christian we all believe Satan is behind a lot of evil and that he has his own evil angels working on our souls; but I wonder if there is such a thing as demons who possess your very being?"

Rafe set his hamburger down and looked curiously at Steph. "What are you trying to say?"

"I wonder if you've ever run across demons who tried to take over someone's body…or already succeeded?"

"Not personally, but at some of my ministerial meetings I've heard stories of demonic possession: how people prayed over the person, and the evil left their body. Again, why do you ask this question?"

She looked hesitantly at him. "I think there is still an evil force in Apartment 1313…just like the number implies. When I went to check on the apartment after my talk with Miss Mattie, I had a difficult time to open the door. That's unusual in itself. With a master key, the door should open easily. I felt a presence in there…a cold presence. There was nothing in the apartment except for the hum of the air conditioner. Then when I tried to leave, I grabbed the door handle and a whoosh of cold air, like the wind, went past me." She shivered and shook her shoulders. "It really frightened me. I got out of the apartment and leaned against the wall. My heart raced, and I said 'Jesus, help me,' and instantly my heart rate went back to normal."

"Steph, why didn't you tell me about this before? Of course, anything is possible with Satan. He's capable of taking so many different forms to tempt you. When did this happen?"

"After I started to attend church with Azalea and Becca." She looked at him curiously. "Why do you ask?"

"First of all, when you moved here, do you remember telling me you wanted nothing to do with church?"

"Yes."

"And when you started to attend church, your heart changed, and you began to believe in the healing power of Jesus."

"Yes."

"Then you went into that apartment…the same apartment

Callie and Jessie used, and where Jessie hid his drugs."

"Yes. And I remember the way Jessie laughed…a maniacal laugh, like a possessed person."

"I think it makes sense, there was or still is evil in the apartment and could spread throughout the building. Right now, hopefully, it's only confined in that one apartment. It was a good move to call on Jesus for help."

"Several years ago we had a building in the process of renovation. A mysterious force kept the contractors from completing their work. The workers came up with really bizarre stories, and we ended up asking a Catholic priest to do an exorcism within the building. That seemed to satisfy the workers, and renovations were completed on time. I thought it all a bunch of mumbo jumbo at the time, but it seemed to work. Maybe we need to do the same thing."

"I agree. Lola's prayer group meets after lunch. I won't mention that particular apartment, but just suggest they pray for relief from all the evil forces in the building. With everything that's happened in the high rise the past couple months, it won't surprise them when I mention it. I will go up to the apartment personally…if you will accompany me…and we can definitely attempt to push those evil forces out."

"I'm with you all the way. I did not like the feeling it gave me to walk into the apartment." She shuddered.

"Just remember we may not be able to force the demons out right away. Satan is a persistent little devil."

"Ha ha. I take it that was a pun."

"Sorry, but I've been told I have a dry sense of humor."

"Good. Me, too." They laughed together.

Lola's prayer team met in the back corner of the dining room.

Miss Mattie and Maude continued to be faithful in their attendance. With over 100 elderly people living in the building, Lola's team had grown to over twenty, and continued to grow almost on a daily basis. Reverend Rafe, pleased with the turnout, agreed to keep it to a half hour. He teased the group and said they were just like children—too antsy to sit still for long periods of time. They laughed and reminded him that he was still a youngster.

After the prayer meeting, Rafe stopped by the office. Steph accompanied him to Apartment 1313.

"Do you want to go in?" She took a deep breath, and tried to steady the shakiness in her voice.

"Let's see if you can open the door this time."

Steph put her key in the lock and again the deadbolt did not want to click open. She looked at Rafe and shook her head.

"I suppose I could force it a little more."

"Don't push it. It's resisting us. Why don't we pray right here?" He held his Bible in his hands and pointed it toward the apartment door. "In the name of Jesus the Christ, Son of God, I command any evil spirits in this apartment to leave." He repeated the phrase a half dozen times.

"Try the lock now," he told Steph.

She put the key in the lock and tried it again. It did not want to budge.

"Okay, that's enough for today. Satan is strong and powerful. They know now we're here, and we'll come back tomorrow and every day and pray in front of the door until we can easily unlock it."

CHAPTER THIRTY-THREE

Lola's prayer group continued to pray, and the positive response from others in need overwhelmed them. They also persisted and prayed for protection from evil in the building, and demanded anything evil to leave in the name of Jesus.

Rafe put aside his other duties, and made a point to be there each day for a short time. Afterwards, he and Steph went to the apartment and prayed over it.

On the fourth day, they rode the elevator as usual and walked with determination to the apartment. Rafe took his Bible, and this time he placed it directly on the apartment door. He then reached for Steph's hand, and placed it on the Bible along with his.

"Father, in the name of Jesus, we come boldly to Your throne of grace. We stand in the gap and intercede, knowing the Holy Spirit within us takes hold together with us against the evils that attempt to hold this building in bondage. Father, You say whatever we bind on earth is bound in Heaven, and whatever we loose on earth is loosed in Heaven. You say for us to cast out demons in the name of Jesus. We say Satan shall not get an advantage over anything in this building. We are not ignorant of Satan's devices. We resist Satan, and we request he leave this building in the name of Jesus. There are others living in this building as residents who also ask that this building be relieved from the powers of darkness, and translated into the Kingdom of Your dear Son. In the name of Jesus. Amen."

"Amen," repeated Steph. "What a powerful prayer."

"Let's see if it worked." He pointed to the key she carried.

As Steph inserted the key into the lock, she repeated, "In the name of Jesus." Click. The door opened. Their eyes swiveled toward each other in astonishment.

The low hum of the apartment air conditioner calmed their nerves as they slowly crept in. Steph still noticed the small blood stain on the carpet and the fingerprint dust still remained. However, the strange atmosphere she felt in the room previously had vanished. The smell of rotten eggs disappeared, and the air smelled like a fresh breeze.

She raised her arms toward Heaven and shouted joyfully, "Thank you, Lord."

"Amen." Rafe smiled with an air of pleasure. "We did it."

"No, you all did it. It couldn't be done without you," she added, "or without Lola's prayer group. The prayers of our little group defeated Satan in this apartment."

The next day Steph prepared all the documents needed for the monthly board meeting. After the standoff with Jessie Maverick, not a single board member stopped by to talk to her. She believed the board members boycotted the building because of their embarrassment over Donald's accusations, and her declaration to resign after her reinstatement. Donald Hanson, the thorn in her side since the beginning, made a deal with her to arrive on Tuesdays and Thursdays to check on the renovation progress, and now he never showed.

"Karen, what are your thoughts about the new hire to replace Callie? I think the job could be filled by either a man or woman. I wonder if a new person could relieve you of some of your duties. Callie never seemed to have enough to do to keep her busy."

"I would appreciate whoever you hire that they train for my job also. It'd be asset when I take vacation. Lola's a gem, but she's too old and only performs the easiest of tasks."

"I'm eager to start interviews. All this extra work puts a strain on everything we do here."

Steph sat in the board room, and browsed through the applications as she waited for the arrival of all the board members. Clarence Larsvig, as usual, arrived first.

He mumbled, "Good morning."

Jake Leddering and Donald Hanson arrived together, and Wendy and Collette followed within minutes.

"I call this meeting to order," started Clarence, after everyone looked over the agenda. "We have quite an agenda this time, so let's begin. Could someone approve the minutes of the last meeting?"

Jake voted to approve the minutes, and Wendy seconded the motion. The motion carried by everyone's "aye."

"We'll let Ms. Runnell take over the meeting from here, but first I want to make a statement. I think we all owe Stephanie an apology. This deal with Callie was an eye opener," he shook his head, "and I'm sorry she had to deal with such a disagreeable employee. My hope is we can find a good employee to replace her."

"I think we all agree with you, Clarence," said Jake Leddering. The other board members nodded in agreement, except for Donald who sat stolid in his seat.

"Thank you," replied Steph, relieved they finally supported her decisions.

She explained the progress of the renovations, and kept it to a brief synopsis.

"I'm also changing the number on apartment 1313 to 1315. So many come to look at the apartment and feel those are unlucky numbers, so Darrin will order new numbers for the door as soon as we're done with the inside renovations."

"I'm also implementing a new key fob system to access the high rise. The quotes are in front of you. I recommend the lowest bid from Security First. They can start immediately. All we need to do is distribute the key fobs to all the residents and explain how to use them. We can also issue fobs to the board members if you want them. Any questions?"

"I don't have any questions. I think this is an excellent idea for better security control," agreed Clarence.

"The company will also set up another security camera at the entrance, so it'll focus on the elevator and on the front door. Right now there's only one camera on the front door."

It was a unanimous vote for the system. Steph knew they would approve, but now she needed to cut some more of the budget to get it done.

"We've received a small donation from the Rotary Club. I propose to order new shirts for the entire staff. Since it's a personal donation, we are able to use it as we see fit. Any objections?"

No one replied.

"The last item on the agenda—hire a new employee." She

briefly held up the applications, but did not pass them around for the board members to view. Her face set in a determined stance. "I will review the applications and start interviews soon. The final decision will be up to me." She wanted no influence from the board.

The meeting adjourned. Donald Hanson lagged behind as Steph gathered all the paperwork in a pile ready to take back to her office.

"Ms. Runnell, I want to talk to you, off the record, about this thing with Jessie Maverick. I understand from some of the deputies he had drugs stashed in the storage room."

Red flags went up as Steph looked at Donald. Mitch mentioned he kept everything as hushed as possible. Even the newspaper did not call her for an interview, but just printed from the sheriff's so-called report. There was no mention of where Jessie stashed the backpack. Mitch still attempted to find the leak in his department. None of the finer details were in the newspaper article.

How do I answer this question? I need to be truthful. He's one of the board members.

Nervously Steph replied, "I'm sorry, but I've been instructed not to talk to anyone about that night," and waited for Donald Hanson to demand an answer.

"Just concerned," he answered nonchalantly. His attitude surprised her. "I...I thought if there were more drugs stashed around the building, maybe we could get a drug canine recruited to check it out."

Good save. Someone leaked information to Donald.

She decided to bait him.

"Thank you. That's a thought to consider. Maybe you could mention it to the sheriff next time you see him."

"Sure. Sure thing." He turned and walked out of the room.

As soon as she returned to her office, she made a call to Mitch on his personal cell phone.

"Mitch, we just finished our monthly board meeting. Donald Hanson started to ask me questions after the board meeting about Jessie Maverick. Has he talked to you at all?"

"No, I've kept everything as quiet as possible. I didn't want anything to leak out to the press. What did he say to you?"

"He asked if there could be more drugs stashed in the building besides the duffle bag found in the storage room. He said some deputies gave him this information."

"No one knows about that backpack except for the deputies who were with me, Callie, Rafe, and you. That's it. I made up a dummy report and left out that information. I instructed Campbell and Burtwell to do the same without telling them the reason. I need to find the leak in the department."

"Okay. Just thought I would let you know."

"Thanks, I'll handle it from this end."

After he ended the call with Steph, he called his secretary, Sally, to reach Deputies Campbell and Burtwell, who were with him that night.

Burtwell was also one of the deputies in charge of the evidence room, and Mitch had seen Donald Hanson downstairs in the evidence room with Burtwell. Close to retirement and on the force long before Hanson retired, it did not surprise him that Burtwell and Hanson remained friends. He never put two and two together until now.

Campbell and Burtwell were both on duty. Campbell was out on patrol and Burtwell in the evidence room. After he questioned both men, Mitch sent Campbell back out on patrol.

"Burtwell, what's your connection with Donald Hanson?" His face, drawn and tense, watched for Burtwell's reaction.

"Why do you ask?"

"Just curious. He seems to know what's going on in our department even though he's no longer on the force. He's receiving his information from someone in the department. I believe you are that person."

Burtwell stammered, "Well...yes, I know him. We've been friends for years. He comes in periodically. We sit and visit while I'm on duty in the evidence room.

"Have you ever left the evidence room while he was there?"

Burtwell stroked his chin and tried to recall. "Yes, sir, several times I ran an errand to bring items to Detective Bishop. Don said he would stay until I returned. He's my friend and a former officer. I trusted him."

Mitch had an instant thought as if a light bulb turned on. "Let's go down to the evidence room. I want to check something out."

Only the officer in charge for the day carried the evidence room keys. The position, a monotonous job, was usually given to the older officers who expected to retire soon. Assigned two to three days a week in the evidence room, they spent the remainder of the week on patrol. Since Burtwell held the keys for the day, he opened the barred door.

"Get the paperwork on the drugs found in River View Towers when Eddie Barkley was found deceased." he demanded.

Burtwell looked in the evidence book. "It says here forty-two small bags of various drugs entered into evidence. It lists the drugs here."

"Okay. Let's find the box with the drugs." Burtwell knew

the system and located the box. They removed the cover, pulled on latex gloves, and Mitch started to count the number of bags. "I only count thirty-six bags here. Would you please count them yourself?"

Burtwell counted. He opened and shut his mouth.

"I know I entered those bags myself. I couldn't have made a mistake."

Burtwell shook his head, his lips tight.

"I'm sure you didn't, but I'm also sure you've passed information to Donald Hanson out of friendship. You know how strict the department is about giving out information that could affect a case."

"Yes, sir. I am aware, but Don is a friend and a former officer. He wouldn't... He couldn't..." Burtwell continued to shake his head in disbelief.

"Now look in the records for the drugs found in the director's desk at the high rise."

Burtwell opened the book again and walked over to the case number on the box and grabbed the evidence box. Six small bags of drugs spilled out of the box.

"If you compare what is missing in the larger stash to what is in the smaller box, I think you will find the same drugs that are missing in the large box are in the smaller box."

Burtwell sorted through the bags in the larger box and then compared them to those in the smaller box.

"Yes, sir, you are right. Those are the exact missing drugs."

"So Steph was indeed set up." Mitch scratched his head as he mumbled to himself.

"No one knows about this. Absolutely no one. If word gets out before we get this solved, you're fired."

"Yes, sir," answered Burtwell, aware his job and pension

were on the line.

Mitch walked past his secretary and ignored the phone call messages she tried to give him. She gave him an exasperated look, walked in his office, and set them on his desk.

He dialed Steve Bishop's number. No answer. He left a message, "Steve, I think we found a break in the Eddie Barkley case. Give me a call as soon as you can."

CHAPTER THIRTY-FOUR

With sweaty hands Jake Leddering carried his briefcase, and walked precariously into the Law Enforcement Center. He was directed to the sheriff's office by the clerk at the front desk. He did not like being there, but Jake was on a mission for his now departed father.

Always a flirt, he leaned over the desk at Mitch's secretary, Sally, and flashed her a smile. Sally was at least ten years older than Jake, but he enjoyed the chase. "You're looking mighty pretty today, Sally."

Over the past years of real estate sales his easy affinity with the ladies helped him close many deals. Just a few compliments here and there to the wife, and they seemed like putty in his hands. Sally, aware of Jake's reputation as a flirt, still blushed. Today he flirted from raw nervousness.

"What can I help you with today, Mr. Leddering?"

"Please call me Jake. Is the sheriff in? I need to speak to him."

"What's this in regard to?"

"It's personal."

"I'll see if he's available." She dialed Mitch's extension. Jake could see the light on, so he knew Mitch was in his office.

"Sheriff," Sally said into the phone. "Mr. Jake Leddering is here to see you. He says it's personal business."

Jake could not hear Mitch's response, but knew their animosity toward each other since high school never changed. It continued into their adult years as they each went their separate ways, but their lives seemed to always collide.

Jake charmed Mitch's ex-wife into the purchase of the house where Mitch now lived. Mitch never wanted the house, but his wife insisted, so to satisfy her he agreed to the purchase. A few months later she left.

"You can go in," Sally replied, as she hung up the phone and pointed to the door.

"Hello, Jake. I'm sorry about your father. How is your mother?" Mitch motioned for Jake to sit.

"Mom is doing fine. She mentioned returning to Germany to visit her sister and several cousins she's kept in contact with over the years. She'd been a caregiver to my dad for the past year and a half. She needs a break."

"I'm glad to hear she's doing okay. What can I help you with today?"

Jake opened his briefcase and extracted a #10 envelope. "Mom went through Dad's things, packed his clothes for donation…saved mementos. You know, the normal things the family does after one departs. She found this letter addressed to you."

"To me!" Mitch looked surprised. "Why would he write a letter to me?"

"I'm not sure. Open it and find out."

"Do you have any idea what's in the letter?"

"No. I thought maybe you would know. I wanted to open it, but my mother was adamant we give the letter directly to you, and hoped you would share the contents with us."

Mitch removed his letter opener from the desk drawer, and with some hesitancy opened the letter.

Dear Sheriff DeVries:

I am writing this letter because I know I will not be with the world much longer and need to confess and ask for forgiveness. I have already asked forgiveness of my Lord Jesus, but now I am going to ask it from my family, friends, and the people I have hurt in the past.

In October 1973 there were four of us out hunting when we saw a group of Mexicans who worked as laborers on the new senior high rise in town. Most of us had recently returned from Vietnam and unable to find employment.

The four of us decided to follow them after they left The Last Stop. We had no intention of hurting any of them, just scaring them into leaving the area.

There were five Mexicans, and they had been drinking, just like us. Their pickup ran into the ditch after they saw us. We covered our faces with bandanas to scare them. They ran like scared rabbits. We decided to chase them. It felt like we were still in the jungles of Vietnam, and our survival mode kicked in.

We cornered two by the river's edge just above the falls. My dogs barked and growled at the two, and one of them drew a knife out of his boot. Afraid he would hurt my dog, my war instinct took over, and I fired the gun. The bullet hit the one holding the knife, and he fell backwards into the river. The other Mexican jumped in to pull him to shore. I shouted for help. Before we could give them any aid, we heard them scream as they went over the falls.

When we arrived at the bottom of the falls, we found they had hit the rocks.

Between the four of us we pulled them out of the river, but both were dead. Then we looked for the others. They had already pulled their pickup out of the ditch and left. What to do we questioned ourselves? Our lives would be in ruins if we reported what happened. We just returned from Vietnam and then this happened. We panicked. It was an accident, but no one would believe us.

I knew the contractors were scheduled to pour concrete the next day at the high rise. We carried the bodies to the construction site. Since the pipes for the boilers had been buried earlier that day, we figured no one would be doing any more excavating. So we spent the remainder of the night digging a grave to bury the bodies in the same place they buried the pipe. We covered everything up so no one would suspect the area had been tampered with.

All these years and no one told, but it stuck in all our hearts and affected our very beings. We did not come away without any scars. We paid dearly with what we knew.

I want to name all of us that were involved and hope that they come forward with the same story. Since I was the one who fired the gun, I first place myself to blame. The others involved were Eddie Barkley, who is now gone, but he suffered from alcoholism. Then George Walters disappeared afterwards. Only God knows where he is now. He gave up a wonderful life with Mattie Turnborn to escape his fears. The last person involved was Donald Hanson. He tried to make up for his mistake by becoming a police officer and then a deputy, but later on alcohol and drugs overtook whatever good he did for the department.

I can only ask posthumously that you forgive me, the families of the two men forgive me, especially Reverend McGowan, who I admire so much, and the other men involved will forgive me for writing this letter. I cannot go to my grave with this sin on my soul. I have already asked God for His forgiveness. It is up to all of you to do the rest. Now I can go peacefully.

Sincerely,

Charles J. Leddering

Mitch's hands shook as he placed the letter on the desk and looked at Jake. His face hot, as if the temperature went up twenty degrees in the room, even though he knew the air conditioner was on. He handed the letter to Jake.

"I think you need to read this."

Jake reached for the letter, and recognized the shaky handwriting of his dad. As he read it, his face turned ashen. He sat in the chair, as if in a trance, and could not believe what his dad wrote.

Mitch pondered how to handle the situation while Jake continued to read the letter.

"No! I can't believe this!" he cried out in horror.

"Neither can I, Jake. However, it sure looks like a confession letter to me."

"This will devastate my mother." He leaned toward Mitch's desk. "Does she have to know about this?"

"That's up to you, Jake. I don't know how you can keep her from finding out. She's going to want to know what was in the letter."

"The only person left in town is Donald Hanson. If he hasn't confessed by now, he's not going to."

"Jake, let's be serious. A crime was committed. Even

302

though it was over forty years ago, it's still a crime. To me it seems like a terrible mistake and there was no intent to do harm. It just happened. We'll have to get Donald Hanson in here for questioning."

We'll have to get him in here for more than questioning right now. Hanson already has two strikes against him and now this. Bishop and I need to put our heads together and figure out what Hanson has to do with a lot of different things going on in town.

He picked up the intercom to talk to his secretary. "Sally, put out an APB for Donald Hanson. He's wanted for questioning. Also, put out a warning that he carries a gun."

CHAPTER THIRTY-FIVE

Donald Hanson heard laughter from inside Steph's house as he staggered to the front door. He parked his vehicle around the corner at the end of the next block to avoid any suspicion. Already dark outside, he leaned against the side of the house by the front door to avoid detection.

I'm the last one left who knows the truth about the bodies buried, except for one person—Wayne Thomas. Who knows how much he remembers? Burtwell said he made a statement to the sheriff. We all knew someone saw us, but didn't know who? After forty years it turned out to be Wayne Thomas. Why didn't he turn us in when he had the chance? We thought we were safe. Did he know who we were?

His body hurt. He used his last fix of marijuana for the pain, and started to drink the last several hours after the board meeting. Mixing drugs and alcohol confused his mind even more, and he decided to pay a call on Wayne Thomas.

Maybe I need to take care of the whole family. Then my troubles would be over. I don't know why I approved the hiring of that woman. I know she picked up vibes when I asked her about Jessie Maverick. She's too smart for her own good. They did not plan on any digging when doing the renovations. But, no, she gave the contractor permission to dig up the pipe. I tried to get rid of her once, but failed. Not this time.

His drug supplier, Jessie Maverick, sat in jail. Jessie gave him free marijuana and sometimes other drugs to help with his pain, as long as he supplied Jessie with information within the Law Enforcement Center.

Donald's mind was riddled with mixed thoughts—bad thoughts—and the liquor dulled his mind and put crazy things in his head. He checked his pocket for his pistol, a small Glock 9mm in a hidden holster inside his pants pocket.

Who knows where Jessie got this gun. It's got to be hot, but I don't want a gun registered in my name, especially tonight. Got to get rid of it soon as I'm done here. Too bad Jessie's in jail. This could be blamed on him.

He laughed, a low humorless vicious sound.

Azalea Rose worked the late afternoon-early evening shift at the Holiday Station and picked up Becca at her grandma's house. As she drove by Steph's house she noticed a man try to hide his body into the shadows against the porch wall by the front door. The street light at the end of the block reflected light toward the front of Steph's house.

Becca used Azalea's cell phone to play games on the way home. "Becca, give me my cell phone, please?"

"But, Mom, I'm right in the middle of a game."

"Doesn't matter, Becca, this is important. I need to make a phone call." Becca sighed and handed the phone to her mother.

Azalea dialed the 9-1-1 operator and asked to be

dispatched to the sheriff.

Informed he left for the day, she asked, "Could you please get a message to him?"

"Yes, ma'am. I sure can," sounded the nasally voice of the operator over the phone.

"This is important. Tell him there is a man outside Stephanie Runnell's house, and it looks suspicious. I may be crying wolf, but I think something is wrong. Ask if he could please check it out."

"Yes, ma'am. Your name please to pass the message on to the sheriff?"

"Oh...yes. It's Azalea Rose."

"Please stay on the phone while I try and locate the sheriff?"

"Yes, I will. In fact, I will circle around the block to keep an eye on what's going on until he can get there." She put her phone on speaker and set it on her center console. Her hands felt clammy on the steering wheel, and she needed to wipe them one at a time on her jeans. She turned the corner at the end of the block and recognized Donald Hanson's vehicle. She'd seen it often enough as he filled up gas at the Holiday Station.

"I see Donald Hanson's vehicle around the corner. I wonder if it's Donald by the front door."

"I will also send a squad car just in case I'm unable to reach the sheriff."

"Thank you," she replied, as she slowed down to turn the corner again. "Becca keep an eye on Steph's house as we drive by. I don't want to drive by too slow."

"Mommy, is Steph in trouble?" Becca asked.

"I sure hope not," she replied calmly to her daughter, and hoped Becca did not notice her own nervousness. "Let's pray everything will be okay."

"Are you still on the line, Ms. Rose?" The dispatch person questioned as Azalea drove by Steph's house again.

"Mommy, he's still there. This time he's looking in the front window," cried Becca.

"Driving by again. Is a squad car on its way?" she asked the dispatch officer.

"Yes, a squad car will drive by the house. I reached the sheriff. He's also on his way. He said he lives about a mile from there."

"Okay. Thanks. I'll drive by again, but I don't want him to get suspicious. He's looking in the window."

"Ten four. A squad is on its way."

With an APB out for Donald Hanson, all the officers on duty recognized the importance to be on the look-out for him.

When dispatch called him at home, it surprised Mitch to hear Donald would be at Steph's house. Of course, Azalea could be wrong.

Donald watched Wayne's and Anne's animated motions through the picture window. Wayne held a Bible in one hand as he gestured with the other. Rafe would page through his Bible, find his passage, and start a discussion. Steph stood, picked up the empty coffee mugs, and walked into the kitchen. She enjoyed the lively conversation between her parents and Rafe. She hurriedly filled the coffee mugs so she could return and listen to their discussion.

Ah, this would be a perfect shot. I should be able to fire easily through the window and hit Wayne.

He pulled the gun out of his pocket. Fuzzy from too much liquor, he shook his head to clear his eyesight so he could focus the gun site on Wayne. He looked to make sure no cars would see him.

Mitch requested the squad refrain from using the siren. That request seemed to be asked a lot lately. Mitch lived on the opposite side of town, so he turned one block before Steph's street and did not want to drive past her house. He preferred an element of surprise, and arrived before the squad car. He parked his vehicle on the opposite side of the street from Donald's car.

He saw Azalea drive by and motioned for her to keep driving. She drove around the block and parked at the end of the street to stay out of the way. Mitch sprinted through the back alley behind Steph's house and slithered around the corner toward the front door.

Mitch arrived in time to see Donald waiver, and with unsteady hands point the pistol toward the window.

Mitch pulled his pistol out of the holster and walked around the corner. "I wouldn't do that if I were you. Drop your gun, Donald," he demanded, as he pointed his own gun in Donald's direction.

Donald turned around and deftly aimed his gun at Mitch.

"I said drop it."

Donald's hand shook, but he dropped his arm to his side and the gun fell to the ground with a hollow thud.

"Put your hands behind your head and spread your feet."

The squad car arrived at the front of the house the same time Donald dropped his gun. The deputy jumped out, stood behind the squad, and aimed his gun over the hood at Donald.

Inside the house the residents finally noticed activity in the yard. Steph and Rafe rushed to the front door to see a deputy in a squad car as he pointed a gun at the front of their house. She flipped the outside light switch to reveal who was out there. It surprised Steph to see the sheriff stand in the shadows as he pointed a gun at Donald Hanson.

The deputy walked over and picked up the pistol. Donald fell to his knees, and then on all fours. He hung his head and broke out in heart-wrenching sobs.

She looked at the gun; her face paled. "Mitch, what's going on?"

"I'd sure like to know that myself," he replied, as he reached for handcuffs. "Donald, I hate to do this to you, but right now you're under arrest." He handed him over to the deputy. "I'll meet you at the jail to question Mr. Hanson." The deputy escorted Donald to the back seat of the squad car. "Oh, also test him for blood alcohol levels." The deputy gave Mitch the "yes, sir" salute.

He turned to Steph and the others who stood in the doorway.

"Azalea saw someone outside your door and thought it looked suspicious. She drove around the block and recognized Donald Hanson's vehicle. There's an APB on Hanson. He pointed a gun at your picture window, and I assume was ready to fire through the window."

"Dad...he and Mom sat on the couch that faced the window. He wanted to shoot at them. What for?" she looked confused.

"Mitch, is there something you're not telling us?" Rafe calmly asked after he realized there was more to the story. Wayne and Anne stood silently clinging to each other.

"Why would he want to hurt my dad?" Steph asked again.

"It's a long story." Mitch holstered his gun. "Let's go inside, and I'll explain as much as I can for right now. I don't know the entire story, but, hopefully, will find out more after we question Donald."

Before they could walk inside, Azalea and Becca pulled up in their car. Becca exited the car before Azalea came to a complete stop and ran into Steph's arms. "I'm so happy you're okay," she cried as she hugged Steph.

"Thank you, God, for keeping them safe," Azalea proclaimed as she walked up the sidewalk. "It worried me when I saw someone skulking around your house."

"Mitch just told us you called 9-1-1. You saved us from a tragedy," Steph put her arm around Azalea's shoulders.

"Just being a good guardian angel. Both of us prayed as we drove around the block that help would arrive in time. What is going on?"

"Come on inside. Mitch was about to give us an explanation."

Mitch explained about the letter from Charles. He also explained he believed Donald was the leak in the department. Even though he was retired, he spent a lot of time at the station and picked up bits and pieces of on-going investigations.

"I guess we trusted him because of his status in the community. We haven't questioned Hanson yet, but I think he's involved in more illegal activities than we know."

"Why would he want to hurt my dad and mom?" Steph questioned again.

"Think about it, Steph," her dad started to explain. "I gave the statement to Mitch. I couldn't remember anything about the men because I was drunk, but he didn't know that part. He thought I could easily turn him in to the sheriff. That's why I don't drink anymore. My mind was so confused that night, and not sure what I saw. Then Charles' letter. I think Donald Hanson finally broke, and, out of desperation, tried to shoot me. He's a broken soul and needs help."

"I agree," commented Rafe. "He's a lost soul and needs forgiveness."

"You're right," agreed Anne as she held her husband's hand. "It's time everyone is healed from all the tragedies of the past, which includes what happened to Stephanie."

"Yes, I believe Donald's involved in that also, but not sure how he pulled it off. Hopefully, we can find out more once he's questioned. I need to go and spend another night at the station. But first I need to get a sitter for Natalia."

"Why doesn't Natalia come and spend the night with us?" suggested Azalea. "She'll probably be bored with a sitter. I'll make sure she gets to school tomorrow."

"I'll see if she's willing," he replied, surprised at Azalea's offer.

After a call to his daughter and her "Oh, yes," Azalea and Becca drove over to pick up Natalia.

"I better get to the jail and see what I can get out of Hanson."

"I'll walk you out," offered Rafe.

When they stepped outside in the back yard, Rafe walked to the fence by the garage with Mitch. "I want to thank you for what you did tonight. You went above and beyond what I would expect a law enforcement officer to do."

Mitch needed to look away and not look Rafe in the eyes. His heart pounded into his throat. "Steph and her parents are special to me. They're like my second parents, and I grew up with Steph always around. I would do anything for them."

Rafe wasn't real sure he wanted to hear his response, but he needed to ask. "Are you in love with Steph?" The words were out.

Mitch turned his attention to Rafe and kept his face composed. "It could be possible, but Steph doesn't see it that way. We're just friends. Another time, maybe, but she wants you, and she's happy. You take good care of her. She's been through a lot this past year."

"I agree. I will do my best."

"That's all I can ask." Mitch walked through the alley to his squad. As he opened the door, his fist hit the hood of the vehicle. "Why, God, why do things work out this way?"

CHAPTER THIRTY-SIX

Rumors traveled around the next few days in River Falls following the arrest of one of the town's leading citizens. The sheriff assigned the case to Detective Bishop, who complained at being overwhelmed with all the recent criminal activity in town.

Steph and her family heard nothing from the River Falls Law Enforcement Center in regard to the arrest of Donald Hanson. Satisfied to remain left out of any more drama, they figured when Mitch and Detective Bishop finished their investigation they would be notified.

Rafe called his mother and related to her Charles' letter and confession, but left out the situation with Donald Hanson. He did not want to worry her. She released her tear as he told her the entire story of what actually happened to her older brother.

"Please come back to the ranch with the remains, so we can bury Jose and Antonio properly," begged his mother.

"I'll come soon, Mother," Rafe agreed.

"I've talked to the Osorio family, and they agree that Jose and Antonio should be buried together, so we'll bury them on the ranch when you return."

"I'm sorry, Mother, that I couldn't leave sooner, but with everything happening here, I didn't want to leave Steph and her parents without any emotional support and spiritual guidance. Steph was in a vulnerable position, but she pulled through as a strong person."

"It sounds like you're serious about Stephanie. You've waited a long time to find someone special."

"Yes, I did. It happened so fast. The first time I saw her, I knew she would be an important part of my life."

"Bring her to the ranch for Christmas, so we can all meet her. The entire family will be here, and there'll be plenty of room in this big house."

A knock sounded on his office door.

"Hang on, Mom." Rafe put his hand over the phone's mic. "Come in," he shouted, then lowered his voice. "I will talk to Steph about Christmas, but someone is waiting for me."

"Love you, Rafael. You take care."

"Love you, too, Mother. Give Dad my love also."

Beth Leddering, along with her son, Jake, and two daughters, Millie and Naomi, stood in the open doorway.

Rafe's muscles tightened, and he took a quick breath of surprise that Beth would show up with children in tow.

"Reverend Rafe, may we take a moment of your time."

"Welcome. How can I help you?" He reached for all his inner strength to embrace this family.

"We vould like to talk to you for a few minutes," requested Beth in her slight German accent.

Rafe had a round table in his office that he used for meetings. "Let's move to the table so we all can sit."

"Reverend Rafe, I vant to apologize for my husband," Beth started with tears in her eyes. "I know he asked for forgiveness in his letter to the sheriff, but I von't rest in peace until I explain many things about Charles."

"Go ahead." Rafe realized Beth needed closure.

"Charles vas a gut man, a loving man. He provided for his family for many years. All our married life he vould have nightmares that continued even days before he died. He never vould talk about them. I thought they had to do vit the war, but now realize they probably vere a combination of the war and vhat happened on the river bank. I loved him. He vas a gut papa and husband. Please, will your family forgive him?"

"Mrs. Leddering … Beth … Charles asked for forgiveness from the Lord before his death. I'm sure the Lord granted his forgiveness. There is nothing for me to forgive. It is already done."

"Danke, Reverend."

Rafe's sermon weeks before on forgiveness seemed to resonate throughout the community. He knew in his heart the Holy Spirit would provide grace to face any demand.

For you, O Lord, are good and forgiving, abounding in steadfast love to all who call upon you (Psalm 86).

Forgiveness seemed necessary for Beth and her family to move on with their lives. They could not be faulted for their husband and father's mistake. He rendered forgiveness to all four men involved. He decided to make sure and remind the entire parish that forgiveness was necessary to enter into the kingdom of God.

Steph, left in a dilemma with one board member short, decided even though Donald Hanson did not officially resign, she knew there would be something in the by-laws to prohibit him from serving on the board. Before the next scheduled board meeting, Jake Leddering stopped by her office and handed in his letter of resignation.

"Why are you resigning?" Steph secretly shouted for joy that she no longer would be forced to work with Jake and Donald.

Jake sat in the chair across from her desk. "I guess it's hard to explain. Even though I know my father confessed the secret he carried all those years, I need some down time before I make any future decisions. When the next term is up for my district, I may run for city council and don't want to remain on this board."

"I understand," Steph sympathized, "but now I'm left with two open board positions, plus a position in the office."

"You know my sister, Naomi, wants to move back to River Falls to stay with Mom. She's worked at the St. Paul Housing Authority and has experience with the housing standards. Maybe you could look at her résumé."

"Interviews start next week. If she gets her résumé to me within the next few days, I'll take a look at it."

"Thanks, Steph. I'm sorry for all the problems we, as a board, caused for you. I hope you continue to stay on in the director capacity."

"Even though the board apologized for the trouble they put me through, I don't think staying on here will benefit me."

"Sorry to hear that. Good luck with whatever plans you have."

Steph watched Jake leave her office, and pondered what her future would bring.

Steph knew there would be extra expenses because of the discovery of the remains. The expense rested on the housing authority. After they re-keyed all the apartments and installed a new security system with camera, Todd Reinhold worked with her to find ways to cut back on the remainder of the apartment remodeling.

Then an angel of mercy stopped by her office in the disguise of Jennifer Williams, the CEO of the Pearl Candy Company. She and her partner built the company from the startup of a gourmet candy business in their kitchens, and grew the company with their innovative sales of boxed candies on their Website to contracts with gourmet stores throughout the United States and Canada. Within five years, they became millionaires. Steph, well aware of her reputation, was surprised when Lola said Jennifer wanted to see her.

"Hello, Jennifer, I'm Stephanie Runnell."

"It's nice to meet you. Could I take a moment of your time?" Jennifer, a tall, big-boned woman, portrayed self-confidence. Steph received a whiff of her expensive perfume as she extended her hand to Jennifer.

"Sure. Come on back to my office." Steph looked at her JC Penney slacks and sweater next to Jennifer's designer suit.

I wish I put on makeup today and worn a suit, she ranted to herself.

"I'll get right to the point," said Jennifer, as she sat down across from Steph and crossed her long legs. "Because of our success in our business, my partner and I decided to help the community with contributions for worthy causes. We are aware of everything that took place at the housing authority since you arrived. Todd Reinhold designed our newest facilities, and when he learned of your struggles, he called us."

"Really! How nice of Todd."

"We would like to purchase new furniture for your dining room, community room and update your kitchen facilities. I know it was on your list for renovations, but cut because of extra expenses."

Steph eyes widened in astonishment. "Wonderful. I don't know how to thank you for your generosity."

"No thanks are necessary. We've received so much success in our business, we want to give back."

"How would you like to proceed with the donation?"

"Order what you need and send the bill to my office." She handed Steph her business card. "I'd like to come by and see it when you get everything in."

"Absolutely. We will definitely invite you for coffee." Steph stood and vigorously shook her hand again.

Jennifer smiled. Steph noticed a small gap between her bleached-white teeth, and it actually enhanced her no-nonsense sculpted face.

"My business partner, Sydney, and I will be delighted to show up for the unveiling."

"Sounds great. I look forward to meeting Sydney."

Jennifer left and Steph excitedly rushed to Karen's office to tell her the good news.

Steph finally received a call from Sally at the Law Enforcement Center to request that her family and Rafe come by the station to discuss the finalization of the case for the remains found in the high rise. The BCA agent would also be present to give them a synopsis.

With mixed emotions, Steph felt relieved they could put the case to rest. She called her parents and then Rafe to enlighten them about the meeting. Even though her mom and dad were not involved except as witnesses, she thought it was a polite gesture on Mitch's part to include them in the meeting.

As the group sat around the table in one of the conference rooms, Mitch, Agent Norman Schmidt, and Detective Bishop walked into the room, each carried a stack of files. With friendly smiles, they looked more relaxed than in the past months.

"I've asked Agent Schmidt and Detective Bishop to attend because of their integral part in this investigation. Without the help of the BCA we would not have been able to solve the mystery as quickly," Mitch began his speech.

Steph noticed his eyes looked less tired and the creases around his eyes not as tight as they had been since the skeletal remains of José and Antonio were discovered.

They all looked at Agent Schmidt, whose face was unreadable except for a slight shade of pink that peaked through.

"Thank you all for coming here today. I want to tell you what we discovered, and what will happen down the road." He hesitated and looked at Mitch, who nodded for him to continue.

"First of all, we've come to an agreement on the names of the five Mexicans harassed one night in October, 1973."

As he read their names it became more evident to those in the room that these were actual people and not just names in a book.

"We've also established that Charles Leddering, Eddie Barkley, Donald Hanson, and George Walters were involved in the deaths of two of the victims. Even though the confession letter of Charles Leddering will be used as evidence in court, we feel the antagonists did not directly cause the deaths of the two men. According to the confession by Charles Leddering and verified by Donald Hanson, they did attempt to save the men from going over the falls. The men could not swim to shore because the current dragged them toward the falls."

He looked to see if Mitch wanted him to continue. Mitch again nodded his consent.

"We questioned Donald Hanson's and gave him a mental evaluation. We found that he is mentally unstable, and unable able to stand trial. It'll be up to the judge what will happen to him. He seems to remember clearly what happened over forty years ago, but then when questioned about his involvement with Jessie Maverick he refused to talk, so we're still working on that angle. He also doesn't remember that he pointed a gun at the window of Ms. Runnell's house. When I questioned him about the missing drugs from the evidence room, he voluntarily told us what he did."

Puzzled by Norman's statement, Steph asked, "What are you talking about? Missing drugs. There's more to this story."

"Oh, yes," Mitch cut in. "He's gathered information from one of our senior officers for several years now and passed it on to some of the drug dealers in town, mainly Jessie Maverick. He traded information for drugs. Prescription drugs did not help his pain, so he resorted to drugs supplied mainly by Maverick." Mitch paused for their reaction.

"Please continue, Mitch," Rafe suggested. "We'd like to know all the details."

"Well, unknowingly, one of our senior officers allowed Hanson access to the evidence room. When we uncovered this fact, we discovered some of the drugs accounted for in the Eddie Barkley murder were missing. When we pulled the missing drugs found in Steph's desk from the evidence box, they appeared identical to the ones missing in the other box. When questioned about the drugs, Hanson broke down and admitted he planted them in Steph's drawer."

"How did he get into my office to plant them? I have the only key to my office."

Mitch pulled on his ear and smiled, "Why don't I show you?"

He stepped out of the room and came back with a suit jacket and carried a handful of small bags.

"This is just candy in these small bags. Remember when he and Clarence came to your office to confront you?" Steph nodded. "He wore a suit on a hot day. He had the drugs hidden in the sleeve of his jacket. Similar to gamblers when they hide cards up their sleeves." He shoved the bags of candy up one sleeve. "When he put gloves on to search your desk, he used one hand to search." Mitch demonstrated using only one hand. "Knowing he wasn't going to find anything, he didn't search very hard until it came to the last drawer."

"My candy stash," she chuckled.

"Exactly. He wanted to make it look good, so he waited until the last drawer was checked. Then he used his other hand and pretended to move stuff around in the drawer...and he shook the drugs out of his sleeve." He demonstrated, and the bags fell out of his sleeve. "No one was any wiser as both you and Clarence stood on the opposite side of the desk."

Anne Thomas finally spoke. "You know I actually feel sorry for the poor man. He must have been desperate to pull those stunts."

"Unfortunately, even as an ex-deputy he messed up."

"How so?" asked Steph.

"When we checked the bags for fingerprints there were no fingerprints from you," Mitch replied. "However, we did find several other prints including those belonging to Jessie Maverick. On one bag there was one single fingerprint that belonged to Hanson. He wore gloves when in your office, so he couldn't leave any fingerprints on any of the bags unless he handled them before."

"We also got a search warrant for his house and found the suit he wore when he came to see you. We found minute traces of drugs on the sleeve lining," added Detective Bishop, "so that verifies his statement to us."

"I need to ask—why did he do this to me?"

"To get rid of you as the Executive Director. He figured if he got rid of you, then the investigation and all the publicity would die down. He wasn't thinking clearly even at that time," added Mitch.

"What he did was reprehensible, but right now he's in no condition to stand trial," commented Norman Schmidt. "Hanson isn't the last person involved in the incident. We are still searching for George Walters. We have some leads and are checking them out right now. But at this time we are not going to press any charges against him for a forty-plus-years mystery. However, he will be charged with filing a false police report and aggravated assault against Mr. Thomas."

"What about the deputy supplying Hanson with information?" pried Rafe.

Mitch replied, "He agreed to take an early retirement, so he can receive the majority of his pension."

"Are Roberto and Hernando needed for Donald's hearing?" Rafe inquired, concerned about their welfare.

"They're back in California. They agreed to return if we need them." Mitch reached into his file folder and pulled out an email and handed it to Rafe. "This is an email from the Denver Police Department about Fernando Osorio who died in the car accident." Rafe scanned the email.

"I guess that's the end to the secrets in the high rise,"

added Rafe. "Good luck in finding George Walters. He's probably changed his name so he won't be found."

"The BCA always gets their man," quoted Norman.

"I thought that was a quote from the FBI," smirked Rafe.

"We like to think our organization started it," grinned Norman with a smug look on his face.

The easy camaraderie relaxed everyone in the room as they giggled over the banter between Rafe and Norman.

"Thank you all so much. I am so glad this is over. Would it be possible to see Donald and tell him I forgive him?" Steph asked. "I also want him to know he needs to forgive himself. Maybe it will help him to heal faster."

Rafe smiled to himself. He was so proud of the change in Steph. His love for her grew day by day. "I'll go with you."

Mitch made arrangements for Steph and Rafe to visit with Donald the following day.

As they left the Law Enforcement Center, Wayne turned to Anne, "I think it's time to head back South."

Her parents looked back to see if Steph and Rafe heard what Wayne suggested. They held hands, completely oblivious and involved in their own world.

"I think you're right," replied Anne, with a smirk on her face as they walked to the car. "They didn't hear a word we said."

They stood as if frozen in front of Steph's car. Rafe focused on Steph's hand as it held onto his. His thumb rubbed across her knuckles. Now was probably not the right time, but with everything happening so fast he did not want to lose her.

"Steph, I really need to make arrangements to take the remains of my uncle and cousin back to Texas for burial." He hesitated and then took a deep breath. "I love you, Stephanie Runnell, and I hope you feel the same way."

Steph nodded enthusiastically. "Oh…I do love you."

His thumb moved to her cheekbone, his eyes softened with tenderness. "Will you please wait for me to return, and we can talk about our future?"

"Yes…oh, yes," and she threw herself into his arms. His mouth covered hers hungrily, his kiss sang through her veins, and brought tears to her eyes.

Oh, Oh, so much for discretion, kissing in front of the Law Enforcement Center. Gossip will fly now.

CHAPTER THIRTY-SEVEN

One Month Later

After a stay of several weeks with his family, Rafe returned to River Falls. No one was happier than Steph. He had returned with a healthy glow to his skin and a refreshed mind. It had been a healing trip for his family with the burial of his uncle José and cousin Antonio.

Steph talked to Rafe's mom several times on their land line. Rafe explained cell phone service was hit and miss on their ranch. If you went up on top of this one particular hill, it worked the best, he told her.

Steph hired Naomi, Jake Leddering's sister, to take Callie's place in the office. She proved to be an asset with her prior experience.

The mayor of River Falls introduced Steph to an investor, who purchased land on the riverfront and planned to build a 120-unit apartment complex. He offered her a contract to work with the architect and oversee the construction. Being unsure of what her future in River Falls held, she felt reluctant to commit to a contract. She asked for time to make a decision.

They were still in the application process for two more board members. Jake agreed to stay on the board until a replacement could be found.

Donald Hanson's court date was the week after Rafe arrived back. With the evidence against him presented to the judge, he pled guilty to all the charges. The judge pronounced him mentally incompetent to stand trial. His alcoholism and drug abuse drained his mind. The judge sentenced him to a drug and alcohol rehab facility for a minimum of twelve months and on probation for a period of five years. He revoked his license to carry, and he would never be able to carry or own a gun again. With a search warrant they confiscated all the guns from his home.

Azalea, in her spare time, started to learn the flower business from her Aunt Aggie and friend, Donna. She felt giddy and excited to start a new adventure in her life.

Wayne and Anne Thomas returned to Corpus Christi, Texas, before Donald's trial. Mitch did not think they would be needed to testify at Donald's hearing. It was a sad parting for Steph to see her parents leave, but she understood this was no longer their home.

Steph decided to put in as many hours as needed to get the high rise renovations completed. Relieved to start a new venture, she planned to accept the position of project manager for the new apartment complex. She did not want to leave without the knowledge of whether or not she had a future with Rafe. Plus, she promised to help Azalea with some of the renovations on the flower shop.

Fall weather fast approached and the nights came on early. Normally, Rafe spent almost every evening with her since his return. Tonight she told him she needed to work a little later. He offered to bring pizza over so she did not have to cook.

Rafe surprised Steph every day with some little something—nothing extravagant as she knew his minister's salary was limited, but some small thing that touched her heart.

A knock sounded on her office door. Rafe stood at the locked door and gave her a smile that sent her pulse to race.

"What are you doing here? I thought we planned to meet later. Where's the pizza?"

"Do you know what day it is?

"Huh," she drew her eyebrows together. "Let me guess? It's not the official beginning of Fall. It's not my birthday. It's not your birthday. Okay, I give up." She threw her arms up and slapped her sides.

"It's the same time of day we first met...almost to the minute."

"What! You remember the exact time we met."

"I sure do, and it's a time I'll never forget. I'm wearing the same shirt the day we met."

She looked and, sure enough, he wore the same Team Jesus t-shirt. She emitted a small gurgle of laughter.

He got down on one knee and pulled a small box out of his pocket.

"I need a partner by my side. Will you marry me and be the wife of a poor minister? I can't offer you the world, but I can offer you all the love you can handle." He opened the box to reveal a single diamond engagement ring.

Tears burned beneath her eyelids. She was filled with passion for this man who stood by her constantly. Love shone in her eyes as she responded, "Yes, yes, and yes."

God has given me this special man to love and cherish for

the rest of our lives. Thank you, Lord, for your gift.

The End or To Be Continued

NOTE TO THE READER

Thank you for reading *Secrets in the High Rise*, Book One in the *River Falls Mystery* series. Even though River Falls, Minnesota, is a figment of my imagination, it is also an accumulation of what I envision in a small town atmosphere. All small towns have their eccentricities in their traditions, as well as the families who live in them. All carry their secrets.

I started writing because of my inability to find many books where the main characters weren't all in their teens or early twenties. My books were created for the adult reader who appreciates a mystery, romance, thriller, and good Christian ethics all at the same time. Most of my characters are not young, but experienced in life, and have their share of baggage. I *do not* do porn, erotica, or blood and guts descriptions. Even though my books are mysteries, they are also filled with love and compassion, forgiveness, and miracles. I write about real life and to entertain.

Because of my love for our Lord, Jesus Christ, I wanted to bring a Christian theme to my writing. Sometimes Satan tries to inch his way into the plot, but he is unsuccessful in the end.

Tithing is important, and a portion of the proceeds from all books sold will be tithed according to the Bible.

No Reasonable Doubt is Book Two in the *River Falls Mystery series.* Azalea Rose purchases her aunt's flower shop in River Falls. Azalea is a struggling single mom who ends up involved in a murder mystery. There is mystery, romance, and miracles surrounding her shop. It's still a work in progress and should be out by early 2018. Many of the same characters from *Secrets in the High Rise* will return and life goes on.

I apologize in advance if you find errors in the book, such as grammar or punctuation. The book has been reviewed many times, edited twice, and it's human error if we missed anything.

Please view my website (https://jarost-author.com) for future books and their launching dates. Hopefully, my readers will leave a positive review and feedback. I can also be reached on my Facebook page at J.A. Rost and email at booksbyjarost@outlook.com.

God bless y'all,
J. A. Rost

ABOUT THE AUTHOR

J. A. Rost was born and raised in Minnesota and her interest in writing began in junior high school. She initially gave up her love of writing to raise a family and continue in other careers. She now resides in Texas with her husband and two dogs, Lightning and Storm, but continues to spend part of the summer in Minnesota. As a retired grant writer and property manager, she now makes her own time to write. She loves to write for the Christian readers with her short stories, fiction and non-fiction. Even though she often writes under different names, she decided to become an Indie author in 2017 and publish her first novel in the River Falls Mystery Series. Her love for Jesus Christ is evident in her books and short stories.

CPSIA information can be obtained
at www.ICGtesting.com
Printed in the USA
LVHW011443190219
608034LV00001B/110/P